P9-DFP-065

CRITICAL PRAISE FOR *Mike, Mike & Me*

"The inventive premise of Markham's winning novel involves
a love triangle in both the past and the present among pretty
Beau, the Mike she married, and the Mike she left behind....
Markham's latest is an appealing, wholly original yarn."
—*Booklist*

"...hilarious...readers will be instantly catapulted back in time,
into their own versions of Very Big Hair
and spandex bike shorts."
—*Romantic Times BOOKclub*

CRITICAL PRAISE FOR *Slightly Settled*

"Readers who followed Tracey's struggles in *Slightly Single*,
and those meeting her for the first time, will sympathize with
this singleton's post-breakup attempts to move on in this fun,
lighthearted romp with a lovable heroine."
—*Booklist*

"Like many women, Tracey needs to figure out when to
listen to her friends and when to listen to herself."
—*Romantic Times BOOKclub*

CRITICAL PRAISE FOR *Slightly Single*

"...an undeniably fun journey for the reader."
—*Booklist*

"Bridget Jonesy...Tracey Spadolini smokes, drinks
and eats too much, and frets about her romantic life."
—*Publishers Weekly*

FEB   2006

WENDY MARKHAM

is a pseudonym for *New York Times* bestselling, award-winning
novelist Wendy Corsi Staub, who has written more than
sixty fiction and nonfiction books for adults and teenagers
in various genres—among them contemporary and historical
romance, suspense, mystery, television and movie tie-in and
biography. She has coauthored a hardcover mystery series with
former New York City mayor Ed Koch and has ghostwritten
books for various well-known personalities. A small-town girl
at heart, she was born and raised in western New York on the
shores of Lake Erie and in the heart of the notorious snow belt.
By third grade, her heart was set on becoming a published
author; a few years later, a school trip to Manhattan convinced
her that she had to live there someday. At twenty-one, she
moved alone to New York City and worked as an office temp,
freelance copywriter, advertising account coordinator and
book editor before selling her first novel, which went on to
win a Romance Writers of America RITA® Award. She has since
received numerous positive reviews and achieved bestseller
status, most notably for the psychological suspense novels
she writes under her own name. Her Red Dress Ink title
Slightly Single was one of Waldenbooks' Best Books of 2002.
Very happily married with two children, Wendy writes full-time
and lives in a cozy old house in suburban New York, proving
that childhood dreams really can come true.

Slightly
Engaged
Wendy Markham

RED
DRESS
I N K
™

If you purchased this book without a cover you should be aware that this book is stolen property. It was reported as "unsold and destroyed" to the publisher, and neither the author nor the publisher has received any payment for this "stripped book."

SLIGHTLY ENGAGED

A Red Dress Ink novel

ISBN 0-373-89564-X

© 2006 by Wendy Corsi Staub.

All rights reserved. The reproduction, transmission or utilization of this work in whole or in part in any form by any electronic, mechanical or other means, now known or hereafter invented, including xerography, photocopying and recording, or in any information storage or retrieval system, is forbidden without written permission. For permission please contact Red Dress Ink, Editorial Office, 225 Duncan Mill Road, Don Mills, Ontario M3B 3K9, Canada.

This book is a work of fiction. The names, characters, incidents and places are the products of the author's imagination, and are not to be construed as real. While the author was inspired in part by actual events, none of the characters in the book is based on an actual person. Any resemblance to persons living or dead is entirely coincidental and unintentional.

® and TM are trademarks. Trademarks indicated with ® are registered in the United States Patent and Trademark Office, the Canadian Trade Marks Office and/or other countries.

www.RedDressInk.com

Printed in U.S.A.

In loving memory of my beautiful mom,
Francella Corsi
April 17, 1942–May 11, 2005
You alone read and loved everything I ever wrote....
And you said you liked the "funny ones" best of all. Here's one
more, written with laughter through tears, especially for you.

*Most of all the other beautiful things in life come by twos and
threes, by dozens and hundreds. Plenty of roses, stars, sunsets,
rainbows, brothers, and sisters, aunts and cousins,
but only one mother in the whole wide world.*
—Kate Douglas Wiggin

Part I
Labor Day Weekend

Chapter 1

I love weddings!

Doesn't everyone?

Um, apparently not.

"Cripes, Tracey, I can't believe this is how we're spending the last Saturday of the summer."

That's my live-in boyfriend, Jack, grumbling as he gazes bleakly through the windshield of our rented subcompact car at the holiday-traffic-clogged Jersey Turnpike. The midday sun is glaring overhead and heat radiates in waves off the asphalt, along with toxic black exhaust fumes.

Thank God for air-conditioning. I adjust the full-blast passenger's-side vent to blow in the vicinity of my navel, lest it muss my fancy upswept do.

It took me almost an hour and a half a can of Aussie Freeze Spray to get my straight, bra-clasp-length brown hair looking this supermodelish. It'll probably wilt the second I get out of the car, but at least Jack got to appreciate it. He was momentarily complimentary about my hair and my slinky red cocktail dress before he went back to grousing about the wedding.

It shouldn't bug me that he didn't mention anything about how I was wearing a similar red dress the night we met.

It shouldn't, but it does.

I can't help it. For the first year or so that we were together, he made a point of noticing details like that. I guess he's gotten less romantic the last few months. Or maybe I've gotten overly sensitive. I shouldn't go around weighing every comment he makes—or noticing the ones he doesn't make anymore.

I shouldn't, but lately, I do.

It's not that I think we've fallen out of love. If anything, we've become closer, our lives interwoven. His friends are my friends; his mother and his favorite sister, Rachel, sometimes call just to talk to me. My friends are his friends; my mother and sister—well, forget about them. The point is, we're still a solid couple. We laugh all the time; we know each other's most intimate secrets; the sex is frequent and good, if I do say so myself.

So what's the problem?

I want more, dammit. I deserve more. I'm finally over the pesky feelings of unworthiness and insecurity that festered in the wake of my arrogant ex-boyfriend, Will, who callously blew me off two summers ago.

It's not as though I've come right out and asked Jack what his intentions are—maybe because I'm afraid of the answer. But lately, I've found myself wondering pretty frequently— all right, constantly—whether Jack is ever going to take the initiative to make our relationship permanent.

Since he hasn't, I tend to secretly look for evidence that he's got the opposite plan in mind. Or, at the very least, that he's losing interest.

All right, maybe the ghost of unworthy, insecure Tracey

has come back to haunt me. But I really should stop nitpicking—even if it's just mental nitpicking. Really. Before I turn into one of those Bitter Shrews.

Which Bitter Shrews, you might ask?

Oh, you know. The Bitter Shrews who nobody wants to marry. The ones who eventually become joyless middle-aged spinsters with mouths that have those vertical wrinkles in the corners from wearing perpetually grim expressions.

Oblivious to the horrific visions careening beneath my divine updo, Jack props his outstretched wrists on the top curve of the steering wheel in frustration as he brakes to yet another stop.

"We should have RSVP'd no, Tracey. This is ridiculous."

"How could we do that? Mike's one of your best friends. Plus he's my boss."

"Soon-to-be ex-boss."

Right. Mike was fired a few weeks ago. Sort of. The command came down from the formidable Adrian Smedly, director of our account group, to Mike's supervisor, Carol the Wimpy Management Rep. But she didn't have the balls—or in her case, the heart—to come right out and ax a soon-to-be groom. Instead, she called him into her office and more or less told him to start looking for a new job as soon as possible.

The thing about Mike is that he's incessantly upbeat in a dopey, wide-eyed kind of way, like a big old happy pup. He trots nonchalantly through life wearing an open, friendly expression, heedless that his shirts are frequently rumpled and his hair is always mussed. If Mike had a tail, it would be perpetually wagging.

So when Carol told him in so many words that he doesn't have a future at Blair Barnett Advertising, Mike seemed pretty unfazed. In fact, from what I can tell, he hasn't started cleaning out his office or even put together his résumé. I should know. He's all but illiterate.

For the past almost three years I've been working at Blair Barnett, my primary purpose in life is to proofread Mike's stuff, both work related and personal. I've doctored his memos, his presentations, even the supposedly impromptu toast he gave at his engagement party. If he were doing a résumé, I'd definitely know about it. I'd probably be writing it.

Never mind that what I should be writing by now—what I fully expected to be writing by now—is ad copy.

Last year I was promoted from my original entry-level account management position, but not into the coveted Creative Department, as promised. No, I was given the title account coordinator on the McMurray-White packaged goods account, which basically means I make a few thousand dollars more per year to remain in my claustrophobic cubicle and officially do administrative stuff while unofficially assisting my incompetent boss with his own duties. Oh, and I get all the freebie product I want, which means I am pretty much stocked for life on Blossom deodorant and Abate laxatives.

I'm supposedly still first in line for the next junior copy-writing position that opens up in the Creative Department.

The trouble is, thanks to the lousy economy, Blair Barnett has been routinely laying off employees, including junior copywriters and account coordinators, for the past eighteen months. Jack, who is a media supervisor at the agency, keeps reminding me that we're both lucky we still have jobs.

But I'm twenty-five years old. I don't want a job; I want a career. And with Mike gone—which, presumably, he soon will be—who's going to push for me to get another promotion? Certainly not wimpy Carol.

"Aside from whether or not Mike's my boss, you still

lived with him for years," I point out to Jack, shoving aside troubling thoughts of office politics. "You can't just not go to his wedding."

"Why not? I should be *protesting* his wedding."

"Protesting?" Amused, I imagine Jack picketing the church in a sandwich board. "On what grounds?"

"On the grounds that I loathe the bride."

"Yeah, well, who doesn't?"

Back when Jack was Mike's roommate and Dianne was Mike's omnipresent girlfriend, Jack referred to Dianne as a one-woman axis of evil.

I have to say, he wasn't necessarily exaggerating.

It's hard to remember that I actually kind of liked her back when she was just a voice on the other end of the phone whenever I answered Mike's line at the office. My opinion changed rapidly when I found myself sharing girl-friend privileges with her in Mike and Jack's tiny Brook-lyn apartment.

Miscellaneous things I hate about Dianne:

1) She's a catty, mean-spirited snob.

2) She talks to Mike in this cutesy-poo baby voice when-ever she isn't bitching at him.

3) She once called Jack an asshole behind his back and probably to his face for all I know.

Oh, and 4) She's getting married.

Hell, *yes,* I'm jealous.

Don't you think it's unfair that she's getting married, and I'm not?

Yeah, so do I.

Ironically, if it weren't for me, Dianne wouldn't be walk-ing down the aisle today. Or, most likely, ever. I mean, who would want a one-woman axis of evil for a wife?

I guess Mike would.

Except that I don't think he really does. He's basically get-ting married by default.

When Jack and I moved in together a year and a half ago, Mike was left without a roommate. He halfheartedly tried to find a new one for a while, then told Dianne maybe they should live together. She said no way. Not without an engagement ring on her finger and a wedding date on her calendar.

Mike swore to me and Jack that there was no way he was getting married. Not to Dianne, not yet, maybe not ever. He supposedly looked for an affordable studio apartment for a couple of weeks to no avail.

The next thing we knew, he had gone over to the dark side and was shopping for diamond rings.

Rather, he was arranging a five-year payment plan with sky-high interest for the rock Dianne had already picked out.

Wuss.

"Are we almost at the exit?" Jack asks, lifting his foot off the brake and creeping the tiny car forward a whopping two or three feet before stopping again with a colorful curse. It isn't the first time he's said that—or worse—since we left Manhattan this morning.

The day started off on the wrong foot at the rental-car place down First Avenue from our apartment on the Upper East Side.

Our Apartment.

Funny how even after seventeen months of living with somebody, you still get a little thrill over the mundane daily reminders of domestic coupledom. At least, I still do.

Anyway, we had reserved a midsize sedan, but for some reason the counter agent couldn't quite express—either because she didn't speak English or because she simply didn't *have* a logical explanation why—we got stuck with a car that's roughly the size of a toilet bowl, give or take.

At least it doesn't smell like a toilet bowl, like the rental car Jack and I had when we went to my friend Kate's wedding in sweltering Alabama last summer.

Then again, the lemon-shaped air-freshener thingy hanging from the rearview mirror in this car isn't much better. It kind of reminds me of that bathroom spray that doesn't really eliminate odors, merely infuses them with a fruity aroma. My parents' bathroom frequently reeks of country-apple-scented poop.

Jack and I keep good old-fashioned Lysol in our bathroom.

Our Bathroom.

In *Our Apartment.*

See? Little thrill.

After said thrill subsides, I consult the contents of the engraved ivory-linen envelope in my lap: an invitation with a tag line that reads *Grow old along with me…the best is yet to be…*a reception card and a little annotated road map of this particular corner of hell.

Er, Jersey.

"I think we're about five miles away from the exit," I tell Jack.

"That means at least another hour. Maybe we'll miss the ceremony," he adds hopefully.

But we don't. We eventually find ourselves driving along a strip mall–dotted highway with fifteen minutes to spare. Unless we're lost. Which, come to think of it, we just might be. I think I might have missed a turn a mile or so back, when I was trying to dislodge my numb feet from the cramped space between my purse and the glove compartment.

Jack's getting crankier by the second, I have to pee, and we're both scanning the sides of the road as if any second now we might see a picturesque white steeple poking up amidst the concrete-block-and-plate-glass suburban landscape.

"What's the name of the church again, Tracey?" he asks, apparently thinking we might have somehow overlooked a place of worship nestled in the shadow of Chuck E. Cheese.

Without checking the invitation again, I quip, to break the tension, "Our Lady of Everlasting Misery."

Jack laughs. "Really? I thought it was Our Lady of Eternal Damnation."

I giggle. "Or Our Lady of Imminent Sorrow." Then, the nice Catholic girl in me adds, "We probably shouldn't be making jokes like that."

"Sure we should. If Mike's asinine enough to get married, we can make jokes about it."

Okay, here I go again.

But the thing is…

Jack didn't say, *If Mike's asinine enough to get married* to Dianne.

He said, *If Mike's asinine enough to get married.*

Period.

Which makes me wonder if he thinks only the Asinine exchange vows.

It's not as if he's ever said anything to the contrary.

"What's wrong?" he asks, looking over at me.

"I have to pee."

"Are you sure?"

I squirm and struggle to cross my legs beneath the skirt of the slinky red cocktail dress he earlier admired but callously didn't remember to relate to the slinky red cocktail dress I was wearing the magical night we met at the office Christmas party, lo, twenty months ago.

"Am I sure I have to pee?" I echo, irritated. "Of course I'm sure."

"I mean, is that all that's wrong?"

No. I have to pee and there's no room in this car for leg-crossing *and* I'm doomed to bitter spinsterdom, thanks to him.

My mother and sister were right. I should never have moved in with Jack so quickly.

Mental note: Next time you are cordially invited to live with someone, request ring and wedding date prior to signing of lease.

Dianne might be a bitch, but she's a brilliantly strategic bitch. Here I am wedged into a citrus-scented Kia, sans ring or any hope of one, while she's lounging in a stretch limo in a tiara with a glass of champagne in one hand and a prayer book in the other, serenely contemplating happily-ever-after with the man she loves.

Yes. Or, more likely, she has her ever-present cell phone wedged under her illusion-layered headpiece as she curses out some hapless florist who dared to put one too many sprigs of baby's breath into the bridal bouquet.

Regardless, what matters—at least to me, and, undoubtedly, to her—is that she's the one who's getting married today.

"Hey, is that it?" Jack asks suddenly, pointing out the window at, you guessed it, a steeple looming above not Chuck E. Cheese, but T.J. Maxx.

That's it, all right. Our Lady of Everlasting Misery is decked out with floral wreaths on the open doors, long black limousines parked out front and elegantly dressed Manhattanites milling alongside the white satin runner stretching down the front steps.

Ah, weddings. Gotta love them.

Grow old along with me...the best is yet to be...

How romantic is it to stand up in front of everyone you ever knew and vow to be with one person all the days of your life?

I experience a glorious flutter of anticipation until I remember that I'm not the bride here. That I may never be the bride anywhere. Not if I stick with Jack.

Given that the alternative to sticking with Jack is breaking up with Jack, and that I happen to be head over heels in love with Jack, my flutter of excitement swiftly transforms into something that calls for Maalox.

"This is going to suck," Jack mutters as we pull into the crowded, sun-steamed parking lot beside the church.

I'm not sure whether he's referring to the challenge of finding an empty space or the big event itself, but in either case, I couldn't agree with him more.

Chapter 2

"And now, ladies and gentlemen, please welcome the new Mr. and Mrs. Michael Middleford!"

We all—me, Jack, my three co-workers and their spouses—stand and clap as the band launches into a rousing rendition of Frank Sinatra's "Fly Me to the Moon." Our table is in the far reaches of the room, a zone that's obviously been designated for Work Friends and Aging Distant Relatives. There's a row of walkers and canes and even a wheelchair lined up beside the adjacent table, where nobody is standing or clapping, presumably because the occupants can neither see nor hear.

Mike and Dianne swoop into the reception hall with their clasped hands held high, resplendent in black tux and white gown. Mike looks dashing, and Dianne…

"She looks like a cockroach," Yvonne observes over the rim of her martini glass.

"A cockroach? Yvonne, that's a terrible thing to say about a bride." Brenda's Joisey accent seems stronger than ever here among the natives.

"Not if it's true," Latisha proclaims.

"Oh, it's true." Yvonne gives her Pepto-Bismol-tinted bouffant a little pat. "She might be all decked out in a tiara and veil but she still has a pinched little face and her eyes are beadier than the bodice of her dress. Cockroach."

"I couldn't agree more, Why-vonne."

Naturally, that quip came from Jack, who is on his third scotch and consumed nary a liquor-absorbing mini-quiche or bacon-wrapped scallop during the cocktail hour. He claimed he lost his appetite when he was forced to kiss the bride in the receiving line.

Yvonne nods, for once choosing not to chastise him for calling her Why-vonne, which he insists is his way of being affectionate. Never mind that Yvonne hates nick-names and generally shows affection for no one. Not even her husband, Thor.

Which doesn't mean she doesn't love us all to death. Af-fection just isn't her style. She's a tough old New York broad who can generally be found steering clear of small children, kittens with yarn balls and potential group-hug sit-uations.

"Gawd, I hope you people weren't trashing me at my wedding," Brenda says with a shake of her big curly black hair. "Did you think I looked like a cockroach, too?"

"Of course we didn't, Bren," I say reassuringly, avoiding Yvonne's and Latisha's eyes in case they, too, remember that we'd all cattily wondered how Brenda, in her billowing se-quin-studded gown and towering rhinestone and tulle headpiece perched atop a mountain of teased hair, was going to fit through the doorway of the honeymoon suite.

"Yeah, I'll bet you didn't." Brenda knowingly shakes her head at me, no doubt reminiscing about how we'd snidely speculated whether Yvonne got a senior citizen discount on the caterer for her green card marriage to her much younger Nordic pen pal, Thor. Oh, and how just last May we placed bets on whether Latisha's enormous lactating boobs would actually pop out of her low-cut bridal bodice when she bent over to cut the cake.

"Babe, what could anyone possibly say about you?" Paulie asks, patting Brenda's shoulder. "Yo-aw go-aw-jus."

It takes me a second to decipher Paulie's accent, and when I do, I have to smile. He and Brenda are so cute together. She's far from gorgeous these days, with perpetual dark circles under her eyes and thirty extra pounds of postpregnancy weight. But Paulie is still madly in love with her after two years of marriage and a colicky newborn.

"When I get married, I don't know if I'll dare to invite any of you," I find myself saying. "There are plenty of things you can say about me."

"Tracey, we would never!" Brenda protests, then asks, nudging Jack's arm, "So when are you guys getting married, anyway?"

Terrific. I don't dare look at him.

"I was thinking a year from next February thirtieth would be good," Jack says without missing a beat.

"Very funny," I mutter as the men chortle and the women bathe me in sympathetic glances.

I reach for my gin and tonic and find that it's empty. I'm about to flag down the passing waiter when I realize somebody's got to drive the lemon-fresh minicar home. Judging by the way Jack's imbibing, I'm assuming he's assuming it won't be him.

"And now, ladies and gentlemen, let's raise a glass as our best man, Mike's brother, Tom Middleford, toasts the bride and groom."

"He better keep it short and sweet," Latisha murmurs as we all obediently lift our champagne flutes. "I'm ready for prime rib and garlic mashed potatoes."

I'm ready for prime rib and garlic mashed potatoes, too.

What a shame that I was compelled to order the poached salmon and steamed baby vegetables.

Yes, I live in constant fear of gaining back all the weight I lost two summers ago. So far, that hasn't happened, thank God. But it might. The second I let down my guard, I'll find myself straining to zip the old fat jeans I keep in the top of my closet as a reminder.

With a sigh, I sip my ice water—which you wouldn't expect would taste like tap water in a fancy place like this, but it does—and turn my attention to the toast.

Unfortunately, Mike's brother Tom is as eloquent a speaker as Mike is a writer. Meaning, his big speech is all but incoherent. Not because he's drunk—at least, he doesn't look drunk. What he looks is distressed. Distressed that his beloved big brother has just been joined for all eternity to a cockroach in a tiara.

Or maybe I'm reading too much into his expression and his rambling, emotional speech. Maybe I shouldn't assume that just because I've never met anyone who actually *likes* Dianne, such a person doesn't exist. Maybe the best man is overcome by joy, and not sorrow.

Nah.

By the time Tom winds down his toast with a dismal, "Cheers," I'm feeling mighty depressed about the evening ahead.

"Anybody want to come to the smoking room with me?" Yvonne asks, snapping open her black clutch and pulling out a pack of Marlboros and a fancy lighter.

All of us women immediately take her up on it, including Latisha, who doesn't even smoke.

The men—Yvonne's husband, Thor, Brenda's husband, Paulie, Latisha's husband, Derek, and my non-husband, Jack—are content to stay put at the round flower-and-candle-bedecked table.

The four of us traipse through the ballroom and out into

the hallway, where a tiny closed-in space has been graciously set aside for those of us who are willpower-challenged, cancer-defiant, and thus still addicted to nicotine. A noxious haze rolls out when we open the door, but we pile into the crowded room and light up.

Rather, three of us light up. Latisha fans the air with a hand that sports the recently bestowed wedding band she claimed not to want or need. As she fans, she asks, "Tracey, is it my imagination, or is Jack not into getting married?"

"Oh, it's your imagination," I tell her breezily. "He's actually got a diamond ring in his jacket pocket and he's just waiting for the right moment to pop the question."

Everyone laughs.

I try to laugh but end up making the kind of sound one might make if an MTA bus rolled over one's pinkie toe.

"Are you okay?" Brenda asks as Latisha pats my arm and Yvonne's eyes take on the deadly gleam reserved for bosses who ask her to start payment reqs at five to five on Friday afternoons and eligible bachelors who refuse to marry their live-in girlfriends.

"Yes," I say, inhaling my filtered menthol. "I'm okay."

When met with dubious silence, I add, "Sort of."

"Are you sure?" Brenda asks.

"Of course she's not okay," Yvonne barks. "Her boyfriend refuses to marry her. She feels like shit. Who wouldn't?"

Maybe somebody who hasn't been told that she should feel like shit, I can't help thinking. I mean, if my friends weren't here to validate my irritation with Jack, I might be able to convince myself that it's just a typical guy thing; that I should just bear with him a while longer.

After all, Jack isn't downright commitmentphobic like my ex-boyfriend, Will, whom I dated for years without his even entertaining the notion of cohabitation.

No, Jack asked me to move in with him practically the second we met.

Then again…

Don't you think that's a little suspicious?

Yeah, me too. But only lately. For the first year of our relationship, I was blissfully happy and oblivious to the idea of ulterior motives.

But that was back when I assumed that Engagement, Marriage and Baby Carriage would be the logical progression of our relationship. That's how it seems to work for everyone else I know, though Latisha swapped the order of Marriage and Baby Carriage, and I seriously doubt there's a Baby Carriage in Yvonne's immediate future.

Meanwhile, now that Jack and I are stalled at phase one, Living Together, I can't help wondering why he wanted to do that in the first place.

Was he merely desperate to get away from Mike's eternal chipperness? Dianne's eternal wenchiness? Brooklyn?

Obviously, he could never have afforded a Manhattan apartment with a roommate, because half the rent on a two-bedroom Manhattan apartment is way beyond a media supervisor's salary.

Half the rent on a one-bedroom Manhattan apartment is just barely within Jack's budget, and mine. So if we weren't living together, he'd still be in a borough and I'd still be in my dingy downtown studio.

Or maybe I'd have given up on New York City by now and moved back to my hometown way upstate. That's what everyone back home always expected me to do sooner or later. The residents of Brookside know that one doesn't leave home without someday regretting it…or, at the very least, paying a terrible price.

I still remember the neighbor's son who notoriously turned his back on his home, his family, his legacy.

In other words, he moved to Cleveland. When he was run over by a snowplow in a freak accident, my parents said he'd gotten what was coming to him.

Yes, I'm serious.

I'm the first person in my family to move more than a few blocks away from my parents. They'll never forgive me for moving four hundred miles away, and I'm sure they're assuming I'll eventually get what's coming to me. That would explain why my mother's always offering up novenas in my name.

Forgiveness doesn't come easily in the Spadolini family. My parents still haven't forgiven me for daring to say that I don't like the abundant fennel seeds in Uncle Cosmo's homemade sausage, for missing Cousin Joanie's first communion, for forgetting to call my grandmother on her birthday.

I sent her flowers.

But I didn't call.

In my family, you call.

You can send somebody three dozen roses, imported Perugina Baci and front-row tickets to see Connie Francis, but if you don't call, you're out.

So yeah, I'm out.

Especially now that I'm living in sin.

In my family, living in sin is one step away from killing somebody.

Actually, it's probably *worse* than killing somebody, considering my parents' pride in our Sicilian roots, and how they've alluded to the fact that our ancestors weren't exactly antigun lobbyists and didn't take any crap from anybody.

My father likes to share a colorful anecdote about his father's *compare* Fat Naso, and what may or may not have happened to Scully, the neighbor who called Fat Naso's mother something so heinous it can't be repeated at Sunday dinner.

Never mind that Fat Naso's mother callously dubbed her own son Fat Naso because of his weight problem and prominent beak. Back then in Sicily, it was okay to insult somebody as long as you gave birth to them. Conversely, it was *never* okay to stand by while somebody else insulted the person who gave birth to you.

Pop never comes right out and says what Fat Naso did, but I do know that he didn't just stand by, and that Scully was never seen again. Pop is real proud of that.

But he definitely isn't proud of me, his daughter, the *puttana*.

Okay, he's never actually come right out and called me a *puttana*. But I know that to him and the rest of my family, a woman who blatantly sleeps with a man who isn't her husband is a whore.

The thing is, I don't feel like a whore. Should I?

I ask my friends just that.

"You? A ho? Get outta here," is Latisha's response.

"A whore is somebody who turns tricks for money, Tracey," Yvonne informs me, in case I didn't know the Webster's definition.

But Brenda, who grew up in an Italian-American Catholic family like mine, gets it. "My parents would have killed me if I lived with Paulie before we got married. They'd have called me a *puttana* and worse."

"What could be worse than *puttana?*" I ask her, and she shrugs.

So do I. Then I say, "I wonder if it's even worth it."

"If what's worth what?" Yvonne asks, releasing a smoke ring that wafts into my face. Funny how my own smoke— the smoke I'm inhaling directly into my lungs—doesn't bother me, but secondhand smoke does.

Mental note: Stop for patch on way home. Time to quit.

This isn't the first time I've thought of that. Jack has been after me to quit smoking for a while now. He even promised me a weekend trip to a fancy spa outside Providence if I can go for an entire month without a cigarette.

So far, I've made it through an entire morning. Several times.

It's the afternoon lull that's a deal-breaker for me. I can never seem to get past the postlunch hump without lighting up. But I swear I will, sooner or later. I'll do it for Jack. I'd do anything for Jack.

"I wonder if living with Jack is worth the grief that my parents give me," I tell my friends. "Maybe if I weren't living with him, I'd already have a ring on my finger. Do you think I would?"

Without the slightest hesitation, they all nod.

Terrific.

I definitely should have held out, like Dianne did. Well, it's too late now.

"What do you think I should do?" I ask the three of them. "And don't tell me to break up with Will, because I know I can't."

"Will?" Latisha echoes, her eyebrows edging toward her cornrows.

"What?"

"You said Will, Tracey," Brenda points out. "Instead of Jack."

"I did not."

"Oh, yes, you did. And I bet it's Freudian," Yvonne informs me. "You're in the same boat with Jack that you were with Will a few years ago."

"I am not," I protest, even though I realize she might be onto something. "Jack isn't Will. Jack loves me. Jack wants to live with me. Jack—"

"Doesn't want to marry you," Yvonne cuts in. "Right?"

"Wrong. He's just not ready yet. It happens all the time with men."

Nobody says anything.

I glance from Brenda (who started dating the devoted Paulie in junior high) to Latisha (who turned down dedicated Derek's repeated proposals for over a year) to Yvonne (who only intended to have a green card marriage and was promptly swept off her feet by dashing Thor).

Well, what do they know? Their relationships are the exception.

"You know what they say, Tracey," Brenda tells me. "If you love something, set it free. If it comes back to you, it's yours. If it doesn't, it never will."

"Was," Yvonne corrects, stubbing out her cigarette. "If it doesn't, it never *was*. Not *Will*."

"Why does everybody keep slipping up and saying 'Will'?" Latisha asks slyly. "Does Brenda have a subconscious thing for him, too? Bren, are you secretly lusting after Will?"

"Yeah, and I'm secretly lusting after Carson from *Queer Eye for the Straight Guy,* too."

Did I mention that all my friends were convinced Will was closeted and I was a deluded fag hag? No? Well, they did. And obviously still do. At least the Will-being-closeted part.

"Look, Tracey, the point is, maybe you need to set Jack free and see what happens."

Maybe Brenda's right. Good Lord, is this dismal, or what?

"Come on," Latisha says cheerfully. "I bet it's time for dinner."

After a ladies' room pit stop, where I ensure that I am still looking ravishing in red—so why doesn't Jack want to marry me?—we troop back out to the ballroom, where the band is playing "Always and Forever." That song, I recall, is supposed to be Mike and Dianne's first dance together. But the dance floor is empty, the newlyweds are nowhere in sight, and the crowd seems vaguely uneasy.

"What happened to the bride and groom?" I ask Jack, sliding into my seat.

He sips his scotch. "Oh, they left."

"They *left?*"

"Yeah, you just missed it. They started dancing and then they had an argument. You should have seen it, Trace," he says almost gleefully. "She was shaking her fist at him and everything. Right out there on the dance floor with everyone watching. Then she went stomping away and he chased after her. Wuss."

"Don't call him that," I say sharply, despite the fact that I silently called him the same thing a few hours ago. "He isn't a wuss. He's a man who's...who's in love."

Oh, please, I think.

"Oh, please." Jack rolls his eyes and tilts his glass again.

I look around the table and see that nobody is listening to our conversation. They're all caught up in the bridal debacle, oblivious to the antibridal one that's brewing between me and Jack right under their noses.

"If you and I were married, I'd hope you'd come after me if we had a fight and I left," I say unreasonably.

Jack feigns confusion. Or maybe, in his pickled stupor, he really is confused. He says, "Huh? What does this have to do with us?"

"It has everything to do with us. I'm talking about marriage, here, Jack. And the future of our relationship."

I am?

Hell, yes, I am. And it's high time I brought it up.

"I'm talking about why you don't want to get married," I go on.

"Who says I don't want to get married?"

"You do."

"No, I don't."

Hope springs eternal. "So you want to get married?"

"Now?"

"No, of course not *now.* Just...someday."

"Sure," he says noncommittally. "Someday."

"When?"

"I don't know. In a few years, maybe."

Hope takes a hike.

"A few *years?*" I echo, supremely pissed. *"Maybe?"*

"What's the rush?"

I'm silent, glaring into the tossed salad that materialized on my place mat while I was gone. I can't believe we're having this conversation here. I can't believe we're having this conversation at all. But now that it's under way, there's no going back. I struggle to think of what I want to say next.

I assume Jack's doing the same thing.

Until he asks, "Do you want your tomato?"

I watch him poke his fork into it without waiting for a reply.

He has some nerve! Aside from the fact that he just side-stepped the issue at hand, everybody knows the tomato is the best part of a salad, and that restaurants and caterers are for some reason notoriously skimpy with them.

Then again, maybe everybody doesn't know. Or care.

But I do, and I do. It's like tomatoes are some rare, expensive delicacy not to be squandered. When I make a salad, I cut up a couple of them so I can have some in every bite. But perhaps I'm alone in my passion. Maybe most people don't *like* tomatoes, and they're only in a salad for a splash of color to liven up the aesthetic.

Who knows?

Who cares?

Me. I care. Because the fact that Jack would blatantly help himself to my lone tomato just shows what kind of human being he is.

"I thought you had no appetite," I manage to spit out between clenched jaws.

"It came back. Can I have your cucumber?"

It, too, is already on his fork, en route to his mouth.

"Take the whole thing." I shove the salad bowl in his direction.

"Don't you want it?"

"I lost my appetite."

He laughs, with nary a care in the world, damn him.

"Really, Trace? Did you kiss the bride, too?"

No. I just realized I'll never become one if I stay with you.

But I don't say it.

What's the use?

It's all out there on the table. Now all I can think is that if you love something, you're supposed to set it free. If it comes back to you, it's yours. If it doesn't, it never will…or never *was*. Or whatever.

Goodbye, Jack, I think sadly, watching him gobble the rest of my salad as though he hasn't a care in the world.

Chapter 3

Call me a hypocrite, but in the broad light of Sunday morning, the major confrontation Jack and I had at Mike's wedding doesn't seem quite so dramatic.

For one thing, Jack was apparently too drunk to even realize we'd *had* a major confrontation, which goes a long way toward diffusing any post-fight tension. Thus, it was particularly hard for me to stay angry at him, especially when he requested that the band play "Brown Eyed Girl" and dedicate it to me.

I guess he was oblivious to the fact that he'd been set free, because he asked me to dance. What could I do but say yes?

I guess I could have said no. But when "Brown Eyed Girl" is playing and it's been dedicated to you and you happen to be a brown-eyed girl, well, you get your ass out on the floor and you boogie.

At least, I fully intended to boogie. But for some reason, Jack seemed to think that particular song called for a slow dance.

If you've ever tried to stay angry at somebody while slow

dancing with them to "Brown Eyed Girl" at a wedding—and really, who hasn't?—then you'll know why I wound up more or less forgiving the poor lug. At least, for the duration of the night—which, in the end, actually turned out to be kind of fun.

The band was great, the food, when I recovered my appetite, was decent, and Mike and Dianne eventually made a reappearance. They had apparently reconciled, although she did seem to take perverse satisfaction in smushing the cake in his face when she fed it to him.

I found myself thinking that I would never smush the cake in my groom's face when I got married; then remembered that I probably wasn't going to be getting married.

Not to Jack, anyway. Not unless I was willing to wait for *years*. Which I wasn't.

But I couldn't dwell on that all night, could I?

Sure I could. And I guess, in the end, I did.

Jack slept the entire drive home while I listened to the day's news over and over again on 1010 WINS, the only radio station I could get on the car's crappy stereo without static, and tried not to hate him.

Now, here it is, Sunday morning, and Sleeping Beauty is still blissfully snoring in the next room.

Normally, I love our cozy apartment, especially on mornings when the sun is streaming in the window and we don't have to be back at our desks for forty-eight more hours.

But today, the place seems a little too...Ikea. Probably because that's where all our furniture comes from. Jack really likes that Scandinavian, boxy, functional style. My taste is more cottage chic.

Since the apartment is strictly boxy/functional without a hint of cottage, let alone chic, his taste won. I was so grateful to be jointly buying anything more significant than dinner that I didn't put up much of a fight. Now here I am, over a year later, feeling like I should change my name to

Helga and learn to make pepperkaker so I won't clash with the decor.

Back when we moved in, the apartment seemed spacious compared to my old studio…at least for the first five minutes. Today, it seems positively claustrophobic. Probably because one can cross the living room in three giant steps, the bedroom in two, and touch all three kitchen walls with one's fingertips by standing on the center parquet tile.

Plus, the place is cluttered.

Everywhere I look, there are piles of stuff. Not just his; it's my stuff, too. But his is more annoying.

Like the twelve novels he's in the middle of reading, and the stacks of freebie magazines he gets as a media supervisor and is definitely going to read as soon as he finishes the twelve novels.

Then there are the suit jackets draped over the backs of every chair. All right, we only have two chairs, but both are draped in suit jackets.

Don't even get me started on the shoes, the CDs and DVDs, the stuff that comes out of Jack's pockets every time he comes home.

It's not like I'm FlyLady, or Will, but at least I'm neater than Jack, and his clutter is starting to bug me. It's so tempting to start tossing it, which, don't worry, I won't do, because Will once threw away a magazine I was reading when I set it down to go to the bathroom. I'm serious; in the space of time it took me to unzip, sit, pee, zip and wash, he not only threw it into the garbage, but carried the garbage down the hall and dumped it into the garbage chute. He didn't do it on purpose, he said, seeming shocked by my disbelief.

Yeah, and he didn't do Esme Spencer, his summer-stock costar, on purpose, either.

Anyway, here I am, curled up on the couch with my second cup of coffee, trying to read the Metro section of the

Times while pondering my non-future with clutterholic, marriagephobic Jack, when the phone rings.

I figure it's probably my friend Buckley O'Hanlon. He mentioned something about me and Jack joining him and his girlfriend, Sonja, for in-line skating in Central Park this afternoon. It sounded like fun when he brought it up the other day.

Now, not so much.

For one thing, I'm exhausted from all that dancing, and Jack will inevitably be hungover. For another, I've never in-line skated in my life. If my ice-skating and roller-skating prowess are any indication of my skill potential, I should probably learn to blade in a private bouncy tent, as opposed to a public park with gravel, roaming humans and other hazards.

Then again, maybe we should go anyway. After all, Buckley and Sonja are the only true peers we have left in New York. Unbetrothed, cohabiting couples seem to be a dying breed.

As I pick up the phone, I am already wondering if perhaps my weak Spadolini ankles have strengthened over the years, and whether the skate-rental place Buckley mentioned also supplies full-body padding that doesn't make you look fat.

"Hello?"

"Tracey?" says a voice that isn't Buckley's. "It's me, Wilma."

"Oh, hi, Mrs. Candell," I say to the wonderful woman who—*sob*—will never be my mother-in-law.

"Call me Wilma," Mrs. Candell urges for the nine hundredth time since we met, and I murmur that I will, but I know that I won't.

For some reason, I just can't. Maybe because the name Wilma conjures an image of a cartoonish red bun, a prehistoric jagged-hemmed dress with a rock pearl choker and dots for eyes.

There's nothing remotely Flintstone-ish about Jack's mother, an elegant yet bubbly brunette with a penchant for designer clothes and chatty conversation. She's the furthest thing from Wilma Flintstone, and the furthest thing from my own mother, that I can imagine.

You wouldn't catch Mrs. Candell in a jagged-hemmed dress and rock pearls, let alone in stretch pants with graying hair and an unappealing line of dark fuzz on her upper lip.

All right, that's mean. My mother might have a mustache, but she has her good points. She makes a mean minestrone, and she…um…

Well, she has some other good points. But it would be nice if she were as laid back and easy to talk to as Jack's mother is.

"How was the wedding?" Mrs. Candell asks, and I marvel at how she always remembers exactly what our plans are on any given weekend.

"It was fun." I tell her the highlights of the ceremony and reception, skipping over the bride and groom's dance-floor fight as well as her son's callous torture.

She asks about the color of the bridesmaids' dresses, the flavor of the cake, the honeymoon destination.

I know! I told you she was great!

Then she says cryptically, "Well, I guess you'll be next."

Excuse me?

Did she just tell me she guesses I'll be *next?*

What does she mean by that?

I'm silent for a moment, my mind racing. Can Jack's mother possibly know something I don't know?

I probably shouldn't ask, but I can't help it. My entire future—or non-future—with her son is hanging in the balance.

"Mrs. Candell?"

"It's Wilma."

Not.

"Oh. Right. Um, Wilma?" I ask, thinking *Mom* has a more natural ring to it.

"Mmm-hmm?"

"What do you mean? When you say I'll be next," I clarify, in case feigned confusion and sidestepping of issues runs in the family.

"You'll be next," she repeats. "You and Jack."

"Next…?"

"Next. To get married."

Next…after whom? Hazel and Phinnaeus Moder?

Okay, either the woman is seriously deluded, or she's privy to some vast Candell conspiracy.

"I don't think so," I say cautiously, testing the waters. "I mean, I really doubt Jack wants to marry me."

"Tracey! Why would you say something like that? Jack loves you."

If those words coming from his mother don't warm my heart, I don't know what will.

Well, yes, I actually do. A proposal on bended knee from Jack himself would definitely be even toastier.

"Well," I tell his mother, trying not to reveal my burgeoning excitement, "regardless of whether Jack loves me or not, I don't think he wants to get married."

"You're wrong about that."

"How do you know?"

"I just know." Her tone is oozing confidence.

I think.

Well, it's definitely oozing something. Hopefully not bullshit.

"Mrs.—Wilma, I'm not sure I get what you're trying to tell me."

Is she trying to tell me something?

Or is she trying *not* to tell me something?

"Tracey, don't worry about Jack. He wants to get

married. He would kill me if he knew I was telling you this—"

I hold my breath.

"—but he's definitely planning on getting married."

Sensing there's more, I'm afraid to exhale; afraid to move; afraid to do anything that might shatter the moment.

"In fact," she goes on, lowering her voice conspiratori-ally, "when he was up here for dinner last week, he asked if I could open the safe-deposit box for him."

I'm turning blue here, trying to figure out what that could possibly mean, certain there's more. There has to be.

But she doesn't elaborate, so I'm forced to let my breath out at last and ask bluntly, "What, exactly, does that mean?"

Silence.

Then, "You don't know?"

Apparently, I don't. But now I'm dying to.

"Know what?" I ask.

"About the stone?"

Stone? What stone?

I rack my brains.

Stone...stone...grindstone? Rolling stone? Pizza stone? Flintstone?

What the hell is she talking about?

"No," I say tautly, "I didn't know about a—er, *the*—stone."

Her flat "oh" might as well have been preceded by "uh" because she's obviously just spilled something she wasn't supposed to. Which would be tantalizing if I could get a handle on whatever it is she supposedly revealed. But here I am, utterly clueless, my mind racing with possibilities.

"I just assumed the two of you had discussed it."

"The stone?"

"Yes."

"See, the thing is, Wilma...I'm just not following you."

It's her turn to take a deep breath. "Tracey, when Jack's father and I separated last year, I had my diamond taken out of my engagement-ring setting, which I never really liked even though I was the one who picked it out—"

Oh...

Oh, wow.

Diamond. As in *rock.* The only kind of *stone* that really matters.

Diamond.

Do you believe this? Are you hearing this? Talk about a bombshell...

"—and I told Emily and Rachel that the first one of them to get married could have it."

Emily is Jack's younger sister; Rachel is the next one up from Jack. They have two more older sisters, Jeannie and Kathleen, who are both married.

"But both of the girls are positive that they'll want their own rings when they get engaged," Mrs. Candell goes on, "so I decided my diamond is there for Jack whenever he wants it. And...he wants it."

Well, slap my ass and call me Judy!

Better yet, slap my ass and call me "Mrs. Candell the Second!"

Tracey Candell.

It has a nice ring to it, doesn't it?

Speaking of rings...

"You're kidding," I manage to squeak to Mrs. Candell the First.

"No...I gave him the diamond before he left. But you can't tell him you know about it, Tracey."

"I won't. I swear." My hands are shaking. My heart is pounding.

"Really, I thought the two of you must have discussed this. I guess my son is more romantic than his father ever was," she adds with a brittle laugh.

I know that the Candells' marriage was never lovey-dovey, and Jack said it was always only a matter of time before they split up. The month after Emily graduated from college and moved to Manhattan, they separated. The divorce will be final next spring, and everybody seems relieved that it's almost over.

Still, sometimes I wonder if his parents' failed marriage has anything to do with Jack's reluctance to commit.

But right now, all I'm wondering is what cut Wilma's diamond is, and when Jack is going to give it to me, and how I could have missed the subtle signs that he had this up his sleeve. Because there must have been subtle signs. There always are.

Do you think his comment that Marriage is for the Asinine was a subtle sign?

Me neither.

"Anyway," Wilma is saying, "if Jack ever knew I'd let this slip to you—"

"I promise I won't tell him."

"Won't tell who what?"

Startled by the voice behind me, I turn to see Jack standing there: boxer shorts, bad breath, bedhead…

Yes. There he is. The man I love. The man who loves me.

The man who apparently has a stone concealed somewhere in this minuscule apartment and is trying to throw me off his trail with all this convincing talk about only the Asinine getting married.

"Who are you talking to?" he asks.

"Your mother," I admit, gazing adoringly at him, wondering how I ever could have thought I had to let him go. I didn't have to let him go to find out that he's mine. He always was. He always will be.

"*My* mother?" He frowns. "You're keeping secrets from me with my mother?"

"Secrets?"

"You just said you won't tell me something."

"Not you," I say as Wilma makes a warning noise in my ear. "We were talking about someone else."

"Who?" he asks dubiously.

"You mean whom," I amend, just to buy time.

He grits his teeth. "Whom are you talking about with my mother, Tracey?"

"Maybe it actually should have been 'who' when you phrase it that—"

"Tracey, come on! Who?"

"Your father."

Judging by Wilma's muffled groan, I'm guessing that wasn't a good choice. But it's too late now.

"Your mother said something not very nice about your father and she doesn't want me to tell him."

I wait for him to ask what she said, but he doesn't. He merely rolls his eyes and says, "What else is new? And since when do you and my father chat?"

True. I've only met the man twice.

"There's coffee," I say brightly, to distract him, and I point at the counter in our kitchenette.

Our Kitchenette. That's right. *Ours.* Forever.

"I'll be off the phone in a second. Unless you want to talk to your mother?"

"Not if she's on the warpath against my father again." Jack pads over to the coffeepot, yawning and stretching.

I feel gloriously giddy. I'm getting married. I'm getting married!

Just as soon as Jack asks me.

Which, I'm assuming, will be soon. Won't it? At least by tonight. Or tomorrow, at the latest.

Of course by tomorrow, I reassure myself, while making forced, self-conscious conversation with his mother for a few more minutes. Jack is listening in now, no doubt ready to pounce on anyone who dares slander his father's good name.

Before the weekend is out, Jack will pop the question, I'll accept, and it will be full steam ahead to the wedding.

I can hardly wait.

I wonder if it's too late to throw together something for three hundred guests, give or take, in October?

Part II

Sweetest Day, Beggar's Night

Previously on Lifestyles of the Poor and Single, Wilma Candell inadvertently—or not—revealed that her son, Jack, had a diamond and would be getting engaged any second.

Presumably to me.

That was over a month ago.

Hearing Jack's key in the lock, I quickly conceal the dog-eared October issue of *Modern Bride*—which I purchased back on Labor Day weekend an hour after Jack's mother spilled the beans—inside this week's *People* and stick it in the center of a towering stack of freebie magazines he'll never touch.

Here comes the groom, I think.

I think this with just a pinch of irony, considering that forty days and forty nights have passed since his mother told me that an engagement was imminent.

Actually, I think it with a dollop of irony and a side of frustration.

What's a girl to do when the man she loves is keeping proposal plans and diamonds all to himself?

All she can do is wait.

Wait, and secretly plan every detail of the wedding so that when The Question—and celebratory champagne corks, and engagement-photo flashbulbs—finally pop, she won't be waylaid by research on reception halls, caterers and honeymoon destinations.

"Hi, honey, I'm home," Jack quips, draping his coat over the nearest chair.

I watch him deposit his keys, wallet, sunglasses, Metrocard, umbrella, comb, handkerchief, a handful of change and a pack of Mentos on the table.

I swear he somehow carries more in his pockets than I do in my purse, which is bigger than this apartment.

"How was the meeting?" I ask him, tilting my head up as he bends to kiss me from behind the couch.

"It went great. She was happy with my plan."

He's talking about the client and a media plan, of course.

I wish he would talk about me and his proposal plan, but short of asking point-blank whether he has one, I have to be patient. As far as he knows, I still think we *might* be getting married in a few *years* and I'm just hunky-dory with that.

If it weren't for Wilma, I would probably be job hunting in Brookside right about now. Thank God her secret-keeping ability is directly converse to her son's.

"I brought you something," he says, and I get my hopes up.

"Here," he says, and hands me a plastic shopping bag that I can feel contains a smallish box, and I get my hopes up even further.

I know what you're thinking. You're thinking that nobody proposes by handing over a ring box in a plastic shopping bag.

Here's my thought: Jack isn't the most traditionally romantic guy in the world. I wouldn't put it past him to give me—

"A Chia Pet?" I say incredulously, pulling it out of the bag.

"I saw it and thought of you."

"Really."

It's a small gnome. A gnome that will presumably sprout a green Afro.

For a moment, all I can do is stare at it.

Then, knowing I might regret it, I ask, "Why did you think of me?"

"Because you were just talking about how gray and dreary and dead everything is now that summer is over," he says, and I can tell by his expression that he didn't think it was this lame a few seconds ago, before he opened his big fat unromantic mouth.

I'm trying to think of something nice to say to bail him out, but all I can come up with is, "Um, thanks."

"I just figured it would be nice to see something green and growing."

"It will be." A gnome with green, growing hair. How...nice.

"Sorry," he says. "I guess it was a stupid idea."

"No," I tell him, feeling sorry for the poor clod. "It was really...sweet."

I pretend to admire my Chia Pet. Then, when enough time seems to have passed, I put it on the table.

"All I want to do now," Jack says, sitting down beside me and taking off his shoes, "is put on sweats, order take-out pizza and watch the Mets get clobbered in their playoff game."

"Oops," I say.

"What?" He looks at me suspiciously. "Don't tell me the cable is out."

"No...but you're close."

"How close? Is the picture fuzzy?"

"No, Raphael is coming over to play Trivial Pursuit. We're making paella. He'll be here in fifteen minutes."

Jack has the courtesy not to groan at that news, but I can tell he wants to.

"How is that close to the cable being out?" he wants to know.

"You know...you can't get more 'out' than Raphael," I crack.

Jack clearly isn't the least bit amused.

It isn't that he doesn't like my friend Raphael, because everyone likes Raphael. Well, maybe not everyone.

Chances are, your average homophobic red-stater isn't going to appreciate a bawdy, wisecracking male fashionista. But in this little corner of the world, everyone—including Jack—likes Raphael.

That doesn't mean he prefers Pursuit and Paella to Pizza and Piazza. Still...

"You hate the Mets," I remind him.

"Right. And I want to witness them *die.*"

Is it my imagination, or is that hint of viciousness directed at me?

"Sorry," I say with a shrug. "But you can still watch the game. Raphael and I will be quiet."

He snorts at that. "Trace, Raphael isn't even quiet in his sleep."

He's right. We shared a room with him at Kate and Billy's Hamptons share in July and the air was fraught with deafening snores and anguished—or perhaps libidinous— shrieks. I probably should have thought to warn Jack that Raphael talks in his sleep. And that he sleeps in the nude.

"Well, lucky you, he isn't sleeping over tonight," I tell Jack.

"Yeah, lucky me. I'm going to change into my sweats."

"Sweats?"

"What's wrong with sweats?"

"Sweats are just too..."

"Too...what?" he asks. "Too comfortable? Too hetero? Too...?"

"Dumpy. I mean, come on, Jack, we're having company. And you know how Raphael is. He'll be dressed up."

"So you want me to dig out my feather boa and hot pants so he and I can be twins?"

I have to laugh. "No, just at least wear jeans, okay?"

"Is a sweatshirt out of the question?"

"Only if you were planning to wear the hooded one with the broken zipper and the bleach stain on the front."

I can tell by his expression that he was.

"What's wrong with that one?" he asks. "Too dumpy?"

"Too Unabomber."

He scowls.

"Don't be mad, Jack. Come on. Cheer up. Do you want to invite somebody over, too?" I ask in my best toddler-soothing voice, thinking maybe poor Jackie wants a play-date, too.

"Like who?"

"How about Mitch?"

Mitch is one of his college buddies who recently moved to Manhattan and doesn't know many people yet. I keep meaning to fix him up with one of my friends, because it's a sin to let a cute single guy go to waste in this town.

"I can't invite Mitch," says Jack, who needless to say doesn't share my views on cute single guys going to waste.

"Why not? He's probably sitting home alone."

"That's better than being pounced on by a horny queen who thinks every single guy in New York is secretly closeted."

"Horny queen?" I echo ominously. "That's really mean, Jack."

"It's also how Raphael described himself in the last personals ad he ran."

That's right. He did. And he meant it in a most complimentary way.

He got a ton of responses, too.

"Don't you remember what happened when you invited Raphael over the night Jeff was in town?" Jeff is an old frat brother of Jack's.

Feigning Alzheimer's, I ask, "No, what happened?"

"For starters, Raphael gave him a lap dance."

"Oh, yeah." I shrug. "I guess you won't be inviting anyone over tonight, then."

"I guess not. You're lucky I'm staying home at all."

I'm *lucky* he's staying home? Is it me, or should he be wearing a wife beater and belching down canned beer when he says something like that?

"I'm going to change," he says, planting a cozy little kiss on my nose, and I promptly decide to let him off the hook.

You can't really blame a guy for being a little cranky under the circumstances. In fact, how many straight live-in boyfriends would shave, and put on a nice polo shirt and clean jeans for a horny queen?

That's exactly what Jack does.

He emerges from the bathroom in a mist of air freshener just as I'm about to open the door for Raphael.

"Is that Lysol?" I ask, sniffing.

"Room spray. Gristedes was out of Lysol."

"Snoopy Sniffer is going to comment," I warn him.

Raphael's nose is even more discriminating about scents—good and bad—than he is about fashion.

Jack shrugs, and I open the door.

First, I should point out that with his Latin good looks, Raphael is a dead ringer for Ricky Martin. Rather, Ricky Martin is a dead ringer for Raphael because, as Raphael likes to say, he himself is still hotter than hot and Ricky is more over than pink tweed bouclé.

I should also point out that Raphael is dressed in red from

head to toe this fine evening. Red leather jacket, tight red T-shirt, tight red jeans, and—

"Are those red patent-leather *spats?*" I ask. *Ay carumba.*

"Yes!" Raphael shouts joyously, and strikes a toe-pointing pose. "Tracey, do you *love?*"

"Hmm…" I tilt my head. "I could *possibly* grow to love. Where did you get them?"

"Either I bought them off a folding table on the Bowery, or at JCPenney when I was in Missouri on business last year. I forget which."

"My money's on the Bowery," Jack says dryly, draping an arm over my shoulders.

"Mmm, I think it was Penney's," Raphael says decisively, and heads toward our kitchenette toting a couple of grocery bags.

"What did you bring?" I wriggle from Jack's embrace and follow him.

"Everything we need for paella, including rum."

"Rum goes into paella?"

"No, Tracey, the rum goes into *us.* We're making mojitos. Oh!" He smacks his head. "I forgot something at the spice market. I knew I would."

"What is it?" I ask, opening the narrow cupboard where we keep your basic salt, cinnamon and garlic powder. "Maybe we have it."

I have no idea *what* we have, since this has become mostly Jack's domain. It's not that I don't cook, or can't cook. It's just that ever since he cooked for me on one of our very significant first dates, it's become our little tradition.

"I need saffron," Raphael reveals. "Got any?"

I glance at Jack, who's lingering on the outskirts of the kitchen because three adults can't fit within the perimeter unless one of them is a waif.

"No saffron," Jack informs Raphael.

"Jack!" Did I mention Raphael's conversational style is

liberally sprinkled with exclamation points and people's first names? "Do you want to double-check? Maybe you have a smidge left somewhere."

"Nope. I haven't bought a smidge of saffron since... hmm, let me think—*ever.* Can your recipe do without?"

"It *can,* but...well, that's kind of like making marinara sauce without tomatoes," he says dramatically.

Moment of silence.

What to do, what to do...

Jack asks, "Would they have it at the Korean grocer?"

"Probably."

"Okay, then I'll go down to the corner and get some."

I shoot Jack my most grateful, loving look. The look I usually reserve for situations involving my family. Or sex.

"Jack!" Raphael screams joyfully. "*Ohmygodthatwouldbe-great!* But...are you sure it's not a problem?"

"Not at all." Jack is already grabbing his keys. "We're low on beer anyway."

"But, Jack, I'm making mojitos," Raphael protests.

"Will you be insulted if I just stick with a Budweiser?"

"Not at all. Will you be insulted if I tell you that I don't really like that cologne you're wearing? It smells a little fruity. Not in a good way."

"I'd be kind of insulted," Jack says, pulling on his coat. "Considering that I'm not wearing any cologne."

"Oops! Sorry. New coat?" Raphael immediately wants to know, buzzing over to Jack like a bee that just discovered a honey slick.

"No, I got it last winter."

"JCPenney, Jack?"

Jack looks insulted. "Barneys, Raphael."

"You're kidding! You know what? It would look really great in a nice tomato red. Or royal blue, with epaulets," Raphael pronounces, rubbing the placket between his thumb and forefinger.

"Right. Well, I'll be back soon with the saffron," Jack says, and manages to extract himself from Raphael's grasp.

"They call it mellow *ye*-llow…ba da, ba da…" Raphael sings, unloading his bags as Jack beats a hasty retreat. "Mellow *ye*-llow."

The minute the door closes behind Jack, he breaks off his ditty to say, "Tracey! I thought he'd never leave!"

"Raphael! Are you telling me you didn't really forget the saffron?"

"No. Well, yes," he admits. "I mean, I didn't *forget* it. I just kind of…you know, ran out of cash."

"What about your credit cards? Maxed out again? I thought you were going to keep the spending in control from now on."

"I splurged on something yesterday. Something big and juicy-licious…and no, it wasn't human so don't even go there."

I presume *there* is the male-escort service I talked Raphael out of patronizing one lonely night last spring when he was captivated by an ad for an escort who billed himself as Lengthy Louie.

"So what was your splurge?" I ask dutifully. "And how much cash did you spend?"

"Two hundred bucks."

"On shellfish and rice?"

He nods. "The saffron would have been forty dollars an ounce."

"Are you kidding? Where? Your dealer?"

"Tracey, you're funny," he says without cracking a smile. He begins unloading his groceries onto the counter. "No, I found it at the spice market."

"Why is it forty bucks?"

"Because, Tracey…" His eyes are round and he pauses significantly before saying in a near whisper, "It's like powdered *gold*."

"Really?"

Raphael shrugs. "Who knows?" He hands me a mesh bag filled with live clams and a red-and-white paper deli carton containing shrimp.

"This stuff was two hundred bucks?"

"Almost."

Raphael suddenly seems very interested in the line of grout between the countertop and the backsplash.

"Okay, spill it," I order. "What else did you buy on your way over? And I'm not talking about food."

He reaches into his pocket and guiltily produces a silk scarf. "I saw it in the window of that little boutique by my subway stop and I had to have it. It matches my eyes, Tracey, don't you think?"

"Your eyes are not plaid."

"Listen, I know what you're thinking—"

"That you've got some major—"

"*Cojones?*" he asks slyly. "So I've been told, many, many times."

"Um, Raphael, can we please leave your *cojones* out of this conversation?"

"Tracey, Jack won't mind getting the saffron for us. He can use some fresh air."

Before I can ask Raphael what makes him think that—or admit that it's probably true—he goes on, "And anyway, I was hoping we'd have a chance for some girl talk."

"About…?"

"About…you might want to sit down for this."

We both look around the kitchen, which consists of a sink, a stove, a fridge and a few inches of free counter space.

"Never mind sitting," Raphael says. "You can hear it standing up."

I lean against the fridge and fold my arms. "What is it?"

"What do you think of a proposal on Sweetest Day? Too provincial?"

"Do you know something that I don't?" I shout, grabbing hold of his shoulders and shaking him slightly.

"What do you mean?"

"Did Jack say something to you?"

"Jack?" He frowns.

"Jack. Tall guy, brown hair, basic-black leather jacket."

"Oh, him." Raphael gives a dismissive wave of his hand. "No, this isn't about that Wilma bling he supposedly has hidden for you."

"Oh." Disappointed, I loosen my grip and reach for the rum. "Then who's proposing on Sweetest Day?"

"Who do you think?"

I rack my brains. "Honestly, Raphael, I haven't a clue. Who?"

"Me!" he cries.

"*You?* To whom?"

"Tracey! Did you forget already?"

It appears that I have.

"Refresh my memory. Do you have a new boyfriend again?"

"Hello-o! Ye-ah!"

"Petrov?"

"We broke up ages ago!"

"Adam?"

"He was before Petrov."

"Then who?"

Raphael looks exasperated. "Donatello! Tracey, you so know him."

I so don't.

But this is how Raphael operates. He has this annoying habit of insisting that you are familiar—sometimes intimately so—with whoever or whatever he's talking about, when you know damn well that you wouldn't know him from Adam. Or Petrov.

"Donatello," he repeats. "Don't tell me that name doesn't ring a bell."

"The only Donatello that rings a bell is in my nephews' toy box. Isn't he a Teenage Mutant Ninja Turtle?"

"Tracey! Donatello is a full-grown, very normal, very juicy-licious human being."

Yes, normal and juicy-licious go hand in hand in Raphael's world.

I think I need a drink.

I reach into the cupboard for a couple of glasses as Raphael prods, "You met him last month when I took you out to lunch at Bacio on my expense account, remember?"

I rack my brains.

All I remember from that lunch is Raphael scolding me for not spending more time with him these days…

Oh, and the divine piece of pumpkin cheesecake that we shared for dessert, which I couldn't pass up once the waiter rolled it over on the trolley and went on and on about—

"Wait, you mean the waiter?" I ask incredulously.

"Yes! Tracey, I knew you'd remember."

"How could I forget? The way you were flirting with him right from the start—and the way he described that cheesecake…" I shudder at the waiter's risqué-in-retrospect description of velvety cream cheese melting on the warmth of the tongue. And here I thought he was talking to me. About dessert. "It was very…vivid."

"Wasn't it just?" Raphael looks dreamy.

A drink, I think. A drink, *and* a cigarette.

I take a fresh pack of Salems out of the cupboard and tap it against my palm.

"So what you're telling me is that you want to get engaged to the waiter from Bacio on Sweetest Day?"

"Absolutely, Tracey. Unless you think that's too cliché?"

"I wouldn't call it cliché in the least."

I pour a couple of inches of rum into a jelly glass and

wonder how to make a mojito, then decide I don't really care at this point.

"I was thinking we could schedule our commitment ceremony for Valentine's Day," Raphael goes on, oblivious to my imminent bender, "and I'd want you as my maid of honor, of course."

Touched, I look up from the cigarette I'm lighting to make sure that he's serious.

Judging by the tear glistening in the corner of his eye, he is.

"That would mean a lot to me," I tell him sincerely. "Thank you. I would be honored."

"And I'll be honored to return the favor someday, Tracey," he says, gently patting my arm as if assuring a maiden aunt that someday her prince will come.

"Jack *has* a diamond, Raphael." I exhale twin trails of smoke through my nostrils and try not to think about the Chia Pet.

"Of course he does."

"I'm serious! He has a diamond, and he's probably just waiting for…for, you know…"

"The right moment?"

"Yes, and for…um…"

"For the jeweler to make a setting?"

"Exactly."

"Speaking of settings, Tracey, what do you think of this?" Raphael pulls a black velvet box out of his pocket and flips it open. "It's my big splurge."

I'll say. I gape at the marquis-cut diamond engagement ring.

"It's beautiful, Raphael, but…" I search for a tactful way to put it. "I mean, isn't that for a woman?"

"Tracey! No!"

"I have to say…" I tilt my head dubiously. "I'm thinking yes."

"The jeweler said it's definitely unisex. And I say it's *uni-sexy*. I love it, and Donatello will love it, and that's all that counts."

Right. Next thing you know, Raphael will be checking out the bridal sample sale at Kleinfeld.

"So what do you think, Tracey? I'm getting married! I'm planning a glorious proposal and an even more glorious wedding!"

Et tu, Raphael? is what I think.

But I give him a congratulatory hug and I try not to be wistful as he talks about cakes and flowers and dance bands.

After all, my whole life doesn't hinge on when—or even *whether*—Jack pops the question. I am *not* one of those so-called New York career women whose secret main goal in life is a diamond ring on her finger and wedding date on the calendar.

Those women are pathetic.

I'm not pathetic. I'm…

Well, I've got a whole lot more going on in my life.

I've got great friends, a semifunctional family, and some-day I'll be promoted to junior copywriter.

But I can't help wondering, as I take another drag off my cigarette, what Jack is waiting for.

Is he uncertain?

Is he falling out of love?

Or maybe it's Sweetest Day.

Maybe he wants to do it on Sweetest Day.

That has to be it.

Chapter 5

"Sweetest Day? Never heard of it," Jack informs me.

We're headed home from work on the third Friday night in October—which, if all goes as planned, will be our rehearsal dinner a year from now—waiting in a rush-hour crowd on the uptown subway platform at Grand Central.

"Sure you have," I say as though he's just claimed he's never once wondered what it would be like to sleep with the *Sports Illustrated Swimsuit Issue* cover model.

"Sweetest Day?" He shakes his head. "I don't think so. What is it?"

"It's a day when you show your appreciation to loved ones," I recite, having looked it up on the Internet earlier so I'd be prepared for this conversation.

"Show appreciation how?"

"You know...cards...candy..." *Diamond engagement rings*...

NOT *Chia Pets*...

"Who invented it? Hallmark? Brach's?"

"Brach's?" I echo in disdain. At least he could have said Godiva.

"Yeah, you know…the candy guys."

"I know," I tell him—or rather, shout at him as the uptown express train comes roaring into the station on the opposite side of the platform. "Brach's. The candy guys."

I must say, this exchange isn't going quite the way I envisioned.

I was supposed to very casually ask Jack how we're going to celebrate Sweetest Day tomorrow, and he was supposed to get a knowing gleam in his eye and feign ignorance.

The ignorance is there all right, but it sure seems authentic, and the knowing gleam is as scarce as the number-six local.

I wait to make my point until the express train has left the station and the noise level has been reduced to the rumble of trains and screeching of brakes on distant tracks, an unintelligibly staticky public-address announcement upstairs, and—right here for our listening pleasure—an off-key portable-karaoke singer and her coin-cup-jangling pimplike male companion.

I ask, again, "How should we celebrate?"

I can tell Jack's thinking the question would work better if I left off the first word and made it a yes/no.

Should we celebrate?

His answer to that would probably be no.

His answer to *How should we celebrate* is merely, "Celebrate?"

Which is no answer. Unwilling to let him off the hook, I say, "Got any ideas?"

"We can watch Game One?"

"Game one?"

"The World Series. Tomorrow night."

"Oh. Right. I forgot," I tell the man who once came dangerously close to derailing our relationship by choosing a Giants playoff game over dinner with me.

He chose me in the nick of time.

He even cooked that dinner, the first of many.

Yet here he is, acting like a dopey dog that keeps trotting back to the electric fence line for another jolt.

Jack asks incredulously, "How could you forget about something like the World Series?"

Same way you can forget to propose when your mother has practically done all the work already, I want to tell him.

I say simply, "I don't know. But it's not like we don't have TiVo. Don't you think we could do something a little more romantic than watch the World Series, in real time, with commercials?"

He has the gall to look alarmed.

Okay, I give up.

"Romantic...like what?" he wants to know.

Time to let him off the hook. "Never mind," I say with a sigh.

After all, I owe him one for being so charitable to Raphael that night with the paella. He played three rounds of Trivial Pursuit and didn't even complain when Raphael kept cheating to avoid the Sports and Leisure questions and land instead on Arts and Entertainment.

Anyway, clearly, Jack isn't planning to propose on Sweetest Day, even now that I've enlightened him.

I'll have to shelve the story I was going to tell our future kids one day about how we got engaged in October, my favorite month of the year. I think it's safe to assume that the only remotely wedding-related thing anybody's asking me to be this month is maid of honor at a gay wedding.

I crane my neck to look for the light at the end of the tunnel.

I'm not speaking figuratively.

I'm looking for the actual light, as in the headlight of the number-six train.

All I want is to get home and take off these stockings

and two-inch heels. Lame, I know, but two inches are two too many for me.

"Hey, I know!" Jack says suddenly. "How about if we go out to dinner tonight? You know…to celebrate Sweetest Day."

"Tonight? You mean…go back out after we get home?"

Now *that,* my friends, is a revolutionary idea. When we first moved in together we came and went at all hours, but we've become proficient nesters lately. Most nights, once we're home, we're home—especially now that we have TiVo and even last-minute Blockbuster video rentals are a thing of the past. I know. Zzzzzzzzzzzzzzzzzzzzzzz.

"I was thinking we could stop somewhere now, on the way," he says with the air of one who plans to zip through a drive-through for a couple of Whoppers.

"I don't know…I'm kind of tired and I don't really want to hang around all night in this." I look down at my trench coat, crepe suit and pumps, which I donned for a client presentation with the futile hope that somebody might recognize me as executive material.

"We can go home first so you can change," Jack offers. "I wouldn't mind getting into some jeans myself."

Jeans?

Okay, who said anything about jeans?

Aren't we talking about a romantic Sweetest Day Eve dinner here?

Apparently, only one of us is. The other has apparently set his sights on the kind of establishment that offers a denim dress code and a tuna-melt special.

I yawn. It's a fake yawn when I start it, but it turns real before it's over.

"I don't think so," I tell Jack. "I'm really wiped out. It's been a rough week."

He's watching me with an oddly intent expression. The platform has grown so crowded with commuters that his face is about six inches from mine and he's looking right into my eyes, frowning slightly.

"Are you okay, Tracey?"

"What do you mean?"

"You just seem kind of…edgy."

I look around at the restless horde of uptown-bound office drones being serenaded by Karaoke Girl, who is now bellowing, "I've Been to Paradise But I've Never Been to Me."

"Who *isn't* edgy?" I ask. "There hasn't been a six train in almost ten minutes."

"No, not about the subway. About…well, I have no idea what. You just seem edgy lately. At home, too."

"I do?"

"You do."

I smile to show him that beneath edgy, things couldn't be more hunky-doodle-dory.

"It's work, I guess—it's getting to me," I tell him, because A) that's partly true, and B) when you're in the advertising industry you can believably blame everything on work. It's second only to PMS in my stress-related-excuse repertoire.

Looking as though he's had a mini-epiphany, Jack puts an arm around me and pulls me close, pressing his forehead against mine. "I know what you need."

So do I.

But Grand Central Station at rush hour is no place for him to go getting down on one knee. If the train shows up he might get trampled right onto the tracks, wiping out our future kids *and* the charming October-engagement story.

"What do I need, Jack?" I ask anyway, per chance we're not on the same page.

"A quiet night at home. We can watch that new Willie Wonka DVD I just bought in wide screen."

Willy Wonka? *That's* what I need? Is he *high?*

Granted, I liked the book and I liked the movie—both versions.

But…

Willy Wonka?

"I'll make that chicken thing you like," he goes on. "And then I'll give you a back rub. It'll get rid of all the stress."

"Oh." Big fake-smile. "That sounds great."

Don't get me wrong, I would ordinarily welcome a back rub after a tough week at work. And having skipped lunch today, I do find my mouth watering at the mere thought of that Chicken Thing. He makes it with tomatoes and peppers and olives and serves it over diet-friendly whole-grain pasta.

But when I weigh the options—engagement ring versus Willie Wonka/back rub/Chicken Thing—guess which one might as well be full of helium?

"Let's get strudel for dessert, too," he suggests.

"Now you're talking," I say, amazed at how the mere mention of strudel can make things brighter.

You've got to stop obsessing over this ring thing, I tell myself as the long-lost number-six train appears in the distance at last. *It's not healthy.*

But I can't seem to help it.

Especially when, in the sudden shuffle of the crowd to get into position precisely where the train's doors will ostensibly open, I spot a huge billboard of a smiling bride and groom beside the tag line *Married People Live Longer.*

Is this a sign, or what?

Okay, intellectually I know it's just part of that high-profile advertising campaign by some abstinence-advocacy group.

But emotionally, I choose to believe it's a sign that I'll be getting an engagement ring in the near future.

But…how near?

And why did his mother have to go and tell me it was coming?

How am I supposed to focus on anything else when

every random morning I wake up wondering if today's the day?

I'm starting to think it would be better if I didn't secretly know he has a diamond. That it would be better if I were back where I was the night Mike and Dianne got married, when I thought Jack thought marriage was only for Assholes. At least then, I had no expectations.

Then again…maybe he still thinks that. Maybe he just accepted the diamond to humor his mother. Maybe he has no intention of giving it to me in this millennium. Who knows? Maybe he's already traded it for an ounce of saffron and a six-pack.

The uptown local is packed, of course.

The reverse tug-of-war begins. A mass of people shove to get off; a mass of people shove to get on.

Yes, we are among the shovers.

Because in New York, you do things on a daily basis you wouldn't dream of doing anywhere else. At least, *I* wouldn't.

Back in Brookside, I wouldn't dream of shouldering my way through the crowded vestibule of Most Precious Mother to snag a primo pew, scattering little old church ladies with limbs akimbo.

But when in Rome—or the subway…

Well, you get the idea. I'm a seasoned Manhattanite after three years here, and I can shove and curse and even flip people off like a native, although only when absolutely necessary.

And only strangers.

When it comes to people I know, I can be oddly complacent in that regard. If only I'd had the nerve to shove, curse and flip off my ex-boyfriend, Will McCraw, before he had a chance to break my heart.

But I was still the old Tracey-sans-*cojones* back then.

As we shoehorn ourselves into the car, I am careful to align the front of my body with the side of Jack's to avoid accidental intercourse with the total stranger crammed in beside me.

"You okay?" Jack asks.

"Fine," I tell him, taking shallow breaths so as not to inhale fresh B.O. from a neighboring straphanger.

"We'll stop at the store on the way home to get the stuff for my chicken thing."

"All right." I feel like I'm going to gag. Does this person not know he's stinking up the whole car? Or does he not care?

"You don't seem very into it."

"I am!" I snap—then repeat sweetly and guiltily at his hurt look.

The train lurches, stalls.

Lurches, stalls.

Then it lurches again, just enough to pull beyond the platform and into the dark tunnel before there's a hiss as the engine dies and a flicker before the lights go with it.

A cry of protest goes up in the car as people curse in every known language.

"Still okay?" Jack asks in the dark, his voice reassuringly close to my ear. He reaches for my hand and squeezes it.

I take a deep breath of disgusting B.O. air. "Uh-huh."

If this were two years ago, when I was in the midst of my panic attacks after Will left, I would be about to throw up or pass out or both.

But the panic attacks subsided somewhere around the time Jack came along, with the help of some little pink pills that were prescribed for me by Dr. Trixie Schwartzenbaum. As a delightful pharmaceutical side effect, I lost my appetite and the remainder of the forty pounds I needed to take off.

I eventually tapered off the pills last winter with nary a panic attack nor added pounds, but Dr. Schwartzenbaum warned me that they could be triggered again.

The panic attacks.

The appetite too, I guess. But at least I can combat that with my old standby weapons: cabbage soup, baby carrots and brisk lunch-hour walks to Tribeca and back.

Fighting the panic attacks is a little more complicated. Sometimes I wonder what might set them off again.

Being trapped underground in a packed subway car in a dark tunnel could very well do it.

I try not to remember the old movie I once saw with my grandfather about a subway hijacking. *The Taking of Pelham 123*.

I squeeze Jack's hand, hard. He squeezes back.

See, that's the thing. I always know that he loves me, to the point where his mere presence is reassuring. Not just in this subway crisis (I know, but to *me* it's a crisis)—but in my life. That's why I want to know—*need* to know—that we'll be together forever.

Because I can't imagine my life ever feeling normal again without him.

Surely he feels the same way.

Surely he's ready to make that final commitment, wouldn't ya think?

The intercom interrupts my speculation, crackling loudly with a seemingly urgent announcement.

The only words I think I can make out clearly are "grapefruit," "Ricky Schroeder" and "explosive."

Or maybe I'm hearing them wrong.

"What did they say?" I ask Jack.

"Who knows?" he replies amid the disgruntled grumbling from similarly stumped commuters.

Okay, I might not have heard *grapefruit* or *Ricky Schroeder,* but I'm pretty sure I heard the word *explosive.*

I try not to think about terrorist attacks and suicide bombers.

Yeah, you know how that goes. Terrorist attacks and suicide bombers are now all I can think about.

In a matter of moments, I am convinced that this is no ordinary malfunction, but an Al Qaeda plot.

We're all going to die, right here, right now. And when we do, we won't even be able to slump to the ground because we're wedged against each other like hundreds of cocktail toothpicks in a full plastic container.

I try to shift my weight, but succeed only slightly.

Great. Now I'm going to die standing up with what I hope is somebody's umbrella poking into my leg. As opposed to a penis or a gun.

I try to shift my weight back in the opposite direction but that space has been filled. I can't move.

To add to the drama, from this spot, even in this dim light, I have a clear view of yet another *Married People Live Longer* ad.

Dammit!

I know it's not as if all the married people on board the train will be sheltered from harm in a golden beam from heaven while the rest of us losers die a terrible death, but...

Well, that stupid tag line isn't helping matters. Not at all.

Married People Live Longer.

It might as well have said: *Single People Die Young.*

My chest is getting tight and my forehead is breaking out into a cold sweat. This definitely feels like a panic attack.

Mental note: place emergency call to Dr. Trixie Schwartzenbaum ASAP.

I'm trapped. Oh, God, I can't even breathe. There's no air in here.

Yes there is. Stop that. There's plenty of air.

I inhale.

Exhale.

See? Plenty of stale, stinky air to go around.

"Come on!" shouts an angry voice in the dark.

"This is bullshit!" somebody else announces.

Another passenger throws in a colorful expletive for good measure.

Then a woman speaks up. "That's not helping."

"Shaddup!"

In no time, a train full of civilized commuters has transformed into a vocal, angry mob. If there were more room, fistfights would be breaking out.

"I can't breathe," I tell Jack.

"Yes, you can," he says calmly.

"No, I can't."

Verging on hysteria, I fantasize about shoving people aside and breaking a window.

Two things stop me. The first is that it's too crowded to get the leverage to shove anyone. The other is that I don't have a window-breaking weapon in my purse.

I guess I can always snatch the umbrella that's still pressed up against my leg. *If* it's an umbrella.

If it's not…

Well, you definitely don't want to grab a stranger's penis in a situation like this.

Then again, if it turns out to be a gun and not a penis, I can always shoot my way out.

Then *again,* if it's a gun, its owner might shoot me.

The thing is, if it's a gun, there's a distinct possibility that any second now, he might go berserk and start shooting. Things like that happen all the time.

Oh, God. I really can't breathe.

"Jack," I say in a shrill whisper, "I'm scared."

"Why? It's fine. We're fine."

See, the thing is, that's easy for him to say. He doesn't know about the freak with the gun.

"I'm really scared, Jack."

"Of what?"

"You know…" Conscious that the fifty or so people standing within arm's length might be eavesdropping, I whisper, "Death."

"Relax. You're not going to *die.*"

"How do you know?"

"Because—well, why would you think you're going to die?" he asks, loudly enough to be heard in Brooklyn.

Terrific. If the guy with the gun/umbrella/penis didn't think of opening fire yet, Jack just gave him the idea.

"I don't," I snap. "I don't think I'm going to die."

"But you just said—"

"I was joking." Before I can muster a requisite laugh, the lights go back on and the engine whirs to life.

The train starts moving again as if none of this ever happened.

Problem over, just like that.

Panic attack averted.

At least for now.

"See?" Jack says. "I told you you'd survive."

"We're not home yet," I point out. "It's not survival until we're safe at home."

"Isn't that a little extreme?"

"Maybe," I say with a shrug. Actually, I've been in a permanent shrug since we got on the train, thanks to the close quarters. "I just really want to get home."

Jack just looks at me for a second, then says, "You really *are* stressed."

"I really am stressed."

And you're the cause of it.

All right, so he had nothing to do with the stalled subway.

But I do find myself thinking life's minor—and major—disruptions would be much easier to handle if we were engaged.

Then I find myself thinking, in sheer disgust, that I really am one of those marriage-obsessed women after all.

I'm Kate, when she was hell-bent on marrying Billy. All she ever wanted to do was speculate on the status of their marital future, ad nauseam. Raphael and I thought she was our worst nightmare then. Little did we know she'd be even scarier once she had the ring on her finger and a formal Southern wedding to plan.

Now here I am, my own worst nightmare.

How did this happen?

As the train hurtles toward uptown, I tell myself firmly that it *didn't* happen—yet—and it *won't* happen. I will not focus my energy on an engagement that may or may not be imminent.

If Jack wants to marry me, great.

If not…

Well, not great. But not the end of the world, either.

Mental note: time to stop dwelling on getting engaged.

This wanna-be-fiancée stuff is getting old. I need to toss my secret stash of bridal magazines and stop asking everyone—except Jack—why he hasn't proposed yet.

Not that I'm going to ask Jack, either.

I'll have more patience than…well, more patience than I had with Will, for whom I waited an entire summer.

In vain, I might add.

Chapter 6

Speaking of Will, guess who calls me at work the Monday morning after the Sweetest Day when I don't get engaged?

Yes, Will McCraw, the man—and I use the term loosely—who left for summer stock and never came back. To *me,* that is. He did return to New York that fall, and he brought with him a souvenir—a blonde named Esme Spencer, with whom he said he had more in common than he did with me. Meaning, she was also a self-absorbed drama queen.

I do not use *"queen"* loosely, despite the fact that I am apparently the only person in the tristate area who believes in Will's heterosexuality.

I should know, right? I slept with him for three years and can attest that not every good-looking, cologne-and-couture-wearing, narcissistic actor is gay.

Then again, Will secretly being gay could make his lack of interest in me easier to bear. Not that I'm still pining away for him in the least. But when you're as insecure as I used to be—and all right, still am in some ways—then you don't easily get over not being desired by your own boy-friend.

Nevertheless, I truly ninety-nine-point-nine percent be-lieve that what Will McCraw *is,* aside from a self-absorbed drama queen and a cheating bastard, is a flaming *metro*sex-ual.

What Tracey Spadolini is, according to said flaming met-rosexual, is sadly bourgeois.

You wanted somebody who would love you and marry you and settle down with you.

That was Will's breakup accusation, and in his opinion, the ultimate insult. It was also true then and still is, only now I'm not ashamed of it.

My breakup accusation was, "You kept me around be-cause I was as crazy about you as you are about yourself."

Also true, and a long time in coming.

How I didn't realize that from the start is beyond me. I guess I was so beyond insecure, so obsessed with being forty pounds overweight and a small-town hick masquerading as a city girl, that I was grateful just to have a boyfriend.

When I think of how I lapped up the slightest attention from Will like melting chocolate ice cream on a ninety-degree day…

Well, it makes me sicker than the ice cream would if it sat out in the sun for an entire ninety-degree day before I ate it.

Will dumped Esme, as all my friends predicted he would, and came crawling back, as all my friends predicted he would, right around the time I met Jack.

Maybe even *because* I met Jack, since Will certainly wasn't interested in me when I was whiling away a solitary New York summer with only cabbage soup and *Gulliver's Trav-els* for company.

Fortunately, I was never the least bit tempted to hook up with Will again.

All right, maybe I *was* tempted just *once.* The night Jack almost chose the Giants playoff game over me, I almost made a huge mistake.

But he didn't choose the game, and I didn't choose Will, and Jack and I are living happily ever after—more or less—while Will the Flaming Metrosexual is still trying to become the next Mandy Patinkin.

He calls often to update me on his progress.

This morning, in response to my fake-jovial "Will! How the hell are you?" he jumps right in with, "Tracey, guess what?"

Will is not the kind of person who requires much conversational feedback, so I don't bother to guess. In fact, I don't bother to stop checking my Monday-morning e-mail, which is what I was doing when the phone rang.

"I've got an audition."

Yawn.

"And it's not stage this time. It's for a film," he adds quickly lest I erroneously assume it's for a stool-softener commercial.

"That's great, Will." So he's given up on becoming the next Mandy Patinkin in favor of becoming the next Johnny Depp. Yeah, that'll happen.

I reach for my cigarettes before remembering that I can't smoke here. Damn. I clutch the pack anyway, planning to make a beeline for an elevator to the street the second I'm done listening to Will spout gems like, "Trust me, Tracey— this role is so *me.*"

"I trust you." So there's obviously an open casting call for a self-absorbed drama queen cheating bastard flaming *met-rosexual?* Talk about typecasting.

"I'm going to blow them away, Trace."

Trace, he calls me, because we're just that cozy.

"That's awesome," I say in a tone that might hint that *awesome* semi-rhymes with *ho-hum.*

"I know!" he exclaims, too caught up in this revolutionary moment in the Life of Will to catch any hint of hohumness on my part. "If I don't get this, I'll be shocked."

"So will I," I say blandly, scanning an e-mailed chain letter on the off chance that forwarding it to five hundred people in the next minute will shrink Will's ego to the size of his—

"It's a romantic lead," he tells me. "That's my thing."

Yeah, not in my life.

"The only thing that could really put a lock on the role for me would be if it involved singing."

"No singing?"

"No, but I've got the acting skills to carry it, you know?"

Naturally, he waits for me to confirm his well-rounded fabulousness. "Yeah, I know," I say unenthusiastically.

"Fifi told me just Thursday that I'm at the top of my game."

He's talking about Fifi La Bouche, an eccentric Parisian choreographer friend of his. She's about eighty and still looks great in a leotard. I know this because that's what she's wearing every time I've ever met her. She wears it everywhere, to lunch, to shop, to stroll—just a leotard under a trench coat, as if at any moment she might be asked to put together a jazzy chorus-line routine.

"That's great," I murmur, finding it hard to believe that I was ever an avid player in the Life of Will, starring Will, directed by Will, produced by Will.

"What film are you auditioning for?" I ask, because apparently it's still my turn.

Dramatic pause. "It's actually really hush-hush. I can't really say."

Okay, ten to one that means he's auditioning for the role of Pizza Deliveryman or Crowd Spectator #4 in one of those Lifetime trauma-of-the-week movies, or something of that ilk.

"Well, good luck," I tell him, methodically deleting spam without bothering to muffle the mouse clicks. "I hope you get it."

"I've got a good feeling about it," says Will, who has a good feeling about everything he's ever done, is now doing, or will someday do. On camera, onstage, in the bedroom, even in the bathroom, because I'm certain Will honestly believes that when he takes a shit white doves fly down from heaven to bear it ceremoniously away.

There was a time when I almost believed that, too.

Thank God, thank God, thank *God* he dumped me.

If he hadn't, would I have found the common sense to dump him?

Or would I still be his girlfriend?

Or, God forbid, his *wife?*

I'll tell you this: I'd definitely rather be *not* engaged to Jack than *married* to Will.

The irony is that just a few years ago, I had this whole vision of our future mapped out, oblivious to the fact that all Will had mapped out was the fastest route to the bright lights of North Mannfield's Valley Playhouse.

When he left New York and then failed to call or write, then cheated, then ultimately dumped me, I had no idea he was doing me the biggest favor of my life.

Which just goes to show you...

Well, I'm not sure exactly what it goes to show *you,* but it showed me that I wasn't always the best judge of character back then.

I am now, of course.

And I'm definitely as over Will as I am My Little Pony, jelly bracelets and slumber parties.

As Will talks on about his latest audition and the hush-hush movie that he can't discuss but it has some major stars and a famous director and if I knew I would just die, I click on through my e-mail, deleting most of it.

Until I get to the most recent one, from my friend Buckley, which just popped up.

"…and they said I absolutely have the look," Will says, *"and that I…"*

With Will, you barely even have to offer an occasional uh-huh to keep the conversation going, so I can to focus all my attention on Buckley's message.

Hey, Trace, writes Buckley, with whom I *am* just that cozy.

Well, maybe not *that* cozy.

Although I'll confess that I wonder occasionally whether Buckley and I might have had a chance together if the timing had been different.

I was attracted to him from the moment we met—and it was mutual. He immediately asked me out to the movies, which was why I logically assumed he must be gay.

I know, but there I was, on the verge of losing Will, overweight and underconfident, certain that no guy as cute and normal as Buckley would possibly want to date me.

By the time I figured things out, he was with Sonja. If he hadn't met her, and I hadn't met Jack, I might be living with Buckley now and wondering why we aren't engaged.

Funny, the way things work out. Or not.

Buckley and I did attempt a fling once.

It was post-Will, and post-meeting but pre-loving Jack. Oh, and mid-Sonja, although she doesn't know. They were temporarily broken up at the time. Buckley and I fell into each other's arms while crying into too many beers one night at a pool hall.

At long last, I discovered the answer to that burning question: *What is it like to make out with cute, boy-next-door-ish Buckley?*

Answer key: hot.

I also quickly discovered—as did Buckley—that we made better friends than lovers.

Not that we ever got *that* far. Lovers, I mean. A couple of passionate kisses—*searing* kisses, mind you—was the extent of our almost affair.

Then Buckley moved on and in with Sonja and I moved on and in with Jack and here we all are, defiant sin-livers, the last of a dying breed.

"...so then I went and changed into a pair of jeans," Will is saying, *"and that cashmere sweater that everyone says matches my eyes..."*

So Buckley and I are destined to be friends who double-date and read the same books and are aspiring copywriters.

Well, *I'm* aspiring.

Buckley is already a copywriter, lucky dog. He free-lances all over the city and whenever he's working near Blair Barnett, we have lunch.

Which is why he's e-mailing me today:

Hey, Trace, are you free for sushi at one? My treat. I'll meet you on the corner of Forty-eighth and Second.

Yes! Lunch with Buckley is just what I need to take my mind off the most unromantic Sweetest Day ever, which Jack and I spent watching Game One of the World Series.

The Yankees were losing from the first pitch, at which moment Jack's euphoria instantly transformed into despondency. By the time Raphael called at what he thought might be "halftime" to inform me that he and Donatello were officially engaged, the Yankees were down by fourteen and Jack was downright miserable.

In the wake of Raphael's phone call, so was I.

Not that I wasn't happy for the happy groom-and-groom-to-be, because I was. And still am.

But Jack's reaction was less than encouraging.

I waited until the commercial break to announce the glad nuptial tidings.

Jack said, "You're kidding, right?"

"Not at all."

"That's crazy."

"Why? Just because it's not legal?"

"That too, but—"

"Just because it's Raphael?"

"That too," he agreed again, "but—"

Because it's crazy to get married, period?

Was that it? I thought it was. I was waiting for him to say it. Before he could—if indeed he was about to—the game came back on, and the Yankees lost spectacularly. End of conversation. All conversation.

The team somehow blew it again last night, and Jack was still glowering when I left him by the elevator a little while ago.

Some weekend. I've never welcomed a Monday morning as wholeheartedly as I did this one.

Hi Buckley! Lunch sounds great, I type jauntily. See you then and there.

It's been a few weeks since I've even seen him. He's been working way downtown on a long-term project since late September. But it must be over, because—yay!—he's back in midtown.

"...and I just gave it everything I had..."

I believe Will is recapping a recent cabaret performance.

"And then somebody requested 'Empty Chairs at Empty Tables...'"

That, or his latest catering gig.

"You know, from Les Mis..."

Oh. Cabaret performance. I should have known. Will likes to pretend he's a full-time actor. Rarely, if ever, does he freely acknowledge that the line he's rehearsed most often in his career is "chicken or steak?"

Toying with my cigarettes, I tune him out again and wonder whether Buckley will be able to shed some male perspective on my situation with Jack.

Then again, as a fellow altarphobic male, Buckley might not be *that* insightful. Nor sympathetic. After all, he's spent the last couple of years evading his girlfriend's frequent ultimatums.

Every time another Sonja-imposed deadline passes without the desired marriage proposal from Buckley, I somehow still expect her to carry out her threat and move out. But she never does. They just go back to living together until the next hysterical fight that results in the next hysterical ultimatum.

It kind of reminds me of my soon-to-be-divorced sister Mary Beth's ineffective single-parenting style. Only instead of a marriage-shy grown man, Mary Beth is dealing with an almost five-year-old who still has potty-training issues.

If you ask me, both Mary Beth and Sonja are wasting their time with ultimatums. And not just because Sonja never follows through by moving out and Mary Beth never follows through by taking away Nino's Game Boy Advance.

"...and I told them of course I can do that, and more," Will drones on. *"And do you know what they said?"*

My nephew's potty-training problem is clearly a psychological response to his parents' messy divorce. Buckley's unwillingness to commit is clearly a psychological response to his father's untimely and tragic death.

You know, sometimes I think I could really give Dr. Trixie Schwartzenbaum a run for her money.

"Tracey?"

Yes, obviously, both Nino and Buckley have control issues.

So what would Dr. Trixie Schwartzenbaum advise?

I have no idea, but the esteemed Dr. Tracey Spadolini would definitely advise both subjects to either shit or get off the pot.

Will breaks into my brilliant psychoanalysis with an exasperated "Tracey! Are you even listening?"

To your monologue on why you deserve to be a great big beautiful star? Trust me, Will, I know it by heart.

I really should say that.

But I don't.

I say, "You know what? I have to go. My, um, boss needs me to do something right away."

There's a pause.

Then a curt "Oh."

Will is obviously miffed that I have work to do while at work. Imagine that.

"Well, call me back when you have time and I'll finish telling you."

"Yeah, okay."

Why don't I just tell him to fuck off? Is that what you're wondering?

Yeah. I'm wondering that too.

I guess it's because there's a part of me that almost enjoys these calls from Will, in a twisted sort of way. It's somewhat—I don't know...*empowering?*

Yes, empowering. That's how it feels for me to maintain this connection—which is maintained, might I add, with zero effort on my part.

I never do the calling; it's always him. And he calls pretty frequently—every few weeks, at least.

Every time we speak, I'm reminded of just what a loser he is and what a winner Jack is and how far I've come since the summer I spent pining away for Will.

Today, however, I can't help thinking as I hang up the phone that I also still have a long way to go.

Yes, I'm in a healthy relationship now…but I want to share more with Jack than a toothbrush holder and a monthly Con Ed bill.

Yes, I have a stable job…but I was aiming to be a copy-writer, not a glorified secretary for someone who was fired a few months ago yet still comes to work every day.

Yes, I've broken a destructive addiction to food and maintained a healthy weight for a couple of years…but I'm still hopelessly addicted to cigarettes.

I drop the pack onto my desk and stare at it, wondering whether I can actually—

"Tracey? Got a minute?"

Wow. Mike has poked his head into my cubicle like a genie who's been summoned in the puff of a white lie to Will.

"Sure. How's it going, Mike?"

And why are you still here?

When he returned from his two-week honeymoon, Carol ever so gently reminded him that he needs to start looking for another position elsewhere. You know, call me crazy, but I'm not convinced he got the message.

Neither was Carol, because she reportedly mentioned it again in so many words before she left on vacation.

I really think she needs to use just two words: *"Leave now."*

But until she says that, I suspect Mike will continue to show up every day in his little suit and tie to do—well, what seems like busywork to me.

What else can he possibly be doing? His client interaction with McMurray-White and his corporate credit card have been cut off, he is no longer invited to meetings, and he never receives phone calls from anyone other than the Fembot he married.

"Can you edit something for me, please?" he asks pleasantly, because he's just the nicest boss ever. Which is most likely why he didn't make it in this business.

That, and the fact that he makes Jessica Simpson look like an intellectual.

"Sure, Mike." I wait for him to hand over his résumé, thinking it's about time he asked me to whip that baby into shape. I'm so ready to roll up my sleeves and dig in.

But he doesn't hand over his résumé. He gives me a draft of some lame memo about something totally unrelated to the fact that he's supposed to be looking for a new job.

"Thanks, chief. No rush on that. Tomorrow's fine," he says, optimistic as Annie.

Tomorrow?

Doesn't he realize that as soon as Carol gets back from her trip to Cabo San Lucas—which she's expected to do *today*—she's going to flat out fire him?

At least, that's what her secretary told Brenda last week.

With any luck, I'll be out to lunch with Buckley when she gets around to giving Mike the ax.

Poor sap. Look at him, lingering in my doorway…

Almost as if he wants to chat.

I mask my pity with a tentative raised-eyebrow, closed-lipped smile.

He returns it wholeheartedly.

Until I ask, "So…how's married life?"

Exit wholehearted smile.

I think he actually winces as he says, "Married life? It's great."

Yeah, he's about as convincing as Will McCraw would be, playing an NFL linebacker.

"Did you get your wedding pictures back yet?"

"No, but I'll bring them in when I do."

Let's just cross our fingers and hope that's sometime this morning, shall we?

Aloud I say, "I can't wait to see them. Jack and I had a great time…"

…*when we weren't drinking ourselves blind to avoid dealing*

*with a silently stewing partner, or silently stewing over a partner
who was drinking himself blind.*

"So when are you guys going to take the big plunge?"
Mike wants to know.

"You'll have to ask Jack," I say lightly.

At least, I have every intention of saying it lightly, but it
comes out sounding like a guttural Gestapo command.

It's a wonder Mike doesn't salute as he responds, "I'll do
that—if I ever see him around. I never do anymore."

"Yeah, well…he's been pretty busy. And I'm sure you
have too."

"Nah, things are pretty quiet around here."

Yes, you idiot, because you've been fired for over a month.

"Oh, I didn't mean around the office," I say. "I meant at
home." I'm all *wink-wink-you-cunning-little-newlywed you.*

Ew. Somebody stop me.

"I haven't really been all that busy there, either."

I can't say I blame you.

He sighs heavily.

Woe is Mike.

I really feel so sorry for him, married to the diabolic Dianne *and* on the cusp of joblessness.

He's…well, he's kind of like…

Me.

Not *now.*

He's like the *me* I used to be in the bad old days, valiantly
plugging away at a doomed relationship with Will.

In fact, now that I think about it, the parallel is astonish-
ing.

Especially when you take into consideration that Will
lacking the *cojones* to just break up with me before he left
for summer stock is to Carol lacking the *cojones* to kick Mike
out of here on his ass.

But she won't do it because Mike is—well, *pathetic*, and
Will wouldn't do it because I was…

Was I *ever* this pathetic?

Tell me the truth.

Oh, God.

I was, wasn't I?

But not anymore.

Not…most of the time, anyway.

Look at how I turned my life around that summer. Look at all the weight I lost and all the confidence I gained.

About my looks, anyway.

But what about everything else? All the things that you could make better in your life if you could just find some initiative?

Okay.

That does it.

Starting right here, right now, I'm going to banish every last wishy-washy instinct, starting with…

I abruptly grab my pack of Salems and toss it into the trash can.

Mike blinks. "Hey, chief…what's up with that?"

"I just quit," I inform him, feeling better about myself already. Wait till Jack hears.

Fancy spa in Providence, here I come.

"You quit smoking?" Mike asks, his face riddled with confusion.

Duh.

"Yup."

"You mean just *now?*" he asks, sharp as a tack.

"Just now."

"Was it something I said?"

No, it was something you are.

All I tell him is, "Because it was time."

"Well…hey, good for you. Good luck."

"Thanks," I say, gazing wistfully at my wastebasket and thinking I'm going to need it.

Chapter 7

As soon as we're seated at a table for two at Sushi Lucy's, our third all-time favorite lunch spot after El Rio Grande and Harglo's, Buckley asks, "So what's new?"

I'm talking the very *moment* we're seated, before napkins are settled on laps and menus are open in hand.

He seems awfully eager for an answer, leaning expectantly across the table as if he's holding a lottery ticket with four winning numbers so far.

What's new? What is he expecting me to tell him? Obviously, something big. But what?

That I've just quit smoking?

Not unless he's psychic. Nobody but Mike witnessed that momentous turning point, and he ominously vanished into Carol's office immediately afterward.

He hasn't been seen since, which I assume means Carol located her *cojones* in Cabo.

I did call Jack's voice mail to leave a message that my longtime love affair with cigarettes is over, lest I grow tempted to fall off the wagon before nightfall. Jack will be all over me if I don't follow through.

But Jack couldn't have spoken to Buckley, because he's been at a client presentation since ten. So Buckley doesn't know about the smoking.

Hmm. Something is definitely afoot. His greenish-brown eyes are so filled with eager anticipation that it's almost as if...

He knows something.

That's it! He's obviously spoken to Jack—not today, but recently—about our getting engaged and he's wondering if it happened yet.

Maybe Jack told Buckley he was planning to give me the ring for Sweetest Day.

So why didn't he?

Maybe he changed his plans when I brought it up on the subway platform because he wanted it to be a total surprise.

"*Should* something be new?" I ask Buckley coyly, my heart rate picking up a bit.

"New with me?"

Puzzled, I say, "No. With *me.*"

Isn't that what we were talking about? Me?

Apparently not.

Buckley looks clueless.

About me, anyway...

Oh, I get it. Sort of. I think.

It seems that we might actually be talking about *him.* That something might possibly be new with *him.*

Yes, that's it, I conclude, watching the cute Japanese waiter fill our water glasses, then our cute Japanese teacups. That wasn't really eager anticipation I thought I saw in Buckley's eyes just now. At least, it wasn't eager anticipation for my non-news.

It was pre-enthusiasm for the news he's going to tell me

as soon as I confirm that nothing's new with me, because unlike Will, Buckley feels obliged to at least feign an interest in his fellow man.

Granted, most of the time Buckley's interest is genuine.

But today, he's clearly merely waiting for me to tell him that nothing is new with me—which I quickly do—and to ask what's new with him.

Which I am about to do, but before I can finish sipping my water and speak up, he says, "Tracey, I have great news."

See? What did I tell you?

What am I doing wasting away my life in an advertising agency when I could give both Dr. Trixie Schwartzenbaum *and* Psychic Suzanna a run for their money?

Hmm…what can his news be?

Still holding my water glass, I gaze into it as if it's a crystal ball, channeling my astral guides or whatever it is that Psychic Suzanna does.

Oh! I know! I'll bet he landed that freelance gig he thought fell through at *Sports Illustrated*…

That, or he just scored Yankee tickets for Game Three.

Or…

"Sonja and I are getting married!"

Thud.

All right, I didn't really fall to the floor. That was my water glass, plunking back onto the tablecloth.

But I might fall to the floor any second now. I am just that stunned.

I am also thinking I'd better keep my day job because Psychic Suzanna, I'm not.

Unless, of course, Buckley's kidding.

"You're kidding," I tell him.

"No," he argues affably. "I'm not kidding!"

"You're really getting married?"

He nods, grinning.

Buckley's getting married.

Buckley's getting married…and he's happy about it?

Clearly, while channeling my astral guides, I inadvertently stumbled into some alternate universe. The next thing you know, I'll be back at the office finding out that Mike just got promoted.

"Aren't you going to congratulate me?" Buckley is asking, beaming.

"Yes! *Ohmygoshyes!*" I leap out of my chair and scurry the two feet around the table to throw my arms around him. "Congratulations! *I'msohappyforyouIcan'tbelieveit!*"

Buckley hugs me back, apparently believing me. "Thanks. I'm really happy, too."

Reluctant to believe *him,* I pull away slightly so that I can assess his expression.

Yep. He's really happy, all right. Reeeeally, really happy.

"This *is* great news!" I tell him, just in case he thinks I'm, oh, bitterly resentful or something.

Because I'm so not.

I'm genuinely happy for my good friend Buckley. Super-de-duper happy.

I also happen to be just a wee bit selfishly sad for myself. I can't help it.

But I'm not going to rain on Buckley's parade. Nosirree. I'm going to march back to my seat and…and order a bottle of champagne.

Do they *have* champagne in Japanese restaurants?

They must.

So, yes, I'm going to order some super-de-duper Japanese champagne.

I will then toast Buckley's rosy future with Sonja.

After which, I will proceed to get piss drunk.

As I return to my chair to get the ball rolling, I realize that other diners are glancing in our direction. I guess I was a little fake-overexuberant.

Move along, folks, nothing to see here.

Nothing but the last single twenty-something female in New York City.

All right, maybe I'm exaggerating slightly, but can you blame me? Does it not suddenly seem as though everyone and their gay lover is headed down the aisle?

"What made you change your mind?" I ask Buckley, and come off sounding like Detective Lily Rush interrogating a perp.

Oops. I really need that champagne. I look around for Cute Japanese Waiter. He's in a tête-à-tête with Cute Japanese Waitress. Probably proposing to her, I think grimly, waving my arms to capture their attention.

"Well," Buckley says as the Cute Japanese Waitstaff ignores me and everyone in a two-table radius stares, "Sonja's really been wanting to get married for a while…"

No, ya *think?*

"…and I realized that if I don't step up to the plate, I'm going to lose her."

"So it was her ultimatum that finally got you."

"I guess."

He *guesses?*

Does he really think he might have stepped up to the plate of his own accord?

Then again…

How does that old adage go?

You can lead a horse to the plate but you cannot make him step up to it? Something like that.

God, I need a drink.

And a cigarette.

Too bad Sushi Lucy, like every other restaurant in New York, is a nonsmoking establishment.

And too bad you *are a newly minted nonsmoker, remember?*

Yeah, screw that.

As God is my witness, I'm lighting up the moment we're back out on the street. Forget the spa in Providence. I can't

be expected to handle all this marital bliss on an empty nicotine tank.

"When I looked at my future," Buckley is saying, "I
couldn't really imagine what it would be like without
Sonja."

He should have asked me. I could have pointed out that
there would be no shrill ultimatums, ticking timers, loom-
ing-deadline threats.

What's going to happen when Sonja decides she's ready
for a baby? Will she threaten to leave him if she doesn't have
a bun in the oven by a week from Tuesday? Will she stand
over him with a turkey baster and porn so he can ante up
sperm, sperm, more sperm?

"I asked myself what I was waiting for," Buckley goes on,
"and I couldn't really answer that question. Sonja was always asking why I didn't step up to the plate. Did I think
somebody better was going to come along? Somebody
who would take better care of me than she does? Somebody with whom I have more in common?"

I bite my tongue to keep from pointing out that he and
I are the only ones we know who would use a phrase like
that. *"Somebody with whom…"*

Most people would erroneously say, *"Somebody who I
have more in common with."*

Because they aren't copywriters and aspiring copywriters like us.

But I don't point that out, because I don't want Buckley
to think there's someone now present who doth protest the
joining of this man and that woman in holy matrimony.

I shall not speak now. I shall forever hold my peace.

While holding my peace, I just happen to be secretly
thinking there might be others with whom Buckley has
more in common than he does Sonja, that's all.

"Sonja told me to take a step back and look at the big
picture…" He trails off, shaking his head with a knowing

expression. "And she was right. Because I did, and that was when I knew it was time to—"

"Step up to the plate?" I supply. Not snidely, I swear.

But step up, step back, step up—I can't help noting that Sonja is choreographing more steps these days than Fifi La Bouche.

"Right. I realized it was time to step up to the plate, and that's what I did."

"Good for you," I tell Buckley in a first-grade-teacher voice, as if it was all his very own gold-star idea.

Then I am compelled to ask, "So when did you propose? Sweetest Day?"

"No, halfway through Game Two last night."

"You asked Sonja to marry you in the middle of watching the World Series?"

He nods. "It was totally spur of the moment. You know how she's not really a Yankees fan?"

Yup, I know. She's from Boston and was spawned by a long line of Satan worshipers—I mean, Red Sox devotees. We're talking her family has box seats at Fenway and threw a catered party for three hundred people after the 2004 series. Buckley refused to attend, which nearly led to yet another breakup.

Now here he is, impulsively pledging his troth to a Beantown babe—and in the middle of a Yankees World Series, no less?

"So what happened, Buckley?" I ask, barely managing to swallow the *to you* I wanted to insert between *happened* and *Buckley.*

"I don't know. It was the craziest thing. The Yankees were getting killed. Absolutely annihilated, you know?"

"I know."

"When Jeter missed that pop fly in the fifth inning, I was devastated. Then I looked over at Sonja, and she was crying. Actually crying."

"Did she get hurt or something?" I ask, not following.

"No, she was crying about the game. For my sake."

"She was faking tears?"

"No, the tears were real. She was caught up in rooting for the Yankees because I was caught up in it."

"Oh," I say like I'm convinced, but I still bet she stubbed her toe when he wasn't looking.

Don't get me wrong. I like Sonja. She's always been nice to me, which shows she hasn't got a clue that I have, at various times since we met, secretly lusted after her boyfriend.

Looking across the table at Buckley, picturing him in a tux on an altar vowing to cherish another woman until death do them part, I wonder whether I'm still a little bit in love with him after all.

Is that why I'm so jealous of Sonja?

Do I wish *I* were marrying Buckley?

"Ready to order?"

Saved by Cute Japanese Waiter, who isn't all that cute close up. But then, who is?

Buckley is, that's who.

Jack, too, but he's not marrying another woman. He's not even marrying me.

Therein lies the problem.

The one that can only be solved with liquor.

Placing the soul-search temporarily on hold, I ask Japanese Waiter about getting some champagne.

"You want saki?" is the disconcerting response.

Did I *say* I wanted saki?

"No," I respond succinctly, "I'd like a bottle of champagne."

"No champagne." He shakes his head with Soup Nazi vehemence.

Does he mean they don't serve champagne? Or simply that he doesn't want me to have any?

Before I can pursue it, Buckley butts in to say, "That's

okay, Tracey. I drank half a bottle of White Star last night with Sonja and it gave me a headache."

Sonja again. It's always Sonja with him now that he's engaged. Sonja, Sonja, Sonja. It's sickening. It really is.

"Plus," Buckley goes on, "I've got a lot of work to do this afternoon. I'll stick with water and tea."

That's fine for him, but I order a double bourbon. Straight up.

And the sashimi deluxe with white rice, not healthy brown, a Philadelphia hand roll with extra cream cheese, a side of edamame, and both the miso soup *and* the green salad with ginger dressing.

"Hungry?" Buckley asks dryly as the waiter leaves.

Depressed is more like it.

Am I in love with Buckley?

I think about our history.

Then I think about Jack, and *our* history.

Jack, who doesn't seem convinced that he is capable of loving, honoring and cherishing me until death do us part.

Still…

Jack, who spent an hour and forty dollars combing the Upper East Side for saffron when he could have been parked in front of the playoff game ignoring me and my flamboyant pal.

If that isn't love, what is?

You need to take this relationship with Jack one step at a time, I think, embracing my inner Sonja and Fifi La Bouche. *You need to stop worrying about what everybody else is doing and what you and Jack aren't doing.*

You need to take control of the things that are within your reach for now…

Like the smoking.

I'm ready to quit.

I really am. In fact…

I already did.

An hour down, seventy-some years to go. How hard can it be?

Hey, maybe I can use it as leverage! Maybe I can tell Jack that I'll agree to quit smoking before I leave to spend Thanksgiving in Brookside (I can't smoke in my parents' house anyway) if he'll agree to propose before then.

Nah. That would be an ultimatum, and despite having embraced my inner Sonja mere moments ago, I don't do ultimatums.

If Jack doesn't propose of his own accord, then I don't want him to propose at all.

Okay, not really.

I don't care whose idea it is...

All I want is for Jack to propose.

Chapter 8

I am all cozy on the couch with Jack on the blustery night before Halloween, watching the newest installment in the latest *Apprentice/Survivor/Big Brother/Amazing Race* hybrid, which we TiVo'd last night.

Do you know how challenging it is not to accidentally find out which contestant got booted off this week before you have a chance to watch something? I swear, it's more stressful than account management at Blair Barnett.

Speaking of which, I was forced to stick my fingers in my ears and run away from two *"Can you believe what happened last night on...?"* watercooler conversations this morning at work. Whatever it was must have been big. To play it safe, I avoided the television section of today's *Post,* and I didn't dare open my AOL sign-on screen because I was afraid it would be right there, photo and all, like it was when I accidentally missed a *Bachelor* episode back when it was on and anyone cared.

Anyway, my clever spoiler-avoidance plan worked. Jack and I still have no idea who gets booted or what drama ensues, and we're closing in on the final fifteen minutes. I am on pins and needles, trying my hardest not to eat the entire bowl of candy corn I set out earlier.

It's here because I spotted it in a big display of cellophane bags full of trick-or-treat candy in the drugstore while I was picking up the Nicorette my doctor prescribed, and how can you resist something when they shove it in your face like that?

Okay, I'll admit that the candy wasn't *exactly* right there on the pharmacy counter. But it was close by.

Okay, not *that* close by.

Okay! Okay! I had to wander up and down the aisles in search of it.

Are you happy now? Jeesh. Can't a person indulge their newly discovered sweet tooth without being made to feel all guilty about it?

I used to be more of a chips'n'dip gal myself. But suddenly, candy is calling my name wherever I go. Sour Gummies, M&Ms, Jujubes, nonpareils—anything I can munch like popcorn while pretending it's better than cigarettes. Which is like pretending a church-choir concert is better than U2 live at Madison Square Garden.

Let me tell you, nothing is better than cigarettes. Not sex (although sex with my fantasy boyfriend Bono might come close); not reclaiming your sense of smell, which you hadn't really noticed was missing until now; sure as hell not Jujubes.

True, Jujubes can't kill you. Not that I've heard, anyway. Yet.

Back when my grandmother started smoking, nobody thought cigarettes were deadly, either. For all we know, the surgeon general might one day see fit to place skull-and-crossbone warnings on Jujubes.

What does that prove, you ask?

I have no idea, other than that I resent quitting smoking. Even though it started out as my idea.

Now it's more Jack's idea. If it weren't for him, I'd have at least cheated, or maybe even started up again before now.

So I suppose I should be grateful to him for helping me kick a deadly habit.

But really, I just want to kick him.

Especially when he clears his throat for the gazillionth time tonight.

"I've got a tickle," he informs me for the gazillionth time tonight, too busy fast-forwarding through the commercial to catch the lethal look I give him.

I shake my head and look away, and my gaze falls on the Chia Pet on a nearby table. The seeds I grudgingly spread over its disgusting scalp As Directed have yet to sprout the promised tiny green seedlings. Every time I see the ugly, defective little gnome, I want to hurtle it out the window.

In case you haven't noticed, my nerves are a little fried. If I could just have a smoke everything would be great, but I can't, so I'm clenched and bitchy and Jack's goddamned tickle and all this who-gets-booted tension isn't helping.

Nor is the tasteless Nicorette I'm chewing while chain-eating candy corn. In fact, the Nicorette tastes better when I chew the corn-syrupy-sweet morsels right into it, although the texture is getting slimier and crumblier by the minute.

I really think smoking is infinitely more appealing, death sentence and all. But Jack is sitting right here like a gestapo guard and I promised him I'd quit and it's been over a week and all I have to do is make it through tonight and then if I really want a cigarette I can sneak one tomorrow.

I jab another couple of candy corn in my mouth. Earlier, I started out eating my way through the bowl one piece at a time, in the usual method: nibbling off the white tip of the triangle, then trying to bite off the orange middle section as evenly as possible along the dividing line with the yellow base so as not to get any yellow with it and not to leave any orange on the yellow, and finally, eating the yellow.

That's *my* usual method, anyway.

But tonight, I keep inhaling the whole triangle at once. Rather, a *couple* of triangles at once. I can't help it. I need to keep my mouth busy so that I won't smoke. Or say something stupid. Because not smoking makes everything and everyone get on my nerves.

Including Jack.

Especially poor Jack, because he's the only one here.

Do you think he has any idea that if he clears his throat one more time and mentions that Goddamned tickle, I'm going to smother him with a throw pillow until he stops flailing?

Mental Note: L.W.C.[1] sucks. Don't ever quit smoking again. Jack presses a button on the remote and the show comes back on, but the cheesy host, Ed, whose teeth are blindingly white as all reality hosts' teeth must be, and who speaks without verbs as all reality hosts must, is in mid-sentence and the players have begun a new stunt leading up to this show's equivalent to the boardroom/tribal council/mostdramaticroseceremonyever.

"Can you back it up?" I ask Jack, irritated. If he'd let me handle the remote this wouldn't be happening but no, he thinks the remote is all his and it pisses me off.

"What?" he asks.

"Can you back it up?" I ask through gritted teeth.

"Why?"

"Because we missed what Ed said."

"We didn't miss anything. Maybe like two words," he goes on, effectively drowning out everything that's being said even now.

"Back it up," I say again. Then add a grudging, "Please."

[1] Life Without Cigarettes. Duh.

He seems like he's about to protest again, God help both of us, but then he obviously thinks better of it and points the remote to back up the scene.

Only it's still not far enough—he gets Ed in midsentence again.

"Jack!" I shriek in dismay, just as the phone rings.

He promptly presses a button on the remote, freezes the picture and looks at me. "Should I get it?"

Is he asking my permission, or does he mean do I want to get it instead of him, or does he mean are we going to let it go into voice mail? What is he doing? What does he want from me?

God, I'm so stressed out!

"I don't care," I snap, *"whatever."*

He picks up the phone.

It's his mother, my beloved and perhaps deluded Wilma. Maybe she's so into having me for a daughter-in-law that she convinced herself it's actually going to happen. Poor thing.

But at least someone is crazy about me.

And, perhaps, just plain crazy.

As I listen to Jack's monotone *Yups* and *Nopes* for a minute and wonder why when he talks to her the conversation is entirely one-sided. Is it because I'm here listening? Is he effusive when I'm not here?

I doubt it. I mean, he's not effusive when he's talking to me on the phone, either. I bet our conversations sound pretty much the same way on his end. *Yup, nope, nope, yup.* Strictly taking care of business, especially now that we live together and see each other all the time.

"No, not yet," he says as I reach into the candy bowl.

I wonder if she's asked him whether we've had any trick-or-treaters for Beggar's Night yet. Beggar's Night, where I grew up, anyway. Around here, though, the night before Halloween is apparently called Gate Night. I have no idea what that means. Beggar's Night is more fitting, don't you think? Not that I'm going to get into that again with Jack. We almost had a huge screaming fight over it a little while ago.

Ironic, since it's a moot point in Manhattan. At least, in our building. We don't even get trick-or-treaters on Halloween.

"But I will," Jack is saying into the phone.

Pause.

Perusing my handful of candy corn, I discard a mutant one that's missing its white tip. If I'm going to eat this stuff, it's going to have white tips intact, dammit.

"I don't know when, Mom. Soon… As soon as I have a chance."

Pause.

I eat the candy in my hand, bored, wanting to get on with the show and see who gets the boot.

I bet it's Didi, the annoying female bartender from Wichita.

Or Heidi Jane, the single mom from Los Angeles. I hope it's her. I feel sorry for her little kids, left behind with some random relative while mommy and her enormously fake boobs go off in search of reality-TV stardom. Give me a break.

"I know, I will. I promise… No, she's right here… Yes."

At that, it's all I can do not to leap off the couch, grab him around the neck and demand to know what he's talking about.

Because it's obviously about me. I can tell by his tone, the way he lowers his voice when he says, "No, she's right here," and his voice goes up for emphasis on the first part of *here.*

Okay, this is exciting.

My inner TiVo instantly rewinds everything Jack just said. No, not yet… But I will… I don't know when. Soon…

As soon as I have a chance… I know, I will. I promise…
No, she's right here… Yes.

He is *so* talking about getting engaged!

I mean, what else can it be?

Especially when he says in obvious and irritated resignation, "Yes, I'll ask her tonight, okay?… Yes, I'm serious….
Because I don't want you to keep bugging me, that's
why…yes, I'll let you know right away…. I know…. I will.
Okay? Goodbye."

He hangs up.

I flash him one of those big Snoopy smiles. If I were a
cartoon, a glint would be pinging off my front tooth.

"So?" I ask.

"That was my mother." He tosses the phone aside and
picks up the remote again.

"How was she?"

"She's fine." He backs up the scene again, blip by blip, in
obvious effort not to miss a word Ed is saying this time.

That's odd.

Did he or did he not just promise his mother he'd propose tonight?

I know! He did!

Which in and of itself is bizarre enough, because don't
you think he'd have decided when and where to do it on
his own? As opposed to spontaneously agreeing because his
mom is imposing a deadline?

Then again, who am I to argue with any logic that will
have a ring on my finger and a wedding in the works before midnight?

"There you go," Jack says, and presses Play.

He presses Play.

I guess he's waiting until after the show so that I won't
be distracted.

Okay, fair enough.

I did say earlier that I would be really pissed if, say, there were a terrorist attack before I got to find out who got booted off that caused such a watercooler stir.

But I wouldn't be pissed if I got engaged before I found out. I guess I should have clarified that to Jack.

Too late now.

He's all *and now back to our regularly scheduled programming,* watching television as though he hasn't a care in the world. Good old calm, laid-back Jack.

Ed, the host, is talking, but I'm not hearing a word he's saying. I'm thinking that I'll always remember that I got engaged wearing these pink sweatpants with the bleach stain on the hip, and a mouthful of soggy Nicorette.

Didi the Wichita bartender gets voted off.

When Ed breaks the news, she kicks him in the *cojones* before storming off the set.

Okay, so that's what all the hype was about.

Me, I barely notice. I'm busy trying to remember if the just-in-case bottle of champagne I stashed in the vegetable bin in the refrigerator a month ago is dry or sweet, because after all that candy corn I definitely can't stomach sweet.

"That was great," I say, stretching. "Why don't we turn it off."

"The TV?" he asks, looking shocked. "Don't you want to see the scenes?"

I always want to see the scenes. He'll be suspicious if I say no.

"Yes," I say a little shrilly, "of course I want to see the scenes."

We sit through the scenes. Next week's episode seems to revolve around Heidi Jane and her tremendous boobage having a series of bouncy adventures in an exotic locale as other contestants scowl and plot to get rid of her behind her undoubtedly aching back.

"Isn't that a repeat?" Jack asks.

"No, it said 'all new.'"

"I was being funny."

"Oh." I snicker. Sort of. "So how was your mom?"

"Fine…remember? You just asked?"

"Oh! Right. I did. Sorry."

Ask me to marry you, dammit!

It is *so* Beggar's Night. At least right here, right now.

I try to calm myself down, lest I accidentally wrap my hands around Jack's neck and start shaking him.

Out of sheer love, of course.

"Listen…" He shifts his weight on the couch. "I need to talk to you about something."

"What is it?" I ask, managing to sound calm, wondering if he's going to get down on his knee.

Here it comes!

OhmyGodOhmyGodOhmyGod!!

This is so exciting! Can you stand it?

Me neither!

Then—hey, wait a minute!—I wonder why he isn't going into the bedroom or something first, to get the ring. Does he have it stashed right here by the couch?

I give the vicinity a quick once-over for a telltale ring box that might have been under my nose all along.

Is it in the philodendron saucer?

No-o.

The messy stack of newspapers and magazines, mostly his?

No-o.

The nearly empty bowl of candy corn, mostly mine?

No-o.

I swear I feel like I'm mentally reading *Where's Spot?*, which was my nephew Nino's favorite book when he was a baby.

Where are you, Spot?

Where are you, sparkling diamond engagement ring?

"First, it was my mother's idea," he says. "Not mine."

Okay, is this the most unromantic proposal preamble in the history of proposals, or what?

"Not that I don't want you to say yes, but…I wasn't sure how you'd feel about it and I don't want you to feel obligated. I was going to wait to ask but my mother's really impatient… She'd ask you herself, but I told her I wanted to."

I'm stunned into dismayed silence.

She'd ask me herself?

Major Oedipal issues, anyone?

Good Lord.

How could I not have noticed until now how unhealthy his relationship with his mother really is?

"Tracey, would you possibly consider…"

His proposal is drowned out by the roar of disbelieving anguish in my brain.

This isn't his idea! This is his mother's idea! Look at him! He doesn't look like a man in love! He looks like a man who ate bad shrimp for lunch!

"What?" I ask dully, shaking my head to clear it.

He repeats the proposal…

Which isn't a proposal!

He's not proposing to me!

Hallelujah!

Make that semi-hallelujah.

I mean, I *want* him to propose…but not like this.

What a relief that this isn't the big moment after all!

What this is, in fact, is an invitation to spend Thanksgiving with Jack's family in Westchester.

The reason it's such a big deal is that I have never *not* gone home to Brookside for Thanksgiving.

In a family where you're excommunicated for forgetting an octogenarian's birthday, you can just imagine the reaction if you skip a major holiday.

That hasn't even been an option for me…

Until now.

But is it, really? My parents would be crushed. My siblings would be pissed. And my grandmother…well, if she hasn't already written me out of her will for moving away, I think it's safe to say this would clinch my not getting her bone china settings for eight and a cut of her passbook savings.

Then again…I'm all grown up.

I have a life of my own now. In New York.

A life with Jack.

Wouldn't it be more natural to spend Thanksgiving with him than with my family, since Jack's the person I share my daily life with now?

There are two ways of looking at that.

One is that Jack's the person I share my daily life with now, meaning I see him daily…so shouldn't I share special occasions like Thanksgiving with the family I rarely get to see?

The other view is that Jack's the person I share my daily life with now, so why would I leave him for special occasions?

"I bought my plane ticket back in July when JetBlue had that sale," I point out, trying to sort through my inner turmoil.

"JetBlue is great. They'll give you a credit if you don't use it."

JetBlue *is* great. But still…

"My parents would freak out."

"I know. That's why I never asked you in the first place. But my mother really wants you there since she's doing the cooking this year. She wants it to be special."

Last year, Thanksgiving was a nonissue, since Jack spent it with his newly separated father. His sisters were off with their in-laws or boyfriends and Wilma was on a cruise with some fellow soon-to-be divorcées. Jack and his dad went to a restaurant, I went home to Brookside, and alternatives were never discussed.

When I made my plans for this year, I *did* ask Jack to come along, but he said he couldn't because his mother was having Thanksgiving at her new condo, and he'd promised her he'd come. It never occurred to me to offer to stay here with him…which I guess it wouldn't, not having been invited.

Until now.

"I don't know…"

"You don't have to say yes," Jack says, reaching over and squeezing my hand. He's so cute. So sweet and earnest and worried because he's met my family and knows how suffocating they can be. I love him so much.

Nothing matters, I realize with a warm gush of emotion, but that.

"Hey," I say, "yes."

"Yes?"

"Yes. I'd love to spend Thanksgiving with you."

"You would?" He breaks out into a grin. "I'm so happy! My mother is going to be so happy!"

"I'm happy, too!" I say, and we hug.

We're happy.

We're happy, we're peppy, we're bursting with love, and it's all so warm and fuzzy that I could just cry.

Wow. I mean, the best moments in life are warm and fuzzy. Nothing beats warm and fuzzy…

Mental note: mold is warm and fuzzy.

Which reminds me…

"Where's the phone?" I ask Jack. "I have to call my mother and tell her."

Why, you may ask, does mold remind me of my mother? I have no idea.

Crocheted afghans, onions and garlic frying in olive oil, vinyl purses, Jean Naté…all those things remind me of my mother.

But mold?

Well, it isn't personal. But a reminder is a reminder, and I tell Jack that I really should call her.

"Do you want me to wait to call my mother until after you call yours?" he asks, handing me the phone.

"Why?"

"Just in case…you know."

"In case my mommy says no, Tracey isn't allowed to have a Thanksgiving playdate at Jackie's house?"

"Well…yeah." He grins.

"I'm a big girl. I'm calling to *tell* her, remember? Not *ask* her."

"Okay. Go for it."

I realize he wants me to call with him sitting right here, listening.

Well, okay. I have nothing to hide.

I dial the number.

Maybe she's not home, I think hopefully.

If she isn't, then I can tell my father, who never hears a word I say because his hearing is going and because he says I talk like an auctioneer.

So, yeah, I'll tell him, and he won't hear, so they won't realize I'm not coming until right before Thanksgiving, in which case I can put off the inevitable maternal explosive reaction for almost another month, by which time I'll either be merrily smoking again or accustomed to L.W.C.

There's only one problem with that plan.

My mother is one of those people who is always, always home. Usually cooking for a crowd, at that. I don't think I've ever called and she's not there. I mean ever.

It's not like she's a recluse or anything, but she's hardly Sally Social Life, either. Not out of the house, anyway. In the house, she's a regular domestic diva.

The only day she leaves for any length of time is Sunday, which is when she goes to morning mass and then on to various relatives' houses for various meals. I know not to call her on Sundays.

I also know not to call on Wednesday mornings, because that's when she goes grocery shopping and gets her hair "done"—she has that old-ladyish kind of hair that I guess you don't "do" yourself with shampoo and a blow-dryer because she's had a standing appointment at Shear Magique every week for as long as I can remember.

Speaking of which, you'd think the Shear Magique people would tactfully suggest that she get her lip "done" too, while they're at it, but maybe they're only about cutting, washing and teasing hair, not removing it with hot wax.

Anyway, I fully expect my mother to be home when I call on this blustery Beggars' Night, and I'm not disappointed.

Rather, I *am* disappointed…because she's home.

Not home would have been so much easier.

"Mom!" I say, as if I'm pleasantly surprised to hear her voice. "How are you? What's new?"

She blows her nose loudly in reply, probably on a tissue she had tucked up her sweater sleeve, then says unnecessarily, "I've got your father's lousy cold."

"Dad's sick?"

"So ab I." She coughs, lest I doubt her.

"That's too bad," I say, and it really is.

For her and for me, because my mother in perfect health isn't going to react well to the news I've got to tell her. My mother with a nasty cold finding out that her youngest child—her "baby"—won't be home for the third most important holiday of the year (after Saint Joseph's Day and Christmas)…well, just imagining her reaction is enough to send clammy chills down my spine.

You know what? I don't think I feel like telling her tonight.

She coughs again.

"Okay," I say cheerfully, "so, I'll let you go…"

Jack looks at me like I'm crazy.

Through her overflowing adenoids, my mother says to me like I'm crazy, "What? You're goig to let be go? You just called be!"

"I know, but…shouldn't you be resting or something?"

"Be?"

"Be resting," I repeat slowly, thinking her ear canals must be clogged, too.

"Be rest?"

"Be rest*ing*," I enunciate, as one might with a person who is practically deaf. Or a clueless moron.

Okay, that was mean.

I know it isn't my mother's fault she can't hear, or that she took so much cold medicine it's left her mentally impaired for perhaps the rest of her life, or at least the rest of this conversation.

I'm just so not equipped to deal with mother-daughter tension at the moment. Necessary equipment being cigs, of course. A cigarette would make all this pesky frustration evaporate. I just know it.

"Doe!" my mother says cryptically, sounding as impatient as I.

I don't think we're talking about a deer, a female deer, here.

"Mom, I'm sorry, I'm having trouble hearing you. Can you just…speak up or something?"

She shouts, "I *said,* doe, I heard that part. I beadt, be, rest? Sidce whed do I have tibe to rest?"

Welcome to the UN and my own personal mental interpreter, who after a few moments manages to translate the gibberish into: *I said, 'no, I heard that part. I meant, me, rest? Since when do I have time to rest?'*

Silly me. I forgot. How can one rest when there are undoubtedly endless sheets to be ironed and abundant brica-brac to be dusted; countless pots to be stirred and dozens upon dozens of cannoli to be stuffed?

"Ma," I say, shaking my head, "the world won't come to an end if you take a break and lie down for a while. You have to take better care of yourself."

"Sabe to you, skiddy middy."

Translation: same to you, skinny minny.

She's been calling me that for months, ever since she saw me in a bathing suit at a family picnic and was horrified.

Get this: she thinks I'm wasting away, all skin and bones.

That's because she dwells in a utopic oblivion where anyone under a size fourteen is force-fed fettucine. A size eight—which I have been for two years now—practically warrants an Alfredo I.V.

"I do take care of myself. And anyway, I'm not the one who's got a lousy cold, Ma," I point out.

She sneezes as if to punctuate that remark.

"God bless you," I say sympathetically. "God, you're so sick."

"No, Daddy's the wud who's really sick. He's already id bed."

Yeah, well, that isn't unusual. My father turns in about nine every night, at which point he's already been snoring in front of the television, on and off, for a couple of hours.

Why is it that middle-aged people either need excessive sleep, or none at all?

I look at Jack and try to picture him with gray hair and corduroy slippers.

No can do.

Grow old along with me...the best is yet to be...

Yeah, I used to think that was true.

At least, to a certain extent.

But I'm starting to think that it might be all downhill after, say, thirty.

Look at my parents. I've known them since they were

about thirty, and I can't ever remember them being happy and peppy and bursting with love.

I mean, they're still married, but they're so boring and tired and sick…not all the time, but they're sick now, and I'm finding all of this infinitely depressing.

If Jack doesn't propose to me soon, we're going to miss all the good stuff and go straight to old and tired and sick. Because as far as I'm concerned, the only time *the best is yet to be* is…well, now.

Which means I should probably be enjoying every minute of it, ring or no ring, instead of wishing my life away.

I'm going to enjoy Thanksgiving. With Jack. Ring or no ring.

"Ma," I say, determined not to let her distract me again from the business at hand, "I need to talk to you about Thanksgiving."

"Oh, Thadksgiving. Cad you pick up a couple of cads of those chi chi beads Joey likes? Because I cad't fide theb adywhere."

Chi chi beans?

I can't be sure about some of what she said, but I know that I definitely heard chi chi beans.

I know I said I wasn't going to let her distract me, but…

What the hell is she talking about?

"Ma…what chi chi beans? And…pick them up where?"

"The wuds that cub id the cad with the red ad greed label. They bust have theb id Little Italy."

"You want me to go to Little Italy, buy cans of chi chi beans with red and green labels, and then fly them to Buffalo on the plane?" I ask, just to be sure I have this straight.

I really think somebody put crack in her Comtrex.

Jack is snickering.

I would be, too, if she wasn't *my* mother.

She affirms my question with a resolute "Yes," as though her request is the most logical thing in the world.

"Ma," I say with remarkable patience for one who is in the throes of nicotine withdrawal, "the thing is…I can't do that."

"Why dot?"

Why dot?

Oh, so many reasons why dot, starting with the one about canned chi chi beans not being allowed in carry-on luggage due to post 9–11 airline-safety regulations.

Okay, I made that up.

For all I know, canned chi chi beans are indeed allowed on commercial aircraft.

Or would be, if anybody in their right mind ever found it necessary to officially establish that particular rule.

FAA guy: Okay, George, we've covered your basic guns and knives, your box cutters, your cigarette lighters, your chi chi beans… yup, I'd say we're good to go.

"Ma," I say, deciding to cite only the most important reason I will not be toting chi chi beans to Buffalo on JetBlue, "I can't get the beans for you because I'm not going to be able to come home this year for Thanksgiving."

I know. I can't help it. I wimped out. I stuck in "able to" at the last minute to make the whole thing seem more…I don't know, involuntary.

Why did I do that?

I look at Jack to see if he caught it.

He's frowning a little.

I guess he caught it.

"What? Why? Tracey!" My mother is freaking out in my ear.

Give me a break, I think ferociously at Jack. *I don't see you on the phone telling your mother you'll have to dash her holiday hopes this year.*

Yeah.

Why don't I insist Jack come with me to Brookside for Thanksgiving? Huh?

Because I don't want to go to Brookside for Thanksgiving, that's why.

I didn't before, and I especially don't now that I know it would involve smuggling legume contraband through JFK.

God, I need a cigarette.

If I can get through this without one, I swear I can get through anything.

"Is it work?" my mother asks. "Is that why you cad't cub hobe?"

"No, it's not work, Ma. It's…"

"You're pregdadt."

It takes me a second to decipher that one.

When I do, I'm incredulous. "I am not pregnant."

Jack shoots me a look.

I shrug at him—then clench my teeth when he clears his throat and whispers something to himself—or maybe to me—about that tickle.

I ask my mother, "But if I *were* pregnant, which, again, *I am not*—what would that have to do with my not coming home for Thanksgiving?"

"You dough…to hide it frub us."

"Do you think I'd actually go sneaking around hiding a pregnancy from you guys?" I ask needlessly, because yes, she clearly does think that. "If I were pregnant—which *I am not*—I would tell you."

To which she says, "Well, I woudd't wadt to dough."

See what I mean about my mother? She's impossible.

"Well, I'm not pregnant, and I don't have to work, and the reason I can't come home—" I glance at Jack and amend, "The reason I'm not coming home, is that I'm spending Thanksgiving here this year."

There. How hard was that?

Excruciating, actually. And it isn't over yet.

"Alode?" my mother wants to know, and her voice is on the verge of breaking.

"No, not alone. With Jack."

"Two people? What kide of holiday is that?"

In the Spadolini family, you see, holidays are all about the head count.

I swear my grandmother approaches Christmas Eve as though her eat-in kitchen were a tiny car and the rest of us are clowns she's determined to cram into it. The more— well, not the merrier, but the more people you serve, the more you get to cook in advance, and complain about it afterward for extra credit.

I debate telling my mother flat out that I will not only be spending Thanksgiving away from my own family, but I will be spending it with somebody else's.

But I honestly don't think I am physically capable of doing that without a cigarette, so I let her think whatever she wants to think. She usually does, anyway.

Finally, and only when she's in tears and inconsolable, I get to hang up.

I look at Jack.

"Bad, huh?" he asks, rubbing my shoulders.

With a brittle laugh, I ask, "What makes you think that?"

"Are you okay, Trace?"

"I'm fine," I lie, trying not to squirm out of his grasp.

It's not that I'm unhappy with my decision, or him.

It's just that I'm wondering if I should be inflicting maternal torture to spend Thanksgiving dinner with a man who isn't entirely committed to spending the rest of his life with me.

Not that one is a prerequisite to the other…

Unless…

Hey, maybe he's going to pop the question on Thanksgiving Day?

Is that what he's been planning?

If it was, then he didn't do a very good job of it, considering that he let me buy a plane ticket to Buffalo and it was his mother, and not him, who put the wheels into motion to get me out of it.

Well, now that I'm all set to spend the holiday with him, maybe he'll realize Thanksgiving would be a perfect time to engage me.

If not sooner.

"So…" I snuggle into his arms after all. "Thanksgiving. Our first one together."

With any luck, the first of many.

"Yeah," Jack says contentedly, leaning his cheek against my head. "It'll be great. I'll call my mother and tell her. Or do you want to do that?"

"No, you tell her," I say, too drained to speak. Even to my beloved future mother-in-law Wilma.

I sink back into the couch cushions and listen to Jack's brief conversation with her. Maybe I should have spoken to her myself, because there is nothing the least bit satisfying about, "Hey, Mom, she's coming…yeah…yeah…no…I will…okay…yeah…bye."

"What did she say?" I ask when he hangs up wearing a satisfied grin.

"She wanted to know if you can bring the chi chi beans."

"What?!"

He cracks up.

I swat him with a pillow.

Then I laugh, too.

And then Jack, whom I love for so many reasons, but especially this one, kisses all the tension and frustration away.

Part III

Thanksgiving

Chapter 9

Ask not for whom the wedding bell tolls, folks...because it sure as hell isn't me.

Nearly four weeks have passed since the whole world got engaged, Mike got fired at last, my Chia Pet refused to sprout and I quit smoking.

Four excruciating, tobacco-free weeks. I may be no closer to a promotion, much less white lace and promises, but I'm definitely closing in on pink lung and Providence.

In fact, that's why my friend Kate and I have embarked on this Sunday-morning excursion to Bloomingdale's. I need some darling—Kate's favorite all-purpose shopping adjective—spa clothes for the Rhode Island trip Jack promised me next weekend. We leave Friday morning, after we spend Thanksgiving at his mother's house on Thursday.

Well, darling spa clothes are why *I'm* here.

Kate is here because a rumor is circulating among Up-scale Young Manhattan Housewives that Bloomingdale's is hosting a pre-holiday Brow Event today.

Yes, a *Brow Event*.

A Brow Event is an event in which brow-challenged shoppers purchase their weight in cosmetics and are then treated to a Professional Brow Reshaping by a Professional Brow Reshaper.

This, I learned just a short time ago, courtesy of Kate, whose brows are reportedly in desperate need of reshaping—as, according to her, are mine.

At first I thought she was talking about how I really could use a *Bra* Event, since her Alabama accent can be a little thick at times. Believe you me, her reference to the extensive plucking and waxing I would undergo at the Bra Event had me confused and more than a little concerned.

But no, it was a *Brow* Event—although I would most certainly benefit from a Bra Event as well.

Losing those forty pounds shrank my grandmother's famed bullet boobs (which had, mid-puberty, materialized on my rib cage) into a third pair of appendages with all the aesthetic appeal of tennis balls in tube socks. I have since become a Wonderbra devotee, and I'm thinking a sexy new push-up is in order for my spa getaway with Jack.

That, according to Kate, can wait until after her own Bloomingdale's agenda has been fulfilled.

Which is a typical Kate reaction.

I only hope Billy won't give in to her longing for a baby before enrolling her in a maternal boot camp where she will learn the intricacies of diapers, bottles and selflessness. I adore Kate, but I can't imagine her deferring her immediate needs to anybody else's, including her own flesh and blood.

Case in point: at Kate and Billy's wedding breakfast last summer, I overheard her instructing her frail old grandmother not to eat or drink anything lest she dribble upon or smudge her pale yellow liquid lamé gown and ruin the pictures. It was enough to tempt Jack to sneak Grandma a powdered-sugar strawberry jelly donut just to spite Kate, but I stopped him, reminding him that all brides are self-centered on their big day.

He in turn reminded me that Kate is self-centered every day. But lovably so, in my opinion. Most of the time.

First on our shopping agenda is first-floor cosmetics where, alas, Kate's Brow Event buzz turns out to be as founded as the rumor that the sleek black Prada bag over my shoulder is the real thing.

Pssst: knockoff.

There is nary a Brow Event under way in the bustling, spot-lit, perfume-scented cosmetics bazaar that encompasses much of Bloomingdale's main floor.

Kate nevertheless winds up purchasing her weight in cosmetics, which isn't as impressive as, say, a person of normal stature purchasing their weight in cosmetics, but still...

My waifish friend piles the counter with countless bottles, tubes, vials and compacts, all the better to accentuate that peaches-and-cream complexion, high cheekbones, wide-set eyes and rosebud mouth Francesca raves on and on about in a fake-sounding Nordic—or maybe French?—accent.

Francesca—I can't help but learn her name due to her towering stature and her nametag being at my eye-level—is a cosmetics saleswoman who apparently takes her job so seriously that she and her fellow scientists—er, saleswomen—are wearing white lab coats.

Francesca enlightens us to the wonders of a brand new age-defying facial lubricant (patent pending).

Kate, a modern-day Ponce de Leon, hangs on her every word.

"You zee?" Francesca asks me, after dabbing some age-defying lubricant in the corners of Kate's eyes and mouth. "No wrinkles!"

I open my mouth to point out that there were no wrinkles before the lotion, but Kate interrupts me with a cheerful, "I'll take three."

Francesca gloats, adding a trio of fifty-dollar tubes to Kate's growing heap of revolutionary beauty products.

"You will look years younger," she promises Kate.

"That would make her a tween," I mention to the amusement of nobody other than myself.

After securing her future children's college tuition and returning Kate's well-worn Bloomies charge, Francesca turns on me with a mad scientist gleam in her painstakingly mascara'd and shadowed blue eyes.

"How about you, my pretty?" she cackles, practically rubbing her manicured hands together, imagining that charming Mediterranean villa she'll be able to afford when she's through with me.

Okay, she doesn't really say *my pretty.* But she definitely cackles.

No, really.

"Would you like to see your cheekbones and your eyes pop right out?" she asks.

No. That would be fun-house frightening.

However, I would like to see my *boobs* pop right out.

But before I can depart for *Destination: Lingerie,* Francesca inquires whether I've sufficiently protected myself against environmental assaults.

If a phrase like that doesn't give one pause in this day and age, I ask you, what does?

"I've got Mace," I tell her, opening my fake Prada bag to show her the can I've been carrying ever since a woman in our building was reportedly mugged in a stairwell last week.

Ignoring the Mace, Francesca bustles around behind the counter, proclaiming, "What you need is…*this.*"

She places a tube of lotion upright on the outstretched palm of her left hand and runs her right fingertips, Carol Merrill–like, along the side to show it off.

"What is it?" I ask reluctantly.

And what the heck is an environmental assault?

"This ointment contains an elixir that will shield your delicate skin from the dangers that lurk all around you," she says ominously, shifting her eyes warily from side to side.

I follow her gaze and spot a pair of elderly female shoppers who look as threatening as milk.

"Environmental aggressors," she clarifies.

"Them?" I ask quietly, watching one old lady stray toward a display table and the other, who is even older, steer her back to the aisle and hook elbows with her. It could be a front. Any second now, they might attack.

Or not.

"Environmental aggressors," Francesca clarifies. "You know...ultraviolet rays, exhaust...that sort of thing. You should be vigilant about laying down a line of defense if you're going to expose yourself to environmental aggressors on a daily basis."

Vigilant...defense...aggressors... Are we talking about my complexion, or Homeland Security?

"I'll think about it," I promise lamely.

Which isn't good enough for our zealous Dr. Francescastein.

Brandishing a vial from the pocket of her white lab coat, she persists with her dramatic claim that she can make me over into a thing of great beauty. Like Kate.

I half expect her to lead me to a granite slab as lightning bolts flash overhead. Or for electrodes and squared-off edges to sprout on Kate's forehead.

"You zee? You zee how your friend's skin is glowing now?" Francesca asks fiendishly.

Well, it *seems* fiendish.

All right, maybe I'm just exaggerating and she merely has good marketing skills. And yes, Kate might be slightly glowing, but at least I can *zee* that she isn't monster-green, thank goodness.

Francesca cups my chin in her hands and says, "You can look just like her if you'll listen to me."

Fiendish. Definitely.

At long last, I summon the fortitude to say thanks but no thanks and flee.

Rather, I attempt to flee, but the glowing Kate, in tow, insists on meandering.

The journey up three escalators to lingerie involves multiple pauses so that Kate can examine "darling little pants" and "darling little tops" and I can examine my reflection in various mirrors, wondering if I'm really as hideous as Francesca would have me believe.

I conclude that I might not be a honey-toned Southern belle, but I'm hardly a hulking Boris Karloffesque creature in need of an on-the-spot mad-scientist makeover. Truly, there's nothing wrong with me that a spa weekend won't fix.

Reaching the fourth floor at long last, I stride efficiently over to the nearest rack and select a black lace push-up bra and matching panties in short order.

"Don't you want to be fitted by the saleswoman?" Kate protests as I march them over to the register.

"Nope," I say breezily.

"But how do you know you've got the right cup size?"

"I just know."

I don't *just know,* but being fitted for a bra and panties by a saleswoman is about as appealing as being grand marshal in a nudist parade down Lexington Avenue.

In other words, I'd rather my C-cup runneth over.

From lingerie, we head back down to Three so Kate can browse a bit in Petites. There, looming amidst the slender Lilliputians, I can't help but feel once again like something conjured by Mary Shelley's worst nightmare.

After Kate purchases a couple of darling size zero outfits, we escalator it back to Two: swimsuit land. We're greeted with a dazzling array of spandex and Lycra in a rainbow of colors and patterns, none of which will flatter me. I can just tell. No matter how much weight I've lost in the past few years, I'm beginning to think I'll never, ever find a bathing suit I like.

Yet I refuse to give up the quest, valiantly moving from swim dress to maillot to two-piece. No, not skimpy bikinis. Nobody looks good in a skimpy bikini.

Nobody but Kate, who buys two before you can say Skeletor.

"I don't know when I'm going to have a chance to wear these," she comments breezily, "but they're darling, and you know me. I can't resist a good buy."

Yup. I know her. And in Kate Land, paying three figures each for a couple of glorified thongs is a good buy.

In Tracey Land, a good buy is anything that leaves cash to spare for lunch and subway fare home.

I am pawing my way through yet another clearance rack of tankinis in my price range when Kate mentions her plummeting blood sugar. She mentions this frantically, wide-eyed beneath her supposedly straggly brows, upon which I have, incidentally, spotted nary a straggly strand.

Sagging against a rack, she says weakly, "Hurry… please…"

Obviously, Kate has decided that it's high time we hightail it to the sixth floor and join the Ladies Who Lunch at Bloomingdale's.

Feeling defiant, I hold up a spiffy red swimsuit and say, "Wait, let me just try this on first."

Kate tilts her blond head, slants her aquamarine eyes, and musters the strength to drawl, "Ah don't know, Tracey… don't you think you'd be better off with black?"

"I look good in red," I remind Kate. "Red is my lucky color. I was wearing a red dress when I met Jack, remember?"

"But this isn't a dress, it's a bathing suit," protests our little sugar Magnolia with the confident air of one who looks better in a string bikini than Gisele Bundchen does. "I thought you liked black bathing suits."

I did…when I was forty pounds overweight.

Maybe I'll never be a size zero, but I've graduated from somber bathing suits that have longer, fuller skirts than my first communion dress did.

"I'm trying this on," I tell Kate stubbornly.

"But, Tracey, I'm starving."

"Have a Mento." I thrust a roll into her hand and make a beeline for the nearest changing room.

There, I discover that the red swimsuit would definitely look better in black. Or on Paris Hilton.

I haven't weighed myself since I quit smoking, but I'd venture to guess that I might have put on a few figure flaws that now require serious camo in the form of memory yarn.

"You're not getting the suit?" Kate asks hopefully when I emerge to find her lounging, in her hunger-weakened state, against a Plexiglas divider.

"No."

"Why not?" She hurries to catch up with me as I stride toward the escalator.

"Too baggy."

At the restaurant entrance, we wait for a table amidst a horde of other shoppers, all of whom belong to one of the following demographics: Upper East Side, European or screamingly gay.

"I'm getting something with noodles," Kate announces. "I'm craving white carbs like you wouldn't believe."

Yeah, who isn't? I would like nothing better than to sit down in front of a steaming plate of pasta. Penne à la vodka. Mmm.

"What are you getting, Tracey?"

"Salad," I say curtly, reminding myself that even if I've

gained a few pounds since I tossed my cigarettes, it's well worth it. Pink, healthy lungs. That's what it's all about. Not pink vodka sauce.

We're seated, and I order my salad and diet soda after Kate orders her noodles with a side of potatoes and a Coke. Full sugar. She never drinks diet.

"So how's Jack?" she asks, somehow managing to break open and butter a roll with elegant grace.

"Jack? He's good." I sip some lemon water and pretend it's a buttered roll.

"Listen, what are the odds you two will be getting engaged soon?"

Hmm, let's see. Either very high, or slim-to-none.

I settle for, "It's hard to say. Why?"

"Because you always said you wanted a summer wedding. And I told you Billy and I are trying for a baby. I don't want to look fat in my bridesmaid's dress."

Okay, that is so Kate for the following reasons: I never said I wanted a summer wedding; I always said I wanted a *fall* wedding. I never invited her to be a bridesmaid in my future wedding, though of course she will be. And even when we're talking about my wedding, it's all about her.

It takes me a moment to figure out what I want to say.

It takes me another moment to keep myself from saying it and instead tell Kate politely, "When I get engaged, you'll be one of the first to know. I promise."

"Well, do you think he really has the ring, like he said?" she presses.

"I guess so. I mean…his mother wouldn't lie. I'm sure he's just waiting for the right moment." Or right woman.

"It would be great if you could prod him a little. I could be pregnant as we speak. I told you, I'm craving carbs and sugar."

"You always crave carbs and sugar. And you just tried on bikinis. I saw you. You definitely aren't pregnant."

"I don't know...we're seriously trying now."

"Seriously trying? As opposed to what? Having casual sex while wearing clown noses and telling jokes?"

"This isn't funny, Tracey. I'm serious."

"I'm sorry. When was your last period?"

"Election Day."

"Election Day?"

"Definitely. I remember the day exactly because Billy was down at campaign headquarters until late and he was supposed to bring me Advil and tortilla chips when he came home and he forgot."

Damn those madcap Young Republicans. You just can't count on them in a PMS emergency.

"That was like two weeks ago, Kate. If you're pregnant, you're maybe a day or two into your first trimester."

"Exactly. And by the time I have the baby, you'll be getting married."

Please, God.

"What do you think is holding things up?" Kate wants to know.

"Jack. Jack is holding things up."

"Well, duh. No kidding. I mean, why isn't he giving you the ring? You've got a wedding to plan. You can't wait around forever."

No, I can't. I've got a wedding to plan. Except...

"Most of it is already planned," I confess. "I did a lot of it back in September, after his mother told me."

"And you didn't tell me?"

"Tell you...?"

"That you were planning the wedding?"

"Sorry. I must have forgotten."

"How could you forget? You can't plan a wedding on your own." Kate shakes her head with the air of a mother who's just caught her six-year-old backing the car out of the driveway. "What's the dress like?"

"White, obviously, with a medium train and a scalloped neckline. And the veil is—"

"Not *your* dress," she cuts in. "The bridesmaid's dress."

But of course. Silly me. How could I have forgotten that this was all about her?

"It's darling," I say pointedly. "A navy blue velvet sheath, off the shoulder."

"Sheath? I can't wear a sheath if I'm pregnant. And velvet? In June?"

"Who said anything about June?"

"You did, Tracey. You've always wanted a June wedding."

"I've always wanted an *October* wedding."

She frowns. "I don't think so."

"You don't think so? Trust me, I've always wanted to get married in October."

Even when I thought I was going to marry Will, in which case October would have ultimately been the only bright spot in the whole occasion. That, and the pumpkin wedding cake with cream-cheese frosting, which I have also always wanted.

"You must have changed your mind," Kate declares, "because I remember you saying you always wanted to get married in June."

"That was you, Kate."

"I know, but it was you, too."

Okay. Uncle. I give up. Let her believe that she listens intently when I speak, and that I've forgotten what I've wanted all my life. Whatever.

"Well, I am definitely getting married in October, not June," I say evenly. "The third Saturday. At Shorewood Country Club, on the water."

"Where's that? Greenwich? On the sound?"

Ha. "No, Brookside."

Pause.

"Brookside? So…the water is…what? A brook?"

This might be fun if I weren't feeling fat and cranky.

"No," I say, "it's on Lake Erie."

"Lake Erie?" She wrinkles her nose as though she smells sewage—or middle class—thus, completing her metamorphosis into one of the Ladies Who Lunch—who are now, incidentally, lunching all around us.

"Yes, Lake Erie. They've cleaned it up a lot the past few decades," I say dryly. "And we'll disguise the floating garbage with floral arrangements."

"You're kidding, right?"

"What do you think?"

"Is the deposit refundable?" Kate wants to know. "Because if it is, you might want to consider the place where Billy and I got married instead. Remember the gorgeous water view?"

Of course I remember the view. I also remember that it was of the Gulf of Mexico.

Maybe it's superfluous to point out, "My family lives near Buffalo, Kate."

I guess it is, because she shrugs as if that's a minor detail. "That doesn't mean you have to get married up there. I mean…I bet it snows in October."

It sure does. May, too. Once, even in June.

But never July. Not that I can recall.

Mental note: rethink fall wedding.

"Is the deposit refundable?" Kate asks again.

"I didn't put down a deposit."

"How could you reserve a country club without a deposit?"

"I didn't technically *reserve* it. I just decided that's where the wedding should be."

She's shaking her head as though some killjoy just told her the world is fresh out of white flour. "You can't just *decide,* Tracey. You need to *reserve.*"

"I will…as soon as Jack officially proposes."

"Yes, and by the time he gets around to that, they'll tell you the next October Saturday is available in the year 2018. Hell, by the time he gets around to that it might *be* the year 2018."

Har de har har, happily married underweight carb queen.

"Here." She hands her cell phone across the table. "Call now."

"I can't call now."

"Why not?"

"Because…"

Hello-o! Because I'm not engaged yet.

But I don't say that.

I say, "Because I don't know the number."

Which is true.

Not engaged yet also true, but why complicate matters?

Kate grabs the phone back, presses 411 and Send, and silently returns it to me.

The next thing I know, I'm dialing Shorewood Country Club.

Yeah, yeah, yeah. I have no spine.

But one can't take chances with the venue confirmation of one's wedding date even when one has yet to receive confirmation from the groom himself. Not unless one wants to risk holding her reception at the Most Precious Mother church hall, where bingo is conveniently held only on weeknights. Father Stefan and the gang are more than willing to push the folding tables apart and cover them with vinyl tablecloths for weekend weddings. I know, because I've been to a number of them, my sister's included.

Yes, and look how *that* turned out.

After being on hold for a few moments, my call is answered by the banquet manager, Charles. From the tone of his hello, I can tell that he is not, nor has he ever been, nor will he ever be, Charlie.

"I, um, wanted to see if the club was available for a wedding in October?"

Are you asking him, Tracey, or telling him?

Channeling Martha Stewart, I add crisply, "Specifically, I'm interested in the third Saturday, a sit-down dinner, for around three hundred."

"Next October?" he asks, and I hear him flipping the pages of his calendar.

Encouraged that he isn't laughing, or asking whether I mean October 2018, I confirm that I am indeed referring to next October.

I don't really say "indeed," though.

In fact, what I say is something along the lines of "Yup."

To which Charles Not Charlie responds, "Yes."

To which I respond, "I'm sorry, I meant yes."

I am thinking that Charles Not Charlie is even more pompous than I thought, yet he can absolutely get away with correcting my grammar because he's the one with the calendar and thus complete control over my future happiness.

Silence.

Then, "Pardon me?"

That doesn't come from me.

But the subsequent blank-sounding "Huh?" does.

If you're noting that Charles and I are clearly not hitting it off conversationally, you are infinitely more perceptive than Kate, who is impatiently hissing, "So is it available or not?"

I gesture to her that I have no idea, but alas, she has swiftly lost interest because our waiter approacheth bearing glad tidings of great noodles. And potatoes. And a wee salad on a serving plate the size of a teacup saucer.

That's my entrée. I'm serious, it's like three lettuce leaves—the dark green, ruffly, limp lettuce that's all fancy pretty but has no satisfying crunch—and two halves, no wait, *three* halves, of a grape tomato. Which, if you've been following your produce trends as I have, you know is much smaller than a cherry tomato.

Three grape-tomato halves.

Again with the tomato dearth.

This bugs the hell out of me, especially now that I've quit smoking and many things bug the hell out of me that were previously just semi-annoying.

Come on. Three grape-tomato halves? Why even bother?

And what did they do with the fourth half? Did some hapless chef drop it on the floor?

Or maybe the rule in this restaurant kitchen is a one-and-a-half-grape-tomato allotment per customer. No more, no less.

Maybe gluttons who want more have to know enough to ask for a side order of grape tomato. I bet the Ladies Who Lunch know to do that.

Not that any of them look like they'd splurge on a side order of grape tomato.

No, the Ladies Who Lunch look as though they'd nibble *half* a grape tomato after a grueling day of trying on size zero couture, declare themselves stuffed and push the plate away *veeeery* carefully so as not to snap their bony wrists.

Me, I sigh inwardly and covet my neighbor's plate.

Damn, Kate's pasta looks good. But then, so does she.

Would I rather look good, or eat pasta? Because unlike Kate, I can't do both. Most humans can't.

I'd rather eat pasta. Definitely. Looks fade. Pasta stays with you. At least until dinner, which Jack and I aren't having until late tonight.

So it's settled. I'm going to order penne with pink vodka sauce as soon as I get off the damn phone.

Turning my attention back to Charles, who is ominously silent and has perhaps even hung up and moved on to better brides, I say, "I'm sorry, I guess I'm confused. Should we start again? I was interested in finding out whether the third Saturday in October is available for—"

Charles, whose thing is obviously grammar and not etiquette, interrupts, "It is."

"It is?"

"Yes."

"It's available for a wedding with a sit-down dinner for three hundred?" I ask, just to be clear.

"Yes," he repeats, and now I get it. When he said *yes* to my *yup,* he wasn't correcting my grammar, he was…

Oh, never mind. The important thing is that it's available!

"It's available!" I tell Kate.

Rapidly twirling pasta around her fork while still chewing her last mouthful, she smiles and nods as though she knew it all along.

"I'd like to book it, then, please," I tell Charles, grateful that for once, things have fallen smoothly into place for me.

"All right…" More pages turning. "Why don't you come in sometime next week and—"

"Oh, I can't," I interrupt, though etiquette is usually my thing. "I'm in New York. Can I just book it over the phone?"

Is *book it* not the right phrase? I wonder belatedly, noting that Charles sounds almost snide when he responds, "I usually *reserve* weddings in person."

"Um, is it possible to reserve it over the phone, though? I'll put down my deposit on a credit card," I add to expedite the conversation because I know that's what's coming next and because I'm getting really hungry for that farfelle.

"It's *possible,*" Charles replies in a tone that reminds me that it is also possible—nay, *preferable*—to ride a scooter through downtown Baghdad in a tutu singing "I Feel Pretty."

"How much would the deposit be?" I remember to ask because I am ever the efficient future-bride-to-be.

Charles responds with a few more questions before informing me that the deposit would be…

Insert pinkie finger…

One million dollars.

Okay, not really.

But it might as well be, because I don't have the kind of money he's asking for—not even in the Total Available Credit box on my monthly Visa statement.

I look up at Kate, who does, and briefly consider asking her for a loan. But that might give her the inalienable right to have a say in everything from bridesmaid's dress to dessert menu.

Might?

She thinks she has a say as it is. No way am I going to hand it to her on a pasta platter.

"How long can you hold it without a deposit?" I ask Charles.

Not long. Not long a'tall.

Sayonara, Chuck.

Farewell, third Saturday in October.

I hang up and pass the phone back across the table to Kate.

Oh, hello there, little sad and skimpy green salad.

I look around for the waiter, but he's nowhere to be seen.

"Are you going to finish your pasta?" I ask Kate, who has moved on to her potatoes.

She nods, mouth full.

Damn. "Well, can I have a taste?"

She finishes chewing.

Asks, "Do you think you should?"

Do I think I *should?* What the hell kind of question is that?

"Yes, I really do," I tell her, wishing the waiter would hurry back from the men's room or Brooklyn or wherever the hell he went off to so that I can order my own pasta and stop begging for Kate's. "Otherwise, I wouldn't have asked."

"I'm just trying to help you, Tracey."

"With…?"

"With…you know. Your diet."

"I'm not on a diet," I inform her.

The look she gives me in return makes it clear that I am not the only one who's noticed the poundage that's crept back on these last few weeks.

I stop watching for the waiter out of the corner of my eye and look my salad directly in the grape tomato.

I can eat this salad. *Just* this salad. Of course I can do it. In the past few years, I've learned to be satisfied with just salad.

My stomach rumbles.

That's the problem, I realize.

I want more than just salad.

I want penne.

Penne, and bread, and a great body. An engagement ring, too.

I want it all.

Now.

I want it now!

So intense is my little Veruca Salt moment that it takes me a moment to realize that I actually have more in common with Charlie Bucket, who has nothing.

Nothing, I recall, but a golden ticket that will bring something fabulous if he clings to his integrity and believes in Willy Wonka.

Okay, so what does that mean? Is Jack my Willie Wonka? Does he hold the key to my future?

What the hell happened to *if Jack wants to marry me, great, if not…well, not great. But not the end of the world, either?*

Isn't that what I decided just weeks ago?

And now I'm right back to wallowing in self-pity?

I shake my head vehemently.

"Okay, so you're not on a diet," says Kate, who is watching me with utter resignation. She shoves the plate of pasta across the table. "Here. Knock yourself out. I'm getting full anyway."

"That's not what I'm thinking about," I tell her, even as I acknowledge that it is now.

I grab a fork and dig in.

Ah. Bliss.

Kate asks, "What *are* you thinking about?"

"I'm thinking that I'm sick of this whole will-he-or-won't-he thing. Why am I letting Jack call all the shots?"

Kate opens her mouth to answer, but I'm on a roll. And anyway, I'm not asking her. I'm asking myself.

"Why is my future his decision?"

"Because, Tracey, that's how it is," drawls our sweet Melanie, shaking her head at headstrong Scarlett's newfangled notion that *she,* and not Rhett, might be in charge of her destiny.

"Why? Why should I sit around waiting for him to ask me to marry him?"

Which is exactly what I've been doing, BTW. For the past two and a half months.

In case you haven't noticed.

"Because the man does the proposing."

My fork is whirling spaghetti faster than a bride and groom in a horah. I shove it into my mouth.

Yummy. Well worth the guilt—and tight waistline—I'm bound to suffer as an immediate consequence.

Then I tell Kate, "Think about it. Why does being engaged matter so much?"

"Because you want to get married."

"Do I *really?*" I ask, shoving in more pasta. *Mmm-mmm-mmm.* "Or do I just *think* I do because everybody else is getting married? Isn't sharing my life with somebody I love all that really counts?"

"Yes…that's why you need to get *married*." Kate is rapidly losing her patience.

"Maybe we don't *need* to get married." I'm speaking for myself and Jack, though I can't help but hope that maybe he does feel at least a smidge of need.

"But if you're not married, he can walk away."

"So can I," I shoot back. "And anyway, he can walk away whether we're married or not."

Exhibit A: Vinnie the Cheat, my soon-to-be-ex-brother-in-law.

Kate shrugs. "Being married makes it harder."

This is pathetic, I think, even as I acknowledge that she's right. Vinnie would have left Mary Beth years ago if it weren't for their wedding vows—or, more likely, if it weren't for the specter of alimony.

Still…

"I can take care of myself," I inform her. "I've been doing it for years now. I don't need an engagement ring."

"I thought you wanted one."

"I did. I do. But if it doesn't happen I won't curl up and die."

I shove Kate's ravaged plate away, sated.

Ah do declare, Miss Mellie, Ah feel better already.

Chapter 10

On Thanksgiving Day, the alarm goes off in the pitch-black chill of 5:30 a.m.

Not because we have to put a turkey in the oven, or catch an early flight.

No, the alarm goes off at five-thirty (an hour that in June might be sun-splashed and tranquil, but in November is always downright depressing) because I am determined to see the Macy's Thanksgiving Day Parade live and in person. After a lifetime of watching it on television, I've finally got the chance to be there, and I'm going, with or without Jack.

Without Jack, Raphael and I will be forced to mingle with the great unwashed as we vie for a sidewalk viewing spot somewhere between the Dakota and Herald Square.

With Jack, however, we will be cordially invited to sit in the VIP viewing stands set up on Central Park West for NBC and its guests.

Network guests tend to include celebrities, families of program staffers and advertising-agency media drones like

Jack. It's just another corporate perk in lieu of actually getting paid a decent salary.

Ask any media planner, and I bet he'll tell you that he'd prefer a beefed-up paycheck to rubbing shoulders with the former cast of *Blossom* beneath a canopy of oversize, inflated cartoon characters that have been known to topple lampposts and maim onlookers.

But me, I love a parade.

As does Raphael.

Or so he claims.

Personally, I wonder if he just wants to keep an eye on Donatello, who's been moonlighting as a so-called "spray model" at Macy's to earn money for their planned African Safari honeymoon. A "spray model" is an attractive being who is paid incredibly well to troll the cosmetics floor assaulting passersby with the latest scents.

Anyway, it seems that Donatello, who is marching today as an official Balloon Handler, is a notorious flirt. I suspect Raphael wants to make sure he isn't cruising the other Balloon Handlers while tethered to the helium-bloated underside of the Honey-Nut Cheerios Bee, because, well, we all know what a turn-on *that* can be.

So yes, Raphael is definitely coming with me. We're scheduled to meet on the subway platform at Grand Central in twenty minutes.

Jack still isn't sure he wants to go, even now that he's showered, shaved and dressed in jeans and a nice gray sweater. He dawdles around by the table, rearranging piles of stuff: newspapers, magazines, the game boxes containing Scattergories and Clue, which we played last night when Buckley and Sonja came over with a bottle of wine.

The board games were my idea. Not that I didn't want to sit around and chat about their upcoming nuptials or anything. I just happen to like board games. Really.

Buckley and Sonja could barely get a word in edgewise

between dice rolls and ticking timers, but they did manage to mention that they're getting married a year from next summer. Now that she knows Buckley isn't going anywhere, Sonja wants time to plan "the perfect wedding." Which will be in Boston, but hopefully without the Red Sox theme she keeps joking about.

At least, I assume she's joking.

The best part about the Sonja-Buckley nuptials being put off for a year and a half is that Jack and I might actually beat them to the altar.

Not that it's a race, or anything.

But if it were, we wouldn't lose…unless, of course, Jack continues to take his sweet time proposing.

Speaking of Jack taking his sweet time…

"Are you coming, or not?" I finally ask him as he drifts aimlessly away from the door again, coming to rest beside the table that holds my Chia Pet. We moved it closer to the window when it developed a severe case of mildew, hoping the sun would cure it. Now it sits there sadly, day after day, growing smelly spores in the gray light. I want to throw it away, but I'm afraid it would hurt Jack's feelings.

"Wouldn't you rather just watch the parade here, on TV?" Jack gazes out the window at the shred of blustery November sky that's visible between the other buildings. "I mean, it's so lousy out."

Today's forecast: rain, sleet, wind, cold. Same as yesterday, same as tomorrow. Ah, November.

"I've watched this parade on TV every year," I say firmly. "I want to see it in person for a change."

For a minute, Jack doesn't say anything.

Then, "Okay."

"You'll go?" I ask, pleasantly surprised.

"I'll go," he confirms with the enthusiasm of one who has just landed a last minute root canal appointment.

He reaches for his jacket, which is, of course, close at

hand, draped over the nearest chair where it's been since he took it off Monday night.

"Are you sure?"

"Positive." He sighs heavily.

Maybe it's just me, but he doesn't sound that into it.

"Come on, Jack," I say, all Rah-Rah, Sis-Boom-Bah, "this is the Macy's Thanksgiving Day Parade!"

"I know."

"It's going to be so great!"

Goooooooooooooo, Macy's!

"Yeah," Jack says, all Eeyore-ish.

Okay, whatever. At least he's going. VIP viewing stand, here I come!

I shove my feet into my sneakers without untying them, then tug the squashed backs up over my heels. I know it drives Jack crazy when I do that, but it drives me crazy when he acts unenthused about festive holiday events, so we're even.

"I wish you could be more excited about this parade," I tell him.

"I was, the first five times I saw it." He pulls on his leather jacket. Then he brightens, like he's just seen the light.

"Hey, what are we having for breakfast?" he asks.

Okay, food is so not the light. Food is darkness. Food is evil.

Because remember that five pounds that crept up on me after I quit smoking?

It's still here, plus two more. Here, there, everywhere: my hips, my thighs, my gut, even my arms. It's as though everything that was once lean and taut—more or less—is now lightly padded in flab.

I'm sure it's nothing that a couple of weeks on Atkins— or a few months at Alderson Federal Prison Camp—won't cure. But it's hard not to feel discouraged, especially when I open my closet each morning and realize the only thing that fits comfortably is my terry-cloth robe.

Today, in addition to sneakers and three unflattering layers of thermal shirts for warmth and camouflage, I've got on my biggest pair of "skinny" jeans, as opposed to my skinniest pair of "fat" jeans, which are tucked away in the top of my closet. I have kept them around strictly as a souvenir of the bad old days, not because I ever in a million years thought I might need to wear them again.

At this rate, though, don't be surprised if you see me in them at the office Christmas party because they're all I can fit into.

God, that's so depressing.

Depressing enough to make me think *no freaking way.*

If I've got the willpower to quit smoking, I've got the willpower to quit eating. Gaining all that weight back again would be a fate worse than…

Well, I really can't think of a fate worse than that. Realistically, anyway. Because what are the chances that I'm going to be taken hostage by a band of militants or terrorists? It goes without saying that that would be a worse fate.

But regaining forty pounds is about as bad as it gets in my world.

"Want to stop off for a couple of ham-egg-and-cheeses at the deli?" Jack asks with callous disregard to my plight.

I bitch slap him across the face.

Okay, not really.

But I do scowl.

"What?" he asks, oblivious. "You love ham-egg-and-cheese."

The thing is…I really don't. I can easily live without ham-egg-and-cheese. Just as I have more or less easily lived without most of the foods I've given up these last couple of years. But that was back when I had cigarettes to take away the hunger pains. Nothing like lighting up and breathing in a lungful of toxic smoke to diminish the old appetite.

Without smoking to fall back on, I have found myself mindlessly munching stuff I never would have dreamed of eating. Mostly Man Food, because I'm usually with Jack when I fall victim to temptation. Burgers, sandwiches, sausage…bulky fill-'er-up food that leaves you feeling bloated and lethargic.

But if I'm going to gain another ounce of weight from here on in—and believe me, I don't *intend* to—it's going to be accomplished with things I really like. Eggplant parmesan, raspberry pie, piña coladas.

Yum, yum and yum.

"Too fattening," I tell Jack, vis-à-vis ham-egg-and-cheeses.

"Okay, so *I'll* get a ham-egg-and-cheese," Jack says reasonably, jangling his keys. "Ready to go?"

"You're going to just eat in front of me?"

"You can get a bran muffin or something."

"Where have you been?"

"What?" he asks with vacant-eyed man-cluelessness.

"Didn't you know that bran muffins have way more fat and calories than, like, six Big Macs?"

"They do?"

I don't know…do they? Inner Tracey asks, ridden with uncertainty.

"Yeah," Outer Tracey says firmly, because I'm sure I read that somewhere, and anyway, who's in the mood to quibble with Jack over fat and calories, and what does he know from bran muffins?

"Besides," I add, "it's Thanksgiving."

"Right." Jack nods. Then asks, "What are you talking about?"

"You know…why would you want to eat a big breakfast on Thanksgiving?"

"Isn't the whole point of Thanksgiving that it's a feast day?"

We head for the door. Jack holds it open for me.

"Exactly," I say. "Why ruin our appetites now?"

"Because we're hungry?"

I shrug. "If I'm going to eat today, it's going to be once. And it's going to be good. I'm having everything I want later, when we get to your mother's house."

"So you're saying, no deli?" he asks as we head toward the elevator.

"We can get coffee, but that's it."

"Yeah, the thing is…I'm not the one on a diet here. Not that you should be either because you look great—" *Ch-ching, ch-ching, ch-ching, boyfriend points adding up rapidly* "—but why do I have to save *my* appetite? It'll be back in an hour either way. By the time we get up to Westchester I'll be starved."

"You know what? Go ahead," I say with a shrug and a martyred expression guaranteed to wring every bit of enjoyment out of future ham-egg-and-cheeses.

"I can't eat in front of you."

"Well, I can't eat, period."

And you know, I can't help thinking that it wouldn't kill him to show some solidarity here.

Especially since, if it weren't for him, I'd be puffing away on my Salem Slim Lights and skinny as ever by now.

I only quit smoking because he wanted me to.

Okay, I originally quit because *I* also wanted to, but I got over that fast.

Now I'm a nonsmoker because Jack apparently wants me to live forever.

Why, I don't know, since he isn't yet willing to guarantee that my immortality will be spent with him.

Regardless of his commitment issues, he doesn't want me to die of lung cancer, so here I am, healthy and fat, and here he is, insensitively going on and on about ham-egg-and-cheeses.

"Okay," he says reluctantly. "I'll skip breakfast. But we still need coffee."

"Coffee's fine."

We get two large ones at the deli on the corner as Jack looks longingly at the cold-cut display case.

"Two coffees…that it?" asks our friendly neighborhood deli man, who knows us well enough to always ask, when one of us is solo, where the other is. Who says New York City isn't a friendly place?

"Two coffees…that's it," I say firmly, tearing my longing gaze away from the Funyuns display. Yes, I know they're chock-full of salt, fat and calories. But I love them. And as soon as I lose a few pounds, I'm going to treat myself to some.

I dump a Splenda packet into my coffee and take two sips from my cup as Jack pays for them both.

"You probably shouldn't have gotten a large," he tells me.

"It's the same amount of calories as a small. Coffee isn't fattening."

"No, I mean, what if you have to go to the bathroom?"

Oh.

I look at Friendly Neighborhood Deli Man. "Do you have a ladies' room?"

He glances around like a spy about to open his trench coat and deliver the goods, then says in a conspiratorial whisper, "Shh, that way."

He points to an unmarked door beside the Fritos display. "Just for you. Okay? You keep it quiet."

"Thank you!" I say with fervent relief, and hand my coffee to Jack. "I'll be right back."

"You have to go already?"

"No, but…there's a bathroom, so I should."

Which makes perfect sense, because New York isn't like other cities. Most public places here don't have rest rooms. I've been a Manhattanite long enough to have scouted out a few that I can rely on—in Grand Central Station, in the Barnes & Noble in the Citicorp Building, in the basement of Trump Tower—but for the most part, preemptive measures are necessary.

The bathroom is surprisingly dirty.

Maybe not *surprisingly*. This is, after all, New York, where cockroaches stroll the walls of the nicest establishments.

Mental note: in future, find new establishment from which to purchase prepared food.

I try to pee, but of course, I can't. Not when I'm half crouched so as not to let my butt cheeks make contact with a toilet seat that's covered in stains and pockmarks.

How does a toilet seat get all beat up like that? I mean, what goes on in here?

I'd rather not picture it, thank you very much. In any case, my brief sojourn into filth alley is disappointingly uneventful. Nothing to do but pull up my fat jeans and hope for the best.

As Jack and I proceed to the subway, I find myself wistfully thinking of home. Not the home we just left, but the home I left a few years ago when I moved to New York.

Right about now, my mother is probably standing at the sink peeling and dicing the contents of four or five bags of potatoes.

When she makes mashed potatoes, she estimates at a pound a person.

My brothers probably eat close to that. I did, too, before I lost weight.

Good thing I'm not home today. I doubt that Wilma will make a pound a person of mashed potatoes or anything else.

Then again, there will be gravy and stuffing and pumpkin pie…which, even in small quantities, is lethal. The holidays are the worst time of year to diet.

I'm hoping the spa visit this weekend will jump-start my efforts. I'm sure it will.

Really. I'm positive I won't end up gaining back all forty pounds I've lost.

Or even, like twenty.

God, I hope not.

Anyway, I'm homesick. Not just for a pound of well-salted mashed potatoes with real butter and heavy cream.

I'm homesick for my parents' house and the way it smells on Thanksgiving morning, when the old-fashioned white enamel electric roaster is emitting its savory aroma from its annual place of honor on the laminate countertop. Homesick for my dad lifting the lid and sneaking bits of the sausage-studded stuffing when he thinks nobody's looking; for my nephews playing with their matchbox cars underfoot; for Mom, official Spadolini Kitchen Slave, wearing an apron over her stretch pants, beads of sweat on her forehead as she bustles and measures and stirs and gives orders.

Usually the orders are directed toward me, as the only daughter without a family of her own to take care of, and thus eternally incumbent Spadolini Kitchen Slave Apprentice. Mary Beth is exempt because she's got kids, and my brothers are exempt because they've got penises.

In Spadolini Land, anything food-related is women's work.

Just as, come to think of it, in Kate Land, anything engagement-related is men's work.

You'd think my mother and Kate might get along great, but I'd be willing to bet they'll take one look at each other and cringe when and if they finally cross paths someday.

My mother will decide Kate's ostensibly bulimarexic influence is the reason I've been "wasting away," and Kate will decide my mother needs an emergency makeover by a Nordic mad scientress in a darling lab coat.

"Are you okay?" Jack asks, peering at me as we wait to cross Third Avenue.

"Me? I'm great."

"You're not homesick, are you?"

"Homesick? What makes you think that?" I attempt to tuck my hand into his, which is in his jacket pocket because it's cold out and he forgot his gloves.

He immediately grabs my hand and pulls it out, with a jerking motion so sudden it's almost as if…

Well, as if there's some reason he didn't want my hand in his pocket.

"What's wrong?" I ask, my mind racing.

Does he have something in his pocket that he doesn't want me to find?

Like…a lizard?

Or…a velvet ring box?

"Nothing's wrong," he says.

Uh-huh. Sure.

Something is afoot in Jack's pocket, folks, and it ain't lint.

The mere notion of what it might be jump-starts a flutter of excitement in my otherwise empty stomach that lasts all the way to Grand Central Station.

Raphael is waiting for us on the platform for the number-seven train. He's wearing black velvet knickers, white knee socks and shiny black shoes with a buckle.

With Raphael, whenever I allow myself to think *now I've seen everything,* it turns out that I haven't. Today is no exception.

"Look, it's Miles Standish," Jack says amiably as Raphael gives me what he refers to as a Big Fat Turkey Day Hag Hug.

"Jack! No! Well, maybe. But only from the waist down," Raphael says slyly, and opens his arms.

Then, noting that Jack isn't exactly eager for his own Big Fat Turkey Day Hag Hug, Raphael opens his jacket instead.

From the waist up, he's…

"Naked?" I ask, frowning. "What's up with that?"

"Tracey, I'm representing both the Pilgrims and the Indians," Raphael informs me.

"Half Miles Standish, half Squanto?"

"It's only fair to be impartial, don't you think?"

"I think I'm glad you decided not to wear a waistcoat on top and a loincloth on the bottom. That's what I think."

Raphael swings his arm and snaps his fingers. "Why didn't I come up with that?"

"Because we all can't be as creative as Tracey is. Or as twisted." Jack shakes his head as though he's glimpsed Raphael's Big Fat Turkey Day future, and there's a loincloth in it.

"I love the holidays, don't you?" Raphael asks, mercifully zipping his coat again as the crosstown train pulls into the station.

Raphael sings gaily—and I mean *gaily*—"It's the *most…* wonderful time…of the year."

"City sidewalks, busy sidewalks, dressed in holiday cheer," I trill in response as we board the train and settle into three adjoining seats on the nearly empty car.

"Joy to the world…the Lord is come!" is Raphael's soprano response, followed by a muttered irreverent aside I don't quite catch but can just imagine.

"Jingle bells, jingle bells, jingle all the way," I reply in my booming alto.

We both look at Jack.

"Yes?" he asks mildly.

"Your turn," Raphael tells him. "We're singing lines from our favorite carols."

"Isn't it too early for that?"

"It's never to early to get the holiday season under way, Jack," Raphael replies, bending over to adjust his knee socks, then the shiny silver buckles of his shiny black shoes.

After watching him for a moment, Jack sings, *"Don we now our gay apparel, Fa la la la la la…laaaaa la la."*

"Jack! You're so funny!"

"So are you, Raphael!" Jack replies good-naturedly.

As the train rattles through the tunnel, I rest my hand on his knee, thinking once again that some boyfriends wouldn't be as tolerant of my flamboyant friend. I mean, I can just imagine how my brothers would react if my sisters-in-law were palling around with a flaming homo like Raphael.

No, I'm not being discriminatory. When Raphael isn't calling himself a horny queen, he's referring to himself as a flaming homo. Not in a self-deprecating way. More like a self-congratulatory way.

Anyway, Jack really is a great guy. I'm so lucky to have him. And right now, as we ride along to the Macy's parade on Thanksgiving Day singing carols and wondering what's in Jack's pocket—well, *I'm* wondering, anyway—my life feels just about perfect.

Two trains, fifteen minutes and three dozen lyrical yuletide lines later, we emerge on the Upper West Side, which has been drastically transformed into a surreal carnival of chaos, shrouded in a gray, misty drizzle. There are countless tour buses, cops on horseback, barricades, tourists. The side streets are lined with high-school bands, floats, Porta Potties and dozens of balloons that are as familiar as elementary-school classmates.

Raphael gestures at a distant, block-filling Bullwinkle hovering flat on its back. "Do you think he's supposed to be that low?"

I follow his gaze. "I don't know. He looks a little…"

"Flaccid?" Raphael supplies. "I thought the same thing." He cups his hands to his mouth and shouts, "Don't worry, Bully, it happens to everyone."

Jack, who would normally have a flaccid-moose crack or two to add, says nothing. He seems distracted. And his hand is, again, quite noticeably lingering in his pocket.

Is it because there's a ring in there?

Is he going to propose to me at the Macy's Thanksgiving Day Parade?

Is he…

Wait! Is he going to propose to me on national television? Is that why he made sure we got these VIP passes from the network?

But he almost didn't come with us today.

Or so he claimed.

Was it all a clever ruse to throw me off his nuptial trail?

I hurriedly pat my hair.

It feels damp and messy. I stuck it back with a plastic banana clip after drying it this morning, figuring the wet wind would toss it around and I could comb it later, before we head up to Westchester.

Why didn't I at least use mousse or gel? Or pull it back in a neat bun?

A bun? Who am I, Wilma Flintstone?

Okay, no bun, but I should have at least gone for a tousled sex kitten look as opposed to a tousled wet dog look.

I tug Raphael's sleeve as we all pause to allow a sequin-bedecked, corn-fed, nude-stocking-wearing female color guard to pass.

Raphael looks at me. "What, Tracey?" he asks loudly enough to be heard by the color guard's extended families gathered around their television sets in Des Moines.

Jack, however, doesn't even glance in our direction. He looks preoccupied with visions of marital bliss. Or something. He's hurrying along with his head bent against the wind, or so I assume. There's something almost furtive about his posture.

He's about to give me a ring. That has to be it.

"Do I look all right?" I subtly ask Raphael, ventriloquist-like.

"What?" he screams. "Tracey, *what?"*

Jack looks up over his shoulder at Raphael, then at me.

I flash an everything's just fine with me but who knows what's up with Raphael smile.

Jack drifts back to thinking about honeymoon locales. Or something.

"Do I look all right?" I whisper frantically into Raphael's ear.

He blinks, then gives me a lingering once-over. Then he asks, "Do you want honesty? Or kindness?"

"If one precludes the other—which I'm assuming it does—then I probably don't need to ask. But I guess I'll take honesty," I add hurriedly, thinking a little constructive criticism can't hurt under the circumstances.

"Well, you pretty much look like hell, Tracey. Why?"

"Give me a comb," I say under my breath, slowing my pace further as Jack strides along a few steps in front of us.

"A comb?" Raphael echoes as though I've just requested a salon chair with drying dome. "I don't have a comb."

"Oh, well, I just thought maybe…"

"How about a brush?" Raphael promptly produces one from the pocket of his Pilgrim knickers. He also hands me a compact mirror.

"I love you," I say, surreptitiously flipping the mirror open.

"Smooches, Tracey," is his cordial response.

I make myself as presentable as I can, what with the gusting wind and the banana clip and no makeup whatsoever. A liquid eyeliner stashed in Raphael's knee sock is probably too much to hope for, but I ask anyway.

"I forgot it on the table at home," is his reply. "Sorry, Tracey."

"It's okay. Do I look better now?"

Again, the once-over.

"Not really," he says. "Why?"

"No reason. I just like to, you know, look good."

Especially when I'm about to be proposed to in front of millions of viewers. I wonder if my nephews are watching the parade at home. I wonder how impossible it would be to sneak in a quick cell-phone call to alert Mary Beth.

Pretty impossible, considering that I left my phone at home with my brush, toiletries and makeup. What was I thinking, leaving home this unprepared and unkempt, wearing sneakers and thermals?

Jack glances back at me as we cover the last block along Seventy-ninth Street single file between the blue barricades, due to the hordes of people. "You okay?"

"Yup. Great!"

"I'm great, too," offers Raphael, two steps behind me. "But these shoes kill."

"Beauty—and historic authenticity—are *pain*, Raphael," I toss over my shoulder.

"You were so right, Tracey. I should have listened to you," is his reply. "Barefoot, loincloth would have been a much better way to go."

Oh, yay. I'll get all the credit for next year's obscene Big Fat Turkey Day attire.

At the viewing stand beside Central Park, where the parade kicks off, Jack shows his ID and presents our VIP passes to the burly security guard.

I watch carefully to see if the guy winks, but he doesn't. He just says, "Go ahead," to Jack, same as he would to a total stranger.

Okay. So maybe Jack didn't tip off the guard. That doesn't necessarily mean the televised engagement is off.

It could still be on.

Or maybe there's a lizard in his pocket.

Which would be *fine,* I hasten to remind myself. I am just *fine* with not getting engaged today…or ever. I wouldn't even be thinking about it if he hadn't yanked my hand out of his pocket that way.

I'd be merrily rolling along, la la la, married or single, who cares, life is great, la la la, from now until forever.

But no, here I am, holding my breath in anticipation of something that may or may not happen today, on live television, or *ever*. Why do I do this to myself?

A second guard at the foot of the bleachers reminds us that we won't be able to leave and reenter the VIP area now that we're in, due to security concerns.

I can't help but feel vaguely claustrophobic at that news. Nor can I help but wonder how letting VIPs come and go as needed would jeopardize security.

But hey, this is post 9–11 New York City, and I'm sure the guards have valid reasons. Even if they don't, who's going to argue with a menacing Wall of Man?

We find seats right behind a woman and a medium-size kid that I could swear are Al Roker's family.

I even nudge Raphael and whisper, "Al Roker's family."

Then they turn around, and they're whiter than I am, and Raphael smirks and says, "Somebody's star struck" in a really annoying singsong voice.

So I stop looking for celebs, even when I'm absolutely positive I catch the guy who played Gunther on *Friends* checking me out.

Good thing I ignore him, because he turns out to be the butch half of a lesbian couple and she looks as though she thinks I'm checking out her girlfriend, and I wish Jack would give me the damn ring so she could see that I have absolutely no interest whatsoever in her girlfriend or her or, for that matter, the guy who played Gunther on *Friends*.

God, I wish I had a cigarette.

That, or a confirmed future with Jack.

But he's currently looking around like a little kid who hasn't been to the Macy's Thanksgiving Day Parade fifty or however-many times, and I'm inexplicably supremely annoyed with him, especially when he says, "Isn't this great? Don't you love these seats?"

"Eh," I say, still feeling claustrophobic and idly wondering what would happen if I had to pee now that we're here in VIP territory—then, of course, immediately realizing that I have to pee. Badly.

I don't suppose they provide, within the cordoned-off area, heated Porta Potties for VIPs with raisin-size bladders.

They don't.

I know, because I just asked Raphael, who asked Jack even though I told him not to, who reluctantly asked the menacing Wall of Man.

"What do I do now?" I ask Jack in the wake of this bad news.

"Hold it?"

"Hold it?" I echo. "For how long?"

"Until Santa passes by?"

"Are you kidding me?"

"I am not kidding you. Santa's the end of the parade. And anyway, I told you to go when we were back at the deli."

"I tried." Is this not the most annoying, least romantic conversation ever? I can't believe we're actually having it on our engagement day. Or not.

"Do you want to leave and try to find a bathroom?"

"By myself?"

"I'll go with you."

"But we can't get back into the bleachers if we leave."

He shrugs. "We'll go home."

But what about the televised engagement?

Is he testing me?

Does he think I'm suspicious and testing him?

"You know what, Jack? Never mind. I'll be fine."

"Good," he says, either believing me and relieved his engagement plans haven't been derailed, or callously unconcerned about my bladder.

What now?

For a few seconds, I watch the parade preparations in the street and try to focus on something else.

But I can't.

"Raphael," I say, turning to him and seeing that he's exchanging winks with a cute homosexual to our left, "I have to pee. And you're engaged, by the way."

"I know. But he's so adorable," he hisses. "I can *look*."

"You winked."

"I can wink."

"I don't know about that."

"Donatello and I discussed it. Winking is allowed. It's harmless."

"Sure it is."

"Tracey, you have a dirty mind."

"So do you!"

"I know!" He is gleeful. "But it's okay, because I love Donatello. If I have lust, it's only in my mind."

"Yeah, yeah, yeah. I have to pee," I say.

I'm not asking for assistance in this matter; I'm merely sharing so that I can receive sympathetic support in my time of need.

"Tell Jack," is Raphael's unsympathetic response.

I notice that Jack is busy turning his back to us and pretending to be very interested in something on the north end of the bleachers. Is he giving the high sign to a waiting camera crew so they can come over and film the engagement?

Play it cool, Tracey.

Further perusal indicates that there is no camera crew in sight on the north end of the bleachers, unless they're disguised as a popcorn-toting Midwestern family of five.

"I did tell Jack," I whisper to Raphael. "He didn't really seem to care."

Unless he was merely acting as though he doesn't care for the sake of preserving his engagement surprise, in which case, I forgive him.

If that's *not* the case, then I have to say I have serious concerns about what kind of husband he'd be. I understand that these are extraordinary circumstances, but I wonder how he'd behave under ordinary circumstances. How many times has my father pulled over at a rest stop five miles into a trip so my mother could visit the ladies' room?

Would Jack do that for me?

I think not.

I shift my weight and shiver. It might be easier not to think about going to the bathroom if a cold rain weren't falling on my face. What if that triggers a biological reflex? Like the old slumber party prank where you put somebody's hand in a bowl of warm water while they're asleep so they'll wet the bed.

It never happened to me, but that's only because I refused to ever go to sleep at a slumber party. I spent many a restless night on faintly mildewed indoor-outdoor carpeted basement floors out of sheer urination dread.

"Come on," Jack says, suddenly turning back to me and taking my hand.

"Where are we going?" I pat my hair with my other hand. Is this it? My big moment? I look around for the cameras.

"To pee," Jack says. "You have to, right?"

That depends.

Is he telling the truth?

And if he is, will peeing now postpone or preempt my engagement?

Then again, do I really want Jack to engage me while I have a stream of urine trickling down my legs?

I look into his face, trying to read his inscrutable expression.

What to do, what to do…

Then I spot it.

A crumb.

A bread crumb!

Holy Hansel and Gretel, Batman, there's a bread crumb in the corner of Jack's lip!

It all falls into place then, just like that.

J'accuse!

I stare at him in disbelief, disappointment, maybe even disgust.

"What?" he asks, all innocence.

So it wasn't a ring in his pocket, and it wasn't a lizard.

It was a ham-egg-and-cheese, smuggled away from the deli counter while I was trying to keep my butt cheeks from making contact with toilet-seat muck.

I just know it, the way I knew last night, right from the start, that it was Colonel Mustard in the Conservatory with the Lead Pipe.

My hopes sag like a Bullwinkle balloon. How could I have gotten all worked up over a stupid sandwich?

But, to keep things in perspective, this doesn't mean it's never going to happen for us.

It just means Jack was hungry.

And sneaky.

He's only human, and humans get hungry.

And sneaky.

I can't hold that against him.

Anyway, maybe we're going to get engaged later, at his mother's house.

If not, I remind myself that I'll still have plenty to be thankful for this holiday…starting with the fact that I didn't wet my pants in the bleachers on Central Park West.

Chapter 11

Wilma Candell moved last year into a brand-new two-bedroom condo not far from the huge Bedford Colonial house where she and her soon-to-be-ex-husband raised Jack and his four sisters.

Don't get me wrong; the condo is really nice. It's much larger and brighter than our apartment, with a deck, a fireplace, an attached one-car garage and access to a community pool, tennis courts and golf course. The fixtures and appliances are brand new and the decor is pleasantly neutral, the better to accentuate her beautiful antique furniture and artwork.

But when you think about the drastic change in Wilma's lifestyle these past few years, you can't help but feel a little sorry for her. At least, *I* can't. It must be depressing to go from six thousand square feet to a fraction of that, and there's just something unsettling about valuable oil paintings hanging on a gypsum wall that has strangers living on the other side.

Wilma greets us looking elegant in a pencil-slim tweed skirt, black cashmere sweater and pearls. She's made up and perfumed, and her shoulder-length dark hair looks as though she just brushed and sprayed it. I can't help but immediately compare her to Audrey Hepburn.

Then to my own mother.

I do that every time I see her, but today, the contrast is more stark than ever because I know that at this very moment, my mother is flushed and exhausted, wearing either an apron or a gravy-and-grease-spattered double-knit pantsuit because she was too frazzled to remember to put on the apron. She always wears the same brown double-knit pantsuit for Thanksgiving. Or maybe it's different brown double-knit pantsuits every year but they always look the same.

Still, she's my mother, and I love her. You can't get more maternal than Connie Spadolini. In the maternal market, she's easily got Wilma Candell beat.

Not that Wilma doesn't love her kids, because she obviously does. She's just quieter, and less traditional about it. She'd never dream of spit-cleaning somebody's face. Not a child's, and certainly not an adult's. Meanwhile, my mother dabbed at my cheek with a saliva-slicked finger the very last time I was home, thinking a freckle was, who knows, dirt or something.

When it refused to budge, she decided it was a precursor to skin cancer and that I'd better wear robes and veils in the sun from now on.

Okay, not robes and veils. But long sleeves, and hats. Not baseball caps, either. Hats. I know this because when I put on my brother Joey's Yankees cap to appease her, she informed me that it was not sufficient protection. I guess she expects me to traipse around Manhattan decked out in a Chitty Chitty Bang Bang motoring hat or something. Like that'll ever happen. But I promised her to take heed against the big, bad, scary sun.

Meanwhile, here's Wilma, all aglow with a natural-looking salon tan in the middle of November. Jack mentioned she's been going daily in anticipation of her Christmas trip to the Caribbean, because she doesn't like to hit the beach looking pasty.

Who does?

And there it is again, the drastic difference between Wilma and my own mother. I can no more imagine my mother in a tanning salon than I can imagine her…well, lying on a beach at a Caribbean resort. Especially at Christmastime.

No, Christmastime is meant to be spent making dozens upon dozens of *cucidati* to give away to family, friends and fellow parishioners under the assumption that what everyone really wants from the Spadolinis this year is a tin of homemade fig-filled cookies that might actually be appetizing if they weren't filled with fig.

My mother hands them out to carolers, mails them to far-off acquaintances, tucks them into my father's lunch pail to share with co-workers, leaves them on shoppers' windshields at the mall parking lot. Okay, I made up that last part but trust me, it's not a stretch.

Maybe it's just me, but I can't imagine why a person would work herself to exhaustion making hundreds of unappetizing cookies from a centuries-old, pain-in-the-ass-to-follow Sicilian recipe, and then give them all away with a vengeance. But that's my mother's yuletide mission and by God, she, like her mother before her, is going to bestow *cucidati* on the masses if it's the last thing she does in this life. Even my sister Mary Beth is on board the *cucidati* train, wholeheartedly pitching in every year to help with the complicated mixing, rolling, stuffing and baking. She even gives tins of them to her babysitters and the boys' teachers, who would probably actually prefer a handy white ceramic World's Best Teacher mug or freshly sharpened pencil.

I'm sure I'll be the one who breaks the family tradition,

barring a brainwashing experience or a sudden onset of more intense guilt than I already have.

"Come in out of the rain! How was the parade?" Wilma asks, greeting both Jack and me with hugs.

I'm afraid to squeeze her too hard because she feels thinner than usual and I don't want to inadvertently snap a bone.

"We didn't really stay for the parade," Jack tells her.

"I don't blame you. The weather was terrible."

"It was," I agree, hoping Jack won't tell her how we were forced to flee the VIP stands, leaving our flirtatious neo-Pilgrim pal behind.

We reached the Porta Potties on Amsterdam Avenue in the nick of time. Afterward, Jack offered to return to Central Park West so that we could watch the parade from the sidewalk, but by then the crowd was enormous. The closest we could get was half a block down West Seventy-seventh Street. From there we could see a sea of people's heads and shoulder-riding toddlers, the tops of a few distant trees in the park, and a floating, bobbing Garfield the Cat as it passed several stories above street level.

Talk about anticlimactic. Jack didn't have to talk me into going home, where I threw together my famous green bean casserole—the one with the Campbell's Cream of Mushroom soup and canned french-fried onions—before we caught an early train to Westchester.

"You beat everyone here," Wilma informs us, taking the foil-covered casserole out of my hands and carrying it to the kitchen area as we slip out of our shoes on the mat before setting foot on the plush ivory carpeting.

She doesn't ask us to take off our shoes; I just know by now that it's expected here and was expected in the Bedford mansion as well. The first time I met her I was wearing a sock with a hole in it and I spent the entire visit trying to keep it folded under so my big toe wouldn't pop through. Now I always wear my best socks when we go to Wilma's.

I wear my best everything, in fact, because there's just something about her that makes you want to be dressed up. I changed into a nice black sweater and I traded my sneakers for boots, but I still have on the same jeans. I could barely button the slimming black pants I intended to wear, much less imagine consuming a feast while wearing them.

"What time is everybody else coming?" Jack asks as his mother leads the way into the spotless living room.

"Jeannie won't be coming until dessert—she and Greg had to go to his parents' house in Rockland to eat with them first. Kathleen and Bob and the twins will be here soon, and they're picking up Rachel on the way."

Plopping onto an antique sofa the way he sprawls on the lovely Ikea couch at home, Jack asks, "What about Emily?"

His mother doesn't make a face or squirm, but she's not exactly making eye contact with him—or me, for that matter—when she admits, "Emily isn't coming."

"Why not?"

That came from Jack, of course. I say nothing, because I don't feel comfortable actively getting into family-based personal business in front of his mother. Maybe I would if I were his wife. Or even future wife.

Which is a status I'm starting to think I may not achieve before this day is over, because Jack seems much too relaxed for a man who's about to pop the question.

He casually helps himself to a handful of mixed nuts from a crystal bowl on the marble-topped coffee table, damn him, and asks again, "Why isn't Emily coming?"

"Because she feels sorry for Daddy. She's going there instead."

"To his apartment? He's cooking?"

"Who knows? Do I know anything?" From the helpless gesture Wilma makes, she does not.

"When did she make this decision?" Jack presses on, oblivious to his mother's heartbreak. At least, I'm assuming it's heartbreak. If I were her and one of my kids blew me off for Thanksgiving, I would be heartbroken.

Then again, I blew off my own mother for Thanksgiving.

I can't help but wonder if, at this very moment, she's helplessly throwing up her hands while talking about me to one of my brothers' wives.

"Because I talked to her last night," Jack goes on, chewing mixed nuts while reaching for a second handful, "and she said she was coming. She said she was bringing two pumpkin pies from some great bakery in Brooklyn."

"She decided this morning, I guess."

"What about the pies?"

"They're coming anyway," his mother zings at him.

Go, Wilma. Go, Wilma.

Jack blinks. "You don't have to be sarcastic."

"Well, what do you mean, 'What about the pies,' Jack? What about them? Do I look like I'm concerned about *pies?*"

Jack says nothing.

I say, because I have this overwhelming need to fill the strained silence, "Don't worry about the pies, Wilma. I'm on a diet anyway."

Why I felt compelled to share that, I have no idea. It makes it sound as if I thought the pies were solely for my benefit.

Not that I don't love pumpkin pie. In fact, I love it so much that the thought of Thanksgiving without it makes me homesick all over again.

My mother always makes homemade pumpkin pie for Thanksgiving dessert. From a real pumpkin, not from a can. She makes six of them, actually. And she serves big slices with real whipped cream that she beats herself with her old handheld mixer that splatters tiny drops of heavy cream all over her hair, her face, the walls, the counters.

She serves the pie from the kitchen but she always brings the whipped cream right to the table in a big yellow earthenware bowl, the same one every year.

She has a green one just like it, a size bigger, in which she always serves the candied yams. I don't like candied yams, but the thought of them in that bowl is putting a sick feeling in the pit of my stomach.

Or maybe that's just acute starvation.

After all, I haven't eaten anything since last night's pizza with Buckley and Sonja. I really could have gone for a turkey dinner with all the trimmings topped off by a quarter of a pumpkin pie slathered in whipped cream.

Or, instead, a cigarette to stave off the hunger pains, because simultaneously going cold turkey on nicotine and food is enough to send a normally sane person over the edge.

Yes, I'm normally *quite* sane, thank you very much.

Meanwhile, Jack, who so far has had not just the purloined ham-egg-and-cheese but cold pizza and several tablespoonfuls of peanut butter before we left home, has resumed gobbling mixed nuts like a protein-deprived reward challenge winner on *Survivor.*

"Do you think the supermarkets are open today, Tracey? Because if they are, we can buy some frozen pies," Wilma offers lamely, apparently having sensed my secret pumpkin-pie-deprivation trauma.

"Don't worry about it, Wilma," I say. "We don't need pie."

That was a little presumptuous, don't you think? Why I feel compelled to be the spokesperson for the entire Candell family when I'm not technically one of them is beyond me. Who am I to decide that a Thanksgiving dinner sans pumpkin pie will suffice for all?

But Wilma doesn't seem fazed. Maybe she thinks I'm using the royal "we."

"Can I get you a glass of wine?" she asks, and I think she's talking to both me and Jack. I'm careful not to answer for him, even when he doesn't answer for himself. I don't want her to think I'll be the kind of pushy daughter-in-law who'll take over her son's life.

I wait for Jack to tell his mother that a glass of wine right now would really take off the edge.

But Jack, who apparently shed his edge at the door, just shakes his head.

"Tracey? How about you?"

"No, thanks," I say reluctantly.

A glass of wine on an empty stomach might lead to my sloppily professing my love for Jack in front of the entire Candell clan—or, even more frighteningly, it might lead to my sobbing on his mother's shoulder in the kitchen because he hasn't given me that diamond ring yet.

"How about a mixed drink?" Wilma persists, the question nearly drowned out by the ferocious growling of my empty stomach, which I cleverly attempt to cover by swiftly changing my position on the sofa. Alas, the shifting cushions do little to drown out my gastro-pandemonium.

"I can make you a vodka and tonic," Wilma goes on, ever the charming hostess. "Or a rum and Coke?"

I'm thinking something more along the lines of a spicy Bloody Mary garnished with plenty of celery and olives: the drink that tastes like a meal.

But she doesn't offer, and I'm afraid to ask, lest I come off as a gluttonous lush.

Instead, I say, "Thanks anyway, but I'm all set. Is there anything I can help you with in the kitchen?"

"No," she says, smiling, "but thank you, Tracey."

I smile back at her.

As I'm smiling, the strangest thought occurs to me.

Speaking of cold turkey…

I smell new paint, Lysol, flowers and Jack's nut breath.

Just new paint, Lysol, flowers and Jack's nut breath.

Shouldn't I also be inhaling the succulent scent of roasting turkey, at the very least?

Not to mention golden gravy bubbling on the stovetop, starchy potatoes boiling in preparation for mashing, savory sage-laced stuffing baking in the oven…

I shoot a questioning glance at Jack, wondering if he can read my mind.

In response to my questioning glance, he says promptly, "Cowboys game doesn't start until four," leading me to conclude that A) mind reading isn't among his many talents and B) his idea of a bended-knee conclusion to Thanksgiving dinner most likely involves pigskin and goalposts.

"Are you sure you don't need help in the kitchen, Wilma?" I ask again, shifting my attention back to the lady of the house in an effort to solve The Mystery of the Absent Cooking Fumes.

"No, thanks." She flashes me a curious look.

"Are you sure?" asks the intrepid Tracey Spadolini, Girl Detective.

"Ye-es," she says, frowning a bit. "I'm positive."

Okay, I'll admit it: I'd make a lousy sleuth despite last night's Colonel Mustard in the Conservatory with the Lead Pipe triumph. But I can't come right out and ask Jack's mother why she hasn't started cooking dinner, can I?

Maybe I can.

Maybe these Candells don't know that it takes six hours to roast a turkey. Maybe somebody should warn them before it's too late.

Maybe that somebody should be Tracey Spadolini, Girl Detective/Kitchen Slave Apprentice.

"Um," I say, always a charming opener.

"Yes?" Wilma asks.

Jack cordially stops munching and leans forward a bit, seeming to sense a provocative note in the scent-free air.

I clear my throat. "I was just wondering...are you sure you'll have time to, uh, cook everything? In time, I mean? To, um, eat?"

"Oh—" Wilma waves a hand and Jack immediately resumes the nut binge "—I did all that yesterday. All we have to do is reheat."

Reheat?

An entire Thanksgiving dinner? Turkey, gravy, stuffing, mashed potatoes, reheated like so many...*leftovers?*

Now I'm really homesick.

"I always do the cooking ahead of time," Wilma informs me breezily. "It's so much easier that way."

Much easier? So is takeout—what the hell, let's just go through a drive-through for Gordita Supremes and Pintos 'n Cheese and call it a feast.

All I can manage aloud is, "Aren't you the clever one!"

At least, that's what I meant to say.

I think it comes out sounding more like, "Huh?"

But the oblivious mother-son duo has turned their attention to more pressing matters. Wilma mentions something to Jack about mini-marshmallows for the canned yams, and my heart sinks even lower. Marshmallows are for hot chocolate, dammit, and yams aren't supposed to be canned. Chi chi beans are supposed to be canned. Yams are meant to be plucked from the rich dark earth, scrubbed and peeled.

All right, plucked from the produce department at Tops supermarket, *then* scrubbed and peeled.

The whole point of Thanksgiving dinner is to work your ass off in a hot kitchen. Isn't it? Well, *isn't* it?

Apparently not. Apparently, Wilma Candell prefers to work her ass off at Curves for Women, and spend Thanksgiving Day lightly tapping the keypads on her microwave so as not to break a nail.

This is…

This is…

This is a travesty. My mother would roll over in her grave if she knew…and, uh, if she were dead. But you get the idea.

And so do I.

I bet the gravy will be Franco-American and the stuffing will be Stove Top.

Connie Spadolini makes homemade everything, in case I neglected to mention it. But whatever.

I smile reassuringly at my culinarily challenged future mother-in-law, to show her that nuked canned goods are just dandy with me.

She smiles reassuringly back at me, to show…*what?*

What is she reassuring me of?

Who knows? But that is definitely a reassuring smile, and there is definitely a knowing gleam in her eye. At least, I'm pretty sure there is.

Hmm. Is she reassuring me that the nuked canned goods will not be the highlight of Thanksgiving Day? That Jack has an engagement surprise in store?

God, I hope so.

Before I can smoke a hint out of her, his two sisters, his brother-in-law and his twin nieces burst noisily in the door.

I know Rachel pretty well because she occasionally calls, and sometimes even comes into the city with her boyfriend. But I've only met Kathleen and Bob St. James on a couple of occasions.

Which was more than enough time for me to realize that they're mired in suburbia the way my family is mired in Brookside. For pretty, brunette Kathleen and preppy, bespectacled Bob, the world revolves around their four-year-old daughters; their house, which they're endlessly remodeling; their cars, both of which are SUVs; and their neighbors, all of whom are presumably complete strangers to the rest of us, though Kathleen and Bob talk about them as if we all know them well. And actually care.

"Sorry we're late," Kathleen says, sinking her size-two hips onto the couch in sheer exhaustion. Clearly, she has spent the day hiking in the Catskills.

Oops, I forgot. She's Kathleen. I bet she slept in and took a rigorous bath.

"Rodney and Sue showed up," she explains inexplicably. "They needed to borrow a pan at the last minute."

Yeah, that'll throw you off by an hour, at least.

I merely smile and, spurred by the ensuing silence that I always feel compelled to fill, ask "Who are Rodney and Sue?"

"They're the ones who live in the Tudor with the three dormers," Bob explains, assuming that, during my lone visit to their house more than a year ago, I took painstaking note of the local architecture.

"Oh, right," I say with a knowing nod, "the nice stucco house. I remember it." I don't really, but I figure this is a safe bet because aren't all Tudors stucco?

Apparently not. Some are brick. Rodney and Sue's place is one of them.

"You're thinking of Kevin and Doreen's place," Kathleen informs me. "That's the stucco one with the newish red-slate roof. And they're the ones with the litter we were telling you about."

When? Back in August at the family barbecue, which is the last time I saw you people?

And...the litter? Are we talking dropped candy bar wrappers or puppies? I don't dare hazard a guess. Instead, I just nod knowingly again. Kevin and Doreen. The litter. Stucco house, newish red slate—not shingled, or thatched, folks—roof. Aha.

"Oh!" Bob slaps his head as though he's forgotten to tell me something important. Like that he brought a bottle of

Grey Goose and it's time for all of us to do shots now. "That's right! Guess what? Chris *finally* got promoted."

"It's about time!" I say triumphantly.

Which begs the silent question, who is Chris and why did it take him/her so darned long to get that promotion anyway?

And, why the heck am I the only one participating in this boring conversation?

Looking around, I see that Rachel is fervently whispering something to her mother, Jack is scarily absorbed in the nut bowl, and the twins, Ashley and Beatrice, are busily crawling around rearranging all the shoes by the door and snickering.

Yes, Ashley and Beatrice. Not Ashley and Mary Kate, or Terry and Kerry, or even Beatrice and Olga.

Ashley and Beatrice.

Guess which one's cuter?

No, go on, guess.

Right. Poor scrawny Beatrice of the limp locks and over-bite is doomed to live a self-fulfilling prophecy, while her cute sister with the cute name will probably be a touring pop princess with a boy-band boyfriend by the time she hits puberty.

Ashley and Beatrice. The cruel implications are staggering. Oh, Kathleen and Bob, what on earth got into you two back on the neonatal-multiples ward?

Jack claims, in all fairness, that each of the twins is named after a special person. Clearly, one after someone's decrepit maiden great-great-aunt, the other after a perky blond starlet.

Fair and square my ass.

Unfortunately, neither of the twins is particularly lovable, though I have tried very hard to have a soft spot for Beatrice.

That pretty much swirls down the proverbial toilet today

as I watch her open the front door and fling one of my leather boots out into the rain before closing it again and looking around to make sure nobody saw.

Nobody did, other than me.

But before I can call her on it, Bob summons the girls to the living-room carpet to recite an original Thanksgiving poem.

It goes: "Turkey is good, cranberries are yummy, and the Pilgrims discovered America." Or something like that.

It's all I can do to muster a smattering of applause as the rest of the family claps wildly and Bob whistles between his fingers—a bit overzealous, in light of the performance.

Hey, nobody says poetry has to rhyme, but…

Oh, never mind.

Bottom line, I suddenly find myself missing my runny-nosed, whiny nephews more than ever.

"How was the parade, Tracey?" Rachel asks in the post-performance lull, and for a brief shining moment, I'm having fun again.

I open my mouth to answer the question, but before I can speak, Bob announces, "Rodney and Sue were there. They watched it from Herald Square. That's why they got such a late start on dinner."

Which you would think might be Wilma's cue to go start warming over the turkey, but it isn't.

It's her cue to say, "Girls, do you have another poem you can recite for us? Or maybe a Thanksgiving song?"

I swear I want to strangle her and those little no-talent twins.

That, or devour the remainder of the bowl of fancy mixed nuts. I'm starving to death, and nobody cares.

Not even Jack. He's too busy smiling and nodding while his nieces serenade us with an off-key duet of some unrecognizable song with ridiculously over-the-top lyrics.

"That was wonderful!" crows their doting grandmother. "I've never heard a better rendition of 'Amazing Grace'!"

I wait for somebody to inform poor deluded Wilma that it wasn't "Amazing Grace," but apparently, it was "Amazing Grace."

Next thing you know, Bob will pull a pitch pipe out of his pocket for an encore: perhaps a rousing rendition of "We Gather Together" followed by several choruses of "Over the River and Through the Woods."

It occurs to me that if Jack ever does pop the elusive question, and I say yes—which, don't get me wrong, I fully intend to do—I will spend many more future Thanksgivings with these people. My kids will have an uncle who will regale them with riveting stories about total strangers re-sodding their lawns; a grandmother whose most crucial kitchen appliance is her can opener; a mismatched set of girl cousins destined for intensive psychotherapy.

It's enough to make me rethink this whole relationship…but only for a split second.

Then Jack catches my eye, raises his eyebrows slightly and grins.

Aw. How cute.

He might suck at mind reading, but I excel at it. Thus, I know exactly what he's telling me: *Yes, my family is a little loony, but I love them…and, more importantly, I love you for indulging them and not complaining about anything, not even your soggy boot.*

Wait.

He doesn't know about the soggy boot.

If he did, he'd love me even more.

Mental note: be sure to tell Jack about soggy boot ASAP.

I smile back at him, a smile that says, *Don't worry, I'm just glad to be spending our first Thanksgiving together, the first of many. Next year, how about if we host it at our place?*

Jack nods slightly, and I know he gets it.

Then he leans toward me and whispers meaningfully, "I'm going to go catch the end of the Detroit game in the other room. Want to come?"

Okay, so maybe he doesn't get it.

Then again, what if he does? What if he not only gets it, but is at last ready for the long-awaited moment of truth?

I have a fleeting moment of wondering if this is it: is he trying to whisk me away so that he can give me the ring in private?

I look into his eyes and common sense quickly takes hold.

No romantic *happily-ever-after* visions there. He really does just want me to watch football with him.

But right now, you know what? Maybe that's okay. Right now, maybe football and Jack are all I really need.

Tomorrow is another day. A day when we'll be alone together at Deux Coeurs Sur La Plage.

A day when anything can happen. Well, anything but a command performance by the woefully inadequate Singing St. James Sisters.

For now the Detroit game awaits.

As I follow Jack toward the spare bedroom that serves as Wilma's den, I make a quick detour to the front entry to retrieve my boot. A chilly blast of wind-driven rain greets me at the door.

I set the boot back on the mat and wonder how long it's going to take to dry. Then I vengefully eye Beatrice's small, unattractive lime-green sneakers (Guess who got the cute pink ones?).

For a moment, I'm tempted to drop one of Beatrice's sneakers into the toilet tank.

But I immediately think better of it, reminding myself that someday, I'll be her aunt Tracey.

Do I really believe that?

Yup. In my heart, I really do.

Someday.

And I, Tracey Spadolini, Girl Detective/Kitchen Slave Apprentice/Future Aunt of Ashley and Not-Mary-Kate, do solemnly swear, here and now, with all my heart, that when *Someday* finally comes, there will be no flower girls at the wedding.

So *there,* you little boot-stealing rug rat, I think as I head into the den where my beloved awaits.

I stop short in the doorway.

Jack is down on bended knee.

Can it be…?

Is this it…?

Nope.

"There it is," he grumbles, retrieving the remote from under the couch. "My mother falls asleep watching QVC and it falls out of her hand onto the floor. She's been doing that for years. Hey, what's wrong?"

"Nothing," I lie, vowing not to get my hopes up again.

Life would be so much easier if I didn't know he had that diamond.

Then again, if I didn't know about it, would I still be here, waiting around for an engagement that might never happen?

At least this way, I know I'm not wasting my time; that there's an eventual engagement and wedding on the horizon.

"I'm so glad you're here," Jack says softly, pulling me close to him as we sink onto the couch.

"Yeah, me too." Suddenly, I'm overwhelmed by an unexpected sweep of emotion. Of pure love.

This is good. Really, really good. Jack and me, I mean. We belong together. He's not going anywhere, and neither am I. I honestly don't need a ring and a promise to realize that.

He kisses me, then pulls back and spots the tears pooling in my eyes.

"Hey," he says in worried surprise, brushing a trickle that's escaped down my cheek. "What's wrong?"

"Nothing," I say again, and this time, it isn't a lie.

Chapter 12

What better place to get engaged than at a luxuriously romantic waterfront New England couples spa?

I don't know, maybe you should ask Jack, because *he* obviously has some other locale in mind.

We've been at Deux Coeurs Sur La Plage for more than twenty-four hours, and call me a pessimist, but I don't think Jack has any intention of proposing this weekend.

My Thanksgiving Day epiphany was unfortunately short-lived.

I'm right back to obsessing over when he's going to pop the question—and wondering why he hasn't yet. He's certainly had plenty of opportunity.

What the heck is he waiting for? Christmas? New Year's Eve? Or—God forbid—springtime?

Doesn't he realize we have little hope of an autumn wedding if he doesn't get his butt in gear?

Yes, I still have my heart set on that.

If he proposes before this weekend is out, we'd still have time to get the plans under way. But I really don't think it's going to happen, regardless of the romantic weekend setting.

Don't get me wrong, I'm glad to be here.

It's just…

Well, as I sit on the bed in a pair of old sweats, watching Jack dig through his suitcase for something to wear to our reflexology session, I can't help but wonder: is this all there is? To the spa, I mean.

Just an antiquated, television-free room with a view of the parking lot; Spartan, albeit healthy, meals that leave me wishing I'd smuggled in Fritos; and hourly seminars with titles like, "Free Your Soul: Who Am I and Why Am I Here?"

All I got out of that one is that I'm Tracey Spadolini and I'm here because this is my reward for quitting smoking. I have no idea what Jack got out of the seminar, but I couldn't help noticing other couples nodding meaningfully at each other and Shalaylah, the female instructor, all clearly moved by some sort of spiritual enlightenment that evaded the two of us.

I conclude that they must all be married—presumably to each other—and that's why we're just not getting it. Our souls—Jack's and mine—are trapped in a spiritual limbo because one of us isn't ready to commit.

But maybe that's not the only problem.

I'm starting to think that maybe spa life just isn't my thing. I guess I pictured more of a self-indulgent, or even decadent, weekend, rather than a hectic barrage of nonstop activity more suited to limber New Age yogini types than to a reformed smoker with a growing paunch and a ravenous appetite.

I don't want to disappoint Jack, though. The weekend has to be costing him a small fortune—one that would have been better spent on a quick, rum-infused jaunt to the Caribbean, in my opinion. I should be enjoying every minute of it.

Not that Jack has any idea I'm *not* enjoying every minute of it. I've become quite the actress, if I do say so myself. Last night, I feigned exhilarated bliss during a hot-stone treatment that smacked of primitive torture methods; this morning, I delivered a joyful Oscarworthy tour de force in response to an excruciating paraffin face mask that I swear removed the epidermis from my neck up.

"Do you think jeans are okay?" Jack asks, holding up the pair he wore yesterday on the train ride up from New York.

"I don't know…they weren't okay for yoga this morning," I point out, remembering how he was forced to trot back to the room and change into sweats. As a result, he endured ten fewer minutes of gravity-defying contortions than I did.

No wonder he's not flinching in pain as he bends over the suitcase again and says knowingly, "Yeah, but that was yoga. This is reflexology."

Yeah, right. As though he has the foggiest notion what "reflexology" is.

Not that I do. But at least if somebody instructs me to roll myself into a ball on the floor, which has happened on more than one occasion since our arrival yesterday, I'll be suitably dressed.

"I'd better wear shorts," Jack concludes, and pulls out a pair of gray fleece ones. "We might need bare legs."

We might? Uh-oh. Maybe I should have shaved better. Or at all, I amend, recalling that my muscles were too sore in this morning's shower to allow me to reach for the razor, let alone bend in half to access a stubbly appendage.

"Maybe you should wear shorts, too," Jack informs me as he pulls his on, again without a discernible wince. Show-off.

"I didn't bring any shorts."

"Why not?"

Because I don't have any that fit, for one thing.

For another, "Um, I forgot."

Yeah, right.

"Do you want to go buy some in the gift shop downstairs?" he offers after glancing at my sweats—which I've worn nonstop since we arrived, in a show of sheer defiance to the hordes of black-spandex-clad spa bunnies in residence at Deux Coeurs Sur La Plage.

"No, thanks. These are fine for reflexology—and the sunset hike," I add quickly, after consulting my mental agenda.

Like I said, these sadistic spa people like to keep you in perpetual grueling motion from dawn till dusk.

The bright side: at least I know what a "hike" is.

And that it will be followed by dinner, with which I am also familiar. Then again, last night's dinner at Deux Coeurs Sur La Plage bore scant resemblance to the average meal back home, which usually consists of a meat, a grain, a vegetable, and of course, a luscious buttery dessert.

The four main food types I've been able to distinguish here at the spa are sprouts, kernels, legumes and greens. All tasteless, yes, but ostensibly very nourishing, very soul-cleansing. I dare say my colon is clean as a whistle as well.

And to think I was complaining mere days ago over the tragic grape-tomato shortage. I woke up this morning so hungry I could eat tree bark, which, for all I know, might be tonight's main course.

Alas, breakfast was meager, steaming, lumpy and unidentifiable. I scraped my bowl clean and it was all I could do not to pull an Oliver.

Please, suh, can I have some mo-ah?

No you can't, you flabby, gluttonous New Yorker! And you can't have any caffeine, either. Mu-wah-ha-ha-ha-ha-ha.

That's right, folks. No coffee here at Deux Coeurs Sur La Plage. As a result, my head is pounding despite the Advil I've been popping all day. At this point, I'd kill for a triple caramel macchiato with an espresso chaser.

Heck, I'd kill for one of Wilma's rubbery turkey drumsticks doused in tepid gravy, accompanied by jelled cranberry sauce with the can rings etched into the curved surface. Mmm-mmm.

But for now, there's only my throbbing skull and hollow, rumbling gut, and nothing but the mysterious reflexology on the immediate horizon.

So off we go, Jack and me, to reflexology.

Which might sound like a clever, bouncy little ditty, but trust me, nobody's singing or skipping along the way.

En route, we manage to get lost twice in the building's rambling corridors.

The spa is located in what was once a turn-of-the-century hotel, perched on the edge of a rocky cliff not far from Newport's famous mansions. Clearly, this is where the middle-class folk stayed back in the Gilded Age. Not much has changed since then. Every possible interior wall is covered in floral wallpaper, the public spaces seem dimly lit, and there's a pervasive musty smell that reminds me of a book left out in the rain, like, twenty-five years ago.

Not that I'm complaining.

Yesterday, I found the place completely charming, musty smell and all.

In fact, it would probably regain much of that charm if a coffee-and-Danish cart appeared around the next bend.

Naturally, that doesn't happen.

Finally, we reach the reflexology room, located in the bowels of the building's annex—a fancy term for "slapped-on concrete-block addition."

We're greeted by Zena and Ted, neither of whom looks a day over twenty-nine, and both of whom have perpetually frozen facial muscles. I'm guessing these two are no strangers to Botox—or the Bobby Sox era, for that matter. Zena has wise old-ladyish eyes that I suspect would be surrounded by wrinkles if not for the miracles of modern poison.

"You can both go ahead and remove your shoes and socks, then lie on the tables," Ted instructs us.

Jack and I exchange glances. Remove our shoes and socks? Mayhap we've wandered into the pedicure wing by accident?

Or the set of a porn flick, I conclude in apprehension when Ted dims the lights, puts on soft music and urges us to lie back and let sensation take over. I half expect him and Zena to strip down and go at it.

But no, we're in the right place after all, and everyone remains reassuringly fully clothed, with the exception of our bare feet.

Reflexology, it turns out, involves Zena and Ted putting pressure on various points in our extremities, ostensibly to reduce stress and send renewed vigor pulsing through our veins. At least, that's what it says on one of the wall charts I can see from my tabletop perch.

I've read only half of it when Zena commences the treatment. The second I feel her cold fingers on the arch of my right foot, I am convulsed in squirmy giggles.

"Sorry," I say when she lifts her hand and gazes questioningly at me. "I guess I'm ticklish."

"It's okay," she says woodenly, clearly never having so much as chuckled in all her sixty-something years. "Let's try again."

We do.

This time when she touches me, I nearly fly off the table in hysteria.

Jack, calmly enduring Ted's kneading of his heel, looks over at me in alarm. "Are you okay, Trace?"

"Yes," I gasp.

Zena sighs and waits for me to compose myself and lie still. Then she presses a forefinger into the base of my pinkie toe, which apparently doubles as my funny bone.

Yowza! This time, I really do bolt from the table.

The moment I've stopped laughing and found my voice, I announce firmly, "I can't do this. It's physically impossible for me."

"Come on, Trace," Jack says, as though I am perfectly capable of detaching the nerve endings in my extremities. "Sure you can. Just stop goofing around."

I glare at him. "I'm not goofing around, I'm laughing. And I can't help it."

"Try to focus," he says, his eyes drifting closed as though Ted's thumb jammed into his instep is the most relaxing thing ever.

"I think I'll go take a nap," I tell Zena, and hand her a good-size tip before retrieving my shoes and socks. "Thanks, anyway."

Zena shrugs and pockets the tip. Easy come, easy go.

Jack's eyes snap open. "You're leaving?"

"Yeah, I'll see you back in the room."

"Wait, I'll come with you," he says, sitting up.

"No, stay. Enjoy your foot, uh, thing."

"No, really, I'll come with you." He swings his legs over the edge of the table.

"You don't have to," I protest, fervently wishing he wouldn't. If I go solo, I can detour back and recheck all the floors for hidden vending machines. You'd think they'd have at least one tucked away somewhere for staffers who need their daily Hostess or No-Doz fix.

Wishful thinking, I know.

Unfortunately for this suffering addict, Jack is already tipping Ted and pulling on his socks.

In no time, we're out the door and heading back to the room.

"You could have stayed," I tell him. "I honestly wouldn't have minded."

"No, I didn't want you to go back upstairs alone," he says quickly—too quickly.

I sneak a peek at him. Hmm.

"Come on," I cajole. "You can't convince me that having that guy Ted poke the soles of your feet actually felt good?"

He hesitates.

Aha!

"No," he admits. "It pretty much sucked, actually."

"Why didn't you say something? Why did you lie there in what looked like ecstasy while I was doing my lunatic-hyena act?"

"It wasn't ecstasy, trust me. It just didn't tickle. It actually kind of hurt. I guess I just didn't get the point."

"Sort of like yoga," I say, having endured two sessions and spent the bulk of both faking poses and checking my watch.

Which I do now, and see that we've got less than an hour before we start that sunset hike. Or not.

"Want to skip the hike, too?" I ask Jack slyly.

"And do what?"

Too bad there's no TV, I think, for the millionth time since we got here yesterday.

"Sleep?" I suggest. "Or send out for coffee and cheese-burgers? Or both?"

He laughs.

"I'm totally serious."

"Really?"

I nod. "I need caffeine desperately, and I'm starved for something I can actually sink my teeth into."

"I guess sprouts and seeds don't qualify?"

"Not unless one is a rodent."

"I have to say, I'm hungry, too."

"Too bad we don't have a car so we could sneak out of here and hit a McDonald's."

Jack contemplates that for a minute, then says, "How about a compromise?"

"Steal a car and hit a Wendy's? I could go for chili and a Frosty, too."

He grins. "No, I was thinking we could sneak out of here and go for a nice long walk on the beach. Alone."

"You mean a nice long walk on *la plage*."

"Is that how you pronounce it? I thought it was *la plage*." As in, rhymes with Madge.

"Nope. It's Deux Coeurs Sur La Plage," I say, shamelessly showing off my year of high-school French.

"That sounds good. What else can you say in French?"

"Voulez-vous couchez avec moi."

He grins. "*Sì*. Later."

"You mean *oui*."

"*Oui oui*. What else can you say?"

"I can say, let's *vamoose*."

"*Vamoose* is French?"

"Who knows?"

And who cares? I'm feeling lighthearted for the first time all day.

Maybe you can't take the "spa" out of Spadolini, but you can definitely take the Spadolini out of the spa…and none too soon.

As we grab jackets and head furtively back outside, feeling vaguely like a pair of truant adolescents, I remind myself that this still hasn't solved my hunger problem.

Well, maybe we can forage on the beach for shellfish.

Do you think Rhode Island's coastal waters are contaminated?

I know.

But do I really care at this point? A few toxins never killed anybody.

All right, maybe I'm wrong about that, but I can't help it. My judgment is clouded by starvation.

We cross the eerily deserted grounds and descend the rickety wooden stairs to a narrow stretch of pebbly bay beach at the base of the rocky cliff. The dense gray sky hangs low over the choppy water and the air is shrouded with mist.

As I look around, I can't help noticing that this would be the perfect setting for a murder...

Or a marriage proposal.

But that's too much to hope for, so I settle for holding hands with Jack as we set out along the packed wet sand left by the outgoing tide.

"This is really nice," I say, watching a gull swoop low over the green-black waves. "Thanks for bringing me up here."

Jack squeezes my hand. "I thought you hated it."

I hesitate. "Not all of it."

"Really? What did you like?"

"This part," I confess. "And..."

I'm afraid I'm drawing a complete blank.

"This part is good," I reiterate.

Jack smiles. "So much for your big reward. I should have brought you to a bed-and-breakfast somewhere instead."

"Or the Caribbean?"

He laughs. "Or the Caribbean. I didn't know you wanted to go there."

"It would be fun," I say. "Don't you think?"

"I guess. My sister went to Anguilla on her honeymoon."

"Kathleen?"

"Jeannie. I remember her raving about the food, and how beautiful it was. I should ask her which resort they went to."

Really? Why should he ask her? Does he want to take me there on *our* honeymoon?

"Yeah, you should definitely find out," I say, and I can feel my heart beating a little faster.

"I will," he says, "when I see her again at Christmas."

My heart lands with a thud.

Christmas.

That was the main topic of conversation last night over dessert, which in absence of pumpkin pie consisted depressingly of Lorna Doones and sliced bananas.

I have long been aware that the Candells have always spent Christmas together in Aspen, where Jack's dad has a ski house. Actually, it used to be the family's house, but he got it in the divorce settlement.

I've seen plenty of pictures and heard countless stories about Candell Christmases, which are always made to seem excitingly Kennedyesque: everybody skis, even the twins, and they all wear three-hundred-dollar parkas accessorized by aviator lenses and those sporty headbands that somehow look great on the snowy, sun-splashed Colorado slopes, but would be ridiculously Olivia Newton-John circa 1982 anywhere else.

When the subject of Christmas came up Thursday, Wilma acted really excited to be going on her Caribbean jaunt with a fellow divorcée while the rest of the family took off for the Rockies with Dad.

But if you ask me, she seemed about as enthusiastic about her trip as I am about spending Christmas in Brookside.

"You mean you're not coming with us?" Rachel asked me, looking genuinely shocked and so disappointed at first I assumed she was talking to her mother.

"Me? No, I have to go home for Christmas," I told her. "My parents would be really upset if I didn't, especially after I missed Thanksgiving."

Everybody seemed to accept that answer, including Jack.

After all, where we would spend our respective Christmases hadn't even been a topic for discussion with us.

But now, as we stroll *sur la* rocky but romantic *plage,* he looks a little wistful as he asks, "Are you sure you can't come with us to Aspen?"

"For Christmas?" I shake my head vigorously. "No way. I've got to go home."

"Are you positive?"

"Positive."

"I hate the thought of us spending the holidays apart."

So do I.

If only...

"We don't have to, you know," I hear myself say impulsively.

He brightens immediately. "You mean you'll come to Aspen?"

"No, you can come to Brookside!" Why didn't I think of it before?

Maybe, I realize on the heels of what I think was an invitation, because it's a really, really bad idea.

Yes, he's visited Brookside before...

But never for Christmas.

If Jack's Aspen Christmases are Kennedyesque, my Brookside Christmases are...well, cross the Sopranos with the Gottis, replace the crime and guns with perpetual chaos and *cucidati,* and you get the idea.

Do I *really* want to subject nice normal Jack to *that*?

Picture this: dozens of opinionated oddball relatives, some with bad colds, some talking loudly and asking too many questions; others not at all because you or somebody in your immediate family offended them last Christmas. Most of them are going to hug and kiss everyone in the house upon arrival and departure, regardless of whether they're speaking to you and whether you happen to be a complete stranger, a.k.a., somebody's visiting boyfriend from New York City. All of these will come bearing utterly useless gifts, which will be opened one by one in an endless ritual that goes on into the wee hours.

Throw in a bunch of bizarre yuletide traditions, too much food, too much steam heat, at least one vomiting kid, cat hair...

And then there's the snow. Incessant, wind-driven snow. Feet of it pile up at a time, and my father would expect Jack to shovel it.

"Are you serious?" Jack is asking.

I feign confusion. "Serious about what?"

Jack: "Me coming to Brookside for Christmas."

Tracey, brightly: "That? Oh, sure!"

I suspect my Oscar nomination just went the way of the reflexology session, judging by the look on Jack's face.

"You don't look like you mean it."

"No, I do! It's just…I mean, I know your dad is probably counting on you to come to Aspen."

"Screw him," Jack says darkly. "Look what he did to my mother. Who cares what he wants?"

Oooh-kay then. I guess it's safe to assume he's not quite over the divorce.

"I'd much rather spend Christmas with you and your family in Brookside," Jack informs me.

You know what? I believe him.

Granted, he knows not of what he speaks.

Still…

"Great," I say, cleverly noting that my chances of becoming engaged over the holidays will be much higher if Jack comes to Brookside than they are if we spend Christmas half a continent apart.

In fact…

Maybe that's why he looks so enthusiastic about this sudden change of plans.

Look at him. Maybe he's plotting right now how he's going to smuggle a ring box into my stocking.

"My sisters are going to be pissed," he says almost gleefully.

Or maybe he's just out for vengeance.

Sigh.

Oh, well.

It's too late to rescind the offer now.

Brookside for Christmas, here we come!

Part IV

Christmas

Chapter 13

"Maybe he sold it for cash to buy drugs, Tracey."

That, of course, is Raphael.

Re: the whereabouts of the diamond Jack has yet to offer.

"F&%# @(★."

That, of course, is me.

Re: Raphael's ridiculous claim.

"Tracey!" His newly dyed-blond eyebrows elevate toward his newly dyed-blond hairline. "That wasn't a nice thing to say."

"Neither was your thing. Jack isn't on drugs."

"You don't know that for sure. Wait, pull over." Grabbing my arm, Raphael steps out of the flow of pedestrian traffic along Saint Mark's Place to examine a sidewalk display of sunglasses.

"I know for sure that Jack isn't on drugs," I argue in frustration, shivering in the brisk night wind blowing off the East River a few blocks away, "but I'm not so sure about you, Raphael."

"If I seem high, it's because I'm madly in love, Tracey."

"Oh, please."

Raphael stops fondling a pair of leopard-spot cat's-eye lenses to rest a hand on my arm. "I know it must be painful for you. Jealousy is a natural reaction in your situation. I'm sorry. I'll try not to mention Donatello any more than is absolutely necessary."

"It's okay. I'm really not jealous."

No, just sick to death of hearing about their Valentine's Day wedding and their safari honeymoon and living happily ever *blah, blah, blah.*

"Of course you're not jealous," he says gently. Then, after a beat, "So do you think Donatello will find me more irresistible in the leopard-print or the zebra-stripe frames for Kenya?"

He pulls on one pair of shades, then the other.

I pretend to debate, while making absolutely certain out of sheer Raphael-induced paranoia that there's not the slightest possibility Jack is, indeed, on drugs.

Of course he isn't.

And I'm an idiot for even bringing up the subject of Jack and our nonengagement to Raphael, the voice of doom. Haven't I learned he has nothing optimistic to say about my chances of becoming Jack's bride?

He keeps telling me I'm the proverbial cow and Jack is getting the proverbial milk for free, and "Sooner or later he's going to become lactose intolerant, Tracey. You'll see."

"What does that even mean?" I made the mistake of asking.

And Raphael told me. Nonproverbially.

Mental note: do not, I repeat, not, mention anything about Jack or the elusive diamond ring for the remainder of the evening.

The only thing is, there's really not much else I care about right now in my life. Everything else—work, finances, Spadolini-family dynamics, pre-holiday madness—is status quo.

I'm sure I'd feel better if I could at least campaign for that promotion at Blair Barnett. But Mike's replacement has yet to be hired, and even if he—or she—were already on board, everybody knows that nothing exciting happens in the agency at this time of year. Everybody's just marking time until Christmas, which is when the agency, like most others in Manhattan, will close until after New Year's.

As a result, there is very little at the office—other than the dreaded annual Secret Snowflake exchange—to keep me occupied.

Not that I'm lacking for distractions on the home front. In fact, there's a lot to do. Cleaning, wrapping, packing...

I look up at the starless December sky, thinking I never should have agreed to come Christmas shopping with Raphael tonight. I should probably be home cleaning. The place is a mess, and to make matters even more depressing, the leg fell off our pressboard dining table when I bumped it earlier. I left it there on the floor because I was late for work. Jack will have to get wood putty or something and fix it when he gets home.

Still, I could be there wrapping the stack of gifts I still have left to wrap, or packing for our trip up to Brookside.

We don't leave for another two days, though. Forty-eight hours. Which is plenty of time.

Plenty of time to go through my drawers and hangers in an effort to find a couple of outfits I can still squeeze into.

No, I haven't lost the post-smoking weight.

If anything, I actually may have gained a few pounds since Thanksgiving—not that I'm willing to step on a scale to find out. Who wants to weigh themselves in December, the height of the holiday-binge season? Better to wait until a cold morning in January, when all that will be available to tempt me might be leftover candy canes and soon-to-expire dip.

"Tracey!"

"The leopard spots," I tell Raphael, who's still waiting impatiently.

"Reason, Tracey?"

"They go better with your tawny new hair."

"You think?"

I nod vigorously.

"Oh, Tracey, I don't know…" Raphael tries to catch sight of his reflection in the mirrored lens of the zebra-striped shades. "You don't think they're too campy?"

"They are, but since when do you care?"

"I wouldn't want to be campy," protests Raphael, who is currently wearing a vintage tweed overcoat on top of an outfit he had custom made by a costume-designer friend who specializes in pirate-wear.

Yes, *pirate*-wear.

I'd be willing to bet he's the only swashbuckler to hit the streets of lower Manhattan in at least three centuries.

Meanwhile, he went platinum—or as he persists in calling it, "tawny"—a few days ago, because "gentlemen prefer blondes." In other words, he caught Donatello exchanging small talk with a strapping, fair-haired mailman en route to mailing their wedding invitations. Talk about paranoia.

"I guess you're right," Raphael decides. "The leopard spots do go much better with my hair, campy or not."

"You're going to buy them?" I ask, even as he puts both pairs of sunglasses back on the display table.

"No, I don't really like them, Tracey," he says airily.

"Because they're campy?"

"Because they squeeze the sides of my head." He extends an arm, gesturing toward the teeming sidewalk. "Shall we?"

I swear, Christmas shopping with fickle Raphael is almost as exasperating as Christmas shopping with fickle Kate, which I did last weekend. I bought exactly one Christmas gift—a pair of gloves for the annual office Secret Snowflake exchange—and spent the remainder of the time watching Kate try on an entire designer line of darling maternity clothes.

No, she's not pregnant yet.

She was "browsing."

The only person I can really shop well with is Jack, but he's in Toledo on business overnight. And anyway, I'm supposed to be buying his gift, something I can't exactly accomplish in his company.

Something I can't exactly accomplish, period.

At least, so far.

That's because every gift item I consider seems all wrong.

A nice scarf?

Too insignificant, especially if he's giving me a diamond ring for Christmas.

A nice Rolex?

Too significant, especially if he's *not* giving me a diamond ring for Christmas.

See what I mean?

"I just wish I knew whether he's going to propose or not," I make the mistake of murmuring to Raphael, after discarding a pile of sweaters at another sidewalk vendor farther down the block, which Raphael has deemed "sub-par cashmere."

His neck snaps around. "Did you just say you wish you knew whether he's going to propose or not, Tracey?"

Okay, obviously I didn't learn my lesson after making that same speculation and subsequent vow not to, ever again, because here I am, once again, watching Raphael shake his head vigorously in response.

"My guess is no, Tracey. He's not."

"Why not?" I ask reluctantly.

"Because he's supposedly had the ring since August, so why wouldn't he have given it to you before now?"

"Because he sold it for cash to buy drugs, remember?"

"Tracey!" He gasps, covering his mouth. "You think?"

"No! I don't *think*. I already told you he's not on drugs."

"Well then, maybe he's involved with somebody else, Tracey, and he's planning on giving *her* the diamond."

On a different night, or a bad-hair day, that suggestion might actually give me pause, but tonight it doesn't. Not on the heels of this morning's rigorously erotic goodbye before Jack left for the airport. Nothing like some good lovin' to leave a gal feeling confident.

So it's my turn to shake my head vigorously. "Nope. No way."

"Well then, maybe he threw it overboard into the sea, like the old lady at the end of *Titanic*."

There are so many things wrong with that scenario that I'm not sure where to start.

I choose, "Last I knew, Jack hadn't gone to sea in at least a couple of years."

"Well, then maybe he tossed it into the East River, Tracey. Ever think of that?"

"No, Raphael. I haven't."

"Well, maybe you should," he says sassily.

I know I'm going to regret this, but…

"Why would he toss the diamond into the East River, Raphael?"

"To destroy the last remaining testament to his parents' failed marriage," he says dramatically, and then, without hesitation, "Ooh! Sparkles!"

He has stopped to cuddle with a turquoise sequined turban, which he then plunks on his flaxen—excuse me, *tawny*—head. "Tracey, do you *love?*"

"It's very…sparkly."

"How do I look in it?"

"Like the Sultan of Oman, if you want to know the truth."

"You say that like it's a bad thing."

"Take off the turban, Raphael."

"But it's adorable, Tracey. And swanky." He sneaks a peek at the white dangling price tag. "And it's an absolute *steal!*"

"Okay, then buy it."

"You think?"

"I do think."

"Well, *I* think you should get one for Jack, Tracey." Raphael closes his eyes and giggles, obviously cracking himself up with the visual. "Can you just see it?"

"No, I can't. Not unless it were Halloween."

His eyes fly open, flickering with sudden interest. "Does Jack dress up in swanky drag for Halloween?"

"Nope. I know you'll find this surprising, but Jack rarely dresses up in drag, swanky or non-swanky."

"That's a crying shame."

"Isn't it just." I watch Raphael take off the turban, start to walk away, then rush back and put it on his head again.

"I can't! I love it, Tracey!"

"So buy it!" I shout back at him.

He calms down, tilts his head in serious thought. "I don't know…I'm not big on impulse buys."

Okay, the thing about that is…he so *is*.

"The way I see it, Raphael, one doesn't acquire a turquoise sequined turban in any other manner."

"True. But…when would I wear it, Tracey?"

"For work?" I suggest, bored out of my non-turban-spangled skull. "For play?"

"It *is* versatile," he muses, examining his reflection in a conveniently located mirror. "I don't know…you don't think it's too…busy?"

Busy isn't the word I'd have chosen, but…

"Not in a bad way, Raphael."

"I'll take two," he announces, and removes a wad of

twenties from his pocket. After counting out six of them, a matched set of turquoise sequined turbans are all his.

"Do you wrap?" he asks the largely unfazed, dreadlocked vendor.

"No, *mon.*"

Disappointed, Raphael asks, "Are you sure?"

"Yeah, *mon.*"

"*Now* you tell me. Can you knock off ten bucks, then? On each?"

The vendor silently isn't amused.

In fact, he's starting to look silently—and ominously—*fazed.*

"Come on, Raphael. They don't wrap. Let's move it."

I'll admit I'm not particularly anxious to top off the evening with an ugly altercation between Dreadlock Dan and our disgruntled little consumer pal, who seems to have forgotten he's not at an accessories counter in Bergdorf Goodman.

"I'll wear mine home," Raphael decides, removing it from the white no-frills plastic grocery sack the vendor hands him. He grumbles loudly over his shoulder as we walk away, "And I guess I'll have to get a box *and* wrapping paper for Donatello's."

Dreadlock Dan has pocketed his cash and gone back to being unfazed.

See, that's the thing about shopping on Saint Mark's Place, as opposed to shopping in a fancy department store. You're not going to walk away with a prestigious paper shopping bag, or gift boxes, let alone fancy wrap, the way you do at Bergdorf.

If I do find Jack's Christmas gift here, I'll have to package it on my own.

Still, this is a great place to find a bargain—though a fifty-seven–dollar turquoise sequined turban isn't it, in my opinion.

"So that's Donatello's gift?" I ask Raphael.

"Tracey! This is just a stocking stuffer."

"Oh, of course." *Silly me.*

"So what else did you get for him?" I ask after a moment, hoping he can give me some ideas for Jack.

He stops walking, rests a fist against his chest and sings in a booming voice: *"Five...golden...rings."*

To which I promptly respond, in song, *"Four calling birds, three French hens, two-oo turtle doves and a partri-idge in a pear tree."*

Then I say in my regular voice, "Your turn."

"Tracey! We're not playing that caroling game again! I'm telling you what I bought for him."

It takes me a moment to regroup and go from trying to remember the ever-elusive second verse of "Good King Wenceslas" to incredulously asking, "You bought Donatello five golden rings for Christmas?"

He nods vigorously. "Just like in the song!"

"Why?"

"Because it's in the song!" he says, as though that makes perfect sense. "You know...*on the fifth day of*—"

"I know!" I cut him off on midnote. "So you're getting him the other stuff, too?"

He looks blank. "What other stuff?"

I sigh. "Four calling birds, three French hens, two-oo turtle doves and a partridge in a pear tree."

"Tracey! Why would I do that?" Raphael asks, as though that's the most ridiculous thing he's ever heard.

"Because it's in the song. You know, a theme gift," I say impatiently. "You got him the five golden rings..."

"Ye-es..." Raphael is still frowning as though he doesn't get my drift.

"But you didn't get him any of the other stuff?"

"Nope. Just the five rings, Tracey. Why would he need any of that other stuff?"

"Oh, I don't know…"

Why would he need five golden rings, dammit?

When I consider the possible uses a man might have for all that bling, I just don't get it.

But that doesn't mean I have to ask, does it?

No. It certainly doesn't.

Tell me to drop the subject.

Hurry. Tell me.

Too late.

"Are they for all five fingers of his hand?" I hear myself inquire.

Because who knows? Maybe that's some new gay style I haven't heard about.

"Nope." Raphael lifts a sly brow. "I bought him one for the ring finger of each hand, one toe ring for the pinkie toe of each foot, and one very large one for—"

"Forget it," I cut in just in the nick of time. "I don't need to know."

Apparently, he thinks I do.

I consequently spend the next few minutes trying to banish *that* unfortunate image from my brain.

"Ooh, this is keeping my head nice and toasty," Raphael comments as the wind kicks up when we stop at the next intersection to wait for a light. "You know what, Tracey? I think I'll give Donatello his early so that we can wear them skiing next weekend. They complement our new parkas."

My squeamish mind's eye finds instant reprieve in a replacement image: Raphael and Donatello sailing along on the slopes in matching turquoise sequined turbans and complementary turquoise sequined parkas.

"Wait," I say. "You're going skiing? Since when?"

"Since Donatello and I rented a château in Vermont for the holidays. Didn't I tell you? Tracey, I know I told you."

"What you told me was that you were going to spend Christmas in Omaha with Donatello's family."

Yes, Raphael's future husband is from Nebraska. Apparently, he was a corn-fed farm boy before he set out for New York to make his fortune as a waiter slash Macy's spray model.

In fact, much to Raphael's delight, Donatello still occasionally wears denim overalls without a shirt underneath, which, as I'm sure you can imagine, goes over much better on Christopher Street than it does, say, on a subway filled with disgruntled construction workers returning home after a grueling day on the job.

Unfortunately, Donatello learned that the hard way.

Thirteen facial stitches and a police report later, you'd think he would have learned.

"Oh, well, we *were* going to spend Christmas in Omaha, Tracey, but that was a while ago. Before Donatello's family disowned him."

"Did they find out he was gay?" I ask, remembering that Raphael's future in-laws are even more staunchly Italian-Catholic than my family is.

"No! He can't tell them *that,* Tracey." From beneath his spangled turban, Raphael looks at me as though *I'm* the crazy one.

"Well, won't they figure it out when they get their invitation to the wedding?"

"They're not invited, Tracey! No family, just friends. It's going to be a secret marriage. Isn't that romantic?"

"Raphael, you put an engagement announcement in the *New York Times.*"

"His family only reads the *Omaha World-Herald,*" he says disdainfully.

"Still…how secret can you make a sit-down reception for three hundred and a twelve-piece orchestra?"

"Eleven-piece, Tracey."

"What? The naked bongo player couldn't make it?" I quip.

"It was always eleven piece, but a naked bongo player isn't a bad idea," Raphael muses, pulling out a notebook he's been carrying around ever since he got engaged, and jotting down a quick note in it.

"So what did Donatello do to get disowned?" I can't help but ask.

"He skipped his great-aunt's retirement party to go to Jones's opening. Give me a break."

See? What did I tell you? In the Spadolini family, he would have been disowned for a lesser crime than that.

"So…what did his great-aunt do?" I ask politely.

"She sent him a family picture in a smashed glass frame. And, Tracey, she drew a pointy beard and devil ears on Donatello."

Ah, revenge, Little Old Italian Lady–style.

"No," I say patiently, "I mean, what did she do for a living?"

Not that I care.

But I'm in this deep, so I might as well know.

"She was a lunch lady, Tracey!"

"What's wrong with lunch ladies? I have an aunt who's a lunch lady, too," I protest. "Don't be a snob, Raphael."

"I can't help it. I am a snob. And these people in Nebraska have no sense of cultural priority."

"One of Donatello's best friends was a featured performer in *Curious George,* and he was supposed to skip it?"

Cultural priority?

"I thought Jones was *your* friend," is all I can think to say.

"We're getting *married,* Tracey. As in forever. As in, all our friends are mutual from this day forward."

I wonder if this means that Donatello's kleptomaniac hag, Nellie, is now part of Raphael's inner circle. If so, I'll be sure to keep a wide berth when she's around. The last time she was over at his place, somebody's wallet went missing.

"So, *Curious George?* You mean the kids' book about the monkey?" I ask, not particularly anxious to linger on the topic of engagement and its consequences, to which I am unfortunately unable to relate, damn that Jack.

"What other *Curious George* is there, Tracey?"

"Snobby and sarcastic, Raphael. How am I supposed to know *Curious George* was a Broadway play now?"

"Because I told you. And it's not Broadway, it's off-off, and it's a musical, not a play. Jones is a *dancer,* remember?"

"Oh, right." Fake lightbulb. "Maybe I'll go see it."

Raphael sighs. "It closed last month, Tracey. Remember?"

"I guess I forgot."

"Of course you did." He looks exasperated. "Unless it has to do with you—or Jack—and whether or not he's going to give you an engagement ring, you're not interested."

Wow. If that's not hypocritical, then I haven't been struck by a sudden fierce craving for nicotine.

"I'm sorry I'm not as culturally enlightened as you are, Raphael," I say loftily, stung by his accusation. "But I've got other things on my plate right now. Things that are more important than *Curious George: The Musical.*"

He mutters something under his breath. I don't catch a word of it, but I'd bet my life that it has to do with that groundless accusation of narcissism.

Suddenly, I've had enough. I really don't need this right now.

"You know what? Let's call it a night, Raphael," I say curtly, all set to spin on my heel and head back to the Astor Place subway.

"Tracey!" He instantly throws his arms around me. "I'm sorry. That was mean. Forgive me?"

I consider it.

"Really, Tracey, I didn't mean to be so bitchy. It's just that between my wedding plans and the holidays, I'm exhausted."

"And bitchy."

"And bitchy," he concedes. "But aren't all brides?"

"I wouldn't know. I've never been one, remember?" I say tartly. "And according to you, I never will."

"Oh, Tracey…" He shakes his head. "I didn't mean that."

"Yes, you did."

"Okay, I did, but…I'm sorry, okay? I take it back."

"Really?" I peer into his face.

"Scout's honor," he says, holding up two fingers.

"Oh, please. You were never a Boy Scout, Raphael."

"No, thank God." He's shifted gears again, going instantly from utter disdain to heartfelt contrition. "But really, Tracey, it would break my heart if you were mad at me."

He *does* look a little weepy.

Then again, he's always been a drama queen.

"Whatever, Raphael."

"You forgive me?"

"I guess." I shrug and cast a longing glance at a couple of passing NYU types who have yummy lit cigarettes hanging out of their mouths.

Yes, even after two months, I'm still not over my addiction. Not entirely, anyway.

But I'll admit that this cold-turkey thing is getting easier. I no longer wake up in the mornings consumed by an instinctive need to light up. And just the other day, when I was hungover from the office Christmas party and caught a whiff of Yvonne's menthol smoke, I felt like I was going to vomit.

I took that as a good sign.

That I was compelled to drink so much at the office party the night before was not a good sign. As you'll recall, Jack and I met at the Blair Barnett Christmas shindig two years ago. Which means the party was our second anniversary, more or less.

More, if you're me.

Less, if you're Jack.

I got him a card, same as last year. Once again, I had to painstakingly explain what it was for. You'd think he would remember the occasion upon which we met. You'd think he'd take a hint after last year, realize that the Office Christmas Party/Anniversary of the Night We Met is an occasion that calls for a card—or even better, a gift.

Like, say, a diamond ring.

But did Jack give me the ring?

You already know he didn't.

Did he even get me a card?

If you guessed *No, Tracey, he did not even get you a card,* you win.

And I lose.

Still, I'm hoping absence will make Jack's heart grow fonder and he'll return from Toledo tomorrow just bursting with the urge to engage me.

Raphael and I spend another hour perusing the wares along Saint Mark's Place.

During that time, he arbitrarily suggests a number of gifts for Jack, none of which is appropriate, much less available here: a beer-making kit, a hammock, an iguana.

"A live iguana?" I ask.

"No, stuffed," he says sarcastically, as though that's any more outrageous. "Of course, live, Tracey. Jeez." He shakes his head.

Choosing my words carefully to avoid another flare-up from Bridezilla, I say, "The thing is, I don't think Jack is really in the market for a live iguana, Raphael."

"How do you know that? Has he ever come right out and said he doesn't want an iguana?"

"No, but—"

"No offense, Tracey, but enough already about you and Jack," he interrupts. "What am I going to get Donatello?"

"I thought you already bought him five golden rings."

"I did, but I need something to go with them. You know, a real showstopper."

If five golden rings—especially number five—aren't a showstopper…

But turnabout is fair play, so I make a few suggestions, all of which are promptly shot down by Raphael. A live iguana. A self-help book for disowned Italian-Catholic homosexuals. A *My Friend Starred in "Curious George: The Musical" And All I Got Was This Lousy T-Shirt* T-shirt.

No, no, and no.

"How about a subscription to the Fruit of the Month club?" I suggest.

"Tracey! He's monogamous now, remember?"

It takes me a moment to get the joke. I laugh.

"What?" he asks, deadpan.

Maybe it isn't a joke?

Then, from Raphael: "Oh! Tracey, you meant *real* fruit? As in kumquats and papayas?"

"Even apples and oranges. And I'm not even going to ask you what *you* meant."

"There's this club that Terry, a drag queen friend of mine, started—"

"I said I wasn't going to ask, Raphael."

"I know, Tracey. I was going to tell you anyway."

And he does.

I tune him out, still trying to figure out what I'm going to get for Jack.

I can play it safe and go with a nice sweater, which is what I did last year. That's a good boyfriend gift. A sweater, a couple of CDs and some books. Perfect.

Unless he's giving me the ring.

Even then, am I obligated to respond with an equally extravagant gift? I mean, a diamond ring is about the symbolism, not the cash value. Correct?

Correct—unless you're Kate, who unapologetically had her solitaire appraised the morning after Billy presented it to her.

Naturally, she told me that she thinks I should get Jack a Rolex.

That's because she can afford one, and in fact got Billy a Rolex the Christmas they were engaged. She bought it with her daddy's money, of course.

My daddy's money would barely buy a Timex, but that's beside the point.

Yes, I have a credit card.

No, it's not maxed out. I still have a few thousand dollars of credit left.

Still, I think I'll play it safe and go with the sweater, CDs and books. Maybe throw in a Chia Pet for good measure, since the one Jack gave me is now beyond hope. I keep waiting for him to notice that it's mildewed and suggest that we throw it away, but he never does.

I know I could just chuck it into the garbage and call it a day, but I can't bring myself to do it.

So there it sits, a disgusting, depressing symbol of our relationship.

Okay, maybe not a symbol of our relationship, but it's definitely depressing.

And disgusting.

"Is that snow?" Raphael asks gleefully, tipping his face up.

I gaze into a streetlight and see a few flakes whirling in the glow.

"Yup," I say, "that's snow."

"Oh, Tracey, it's beautiful, isn't it?" he rhapsodizes.

Actually, it isn't.

I mean, it's not like this is a sugar-frosted Dickens scape.

It's a few measly flakes, just enough to make us colder and collapse our hairdos.

Well, my hairdo, anyway.

Raphael's used so much gel in his tawny locks that it would take a steamroller to flatten them.

"Ooh, I caught one on my tongue, Tracey!" Raphael exclaims.

"You'd better hope that was a snowflake," I say ominously, glancing at the overhead windows of a run-down apartment building.

"Tracey! Why are you being so scroogy?"

"Sorry, I'm just cold," I say apologetically, putting my icy hands into my pockets and turning up the collar of my old blue pea coat that goes in and out of style every other season.

Yes, it's currently *out,* but my other halfway decent coat—a five-year-old long wool dress coat—is at the cleaner's with Jack's suits, which I forgot to pick up yesterday as promised before his trip. Oops.

Mental note: pick up dry cleaning after work tomorrow, before Jack gets home.

"You really should have bought one of these, Tracey," Raphael says, gesturing at his toasty turban. "It's festive *and* warm."

"I'd rather buy a ticket to Anguilla," I say impulsively.

In fact…

"I'd rather buy two tickets to Anguilla!"

"Oh, Tracey, that's so sweet." Raphael gives me a quick, fervent hug. "But if I take any more time off from work between now and the safari, I'll end up an unemployed desperate housewife."

"Not two tickets for you and me, Raphael. For Jack and me." I can't resist adding, "Because, after all, you know my world is all about Jack and me."

"To each his own," Raphael murmurs demurely, busy trying to catch sight of his reflection in a plate-glass window as we pass.

Why didn't I think of this before?

I'll get Jack a Carribbean vacation for Christmas!

It's the perfect solution. He might open it on Christmas morning, but it'll be the gift that keeps on giving…to both of us.

Plus this way, if he doesn't propose for Christmas, he'll have the perfect romantic setting where he can do it later.

But not *much* later.

I'm thinking January. That's the absolute cutoff if we're going to have that October wedding.

Meanwhile, if Jack *does* propose for Christmas, then our trip will be to celebrate our engagement.

I know what you're thinking.

You're thinking Jack probably has his heart set on taking me to Anguilla for our honeymoon.

I know, I'm thinking the same thing.

But with this plan, I can't lose. We can get the Caribbean out of the way now, and he can take me to Europe or the South Pacific for our honeymoon.

See how it all falls into place?

"How much do you think an all-inclusive week in Anguilla would cost?" I make the mistake of asking Raphael.

"More than you make in a month," is the prompt response.

Point taken.

I reconsider.

Then ask, "How about a long weekend?"

"More than you make in a month."

"What if I cut the all-inclusive part?"

Raphael sighs. "I have a question for you, Tracey. If you have to pay for every last dirty banana, what's the point of going at all?"

I just know I'm going to regret asking this too, but…

"I have a question for you, Raphael. What the heck is a dirty banana?"

"One part crème de cacao, one part crème de bananes, one part Kahlúa. Add ice, a heap of vanilla ice cream, and blend till smooth."

What a relief. It's merely a frozen cocktail, and not…

Well, you can just imagine the connotation "dirty banana" might take on in Raphael's lurid little world.

"So they make dirty bananas in Anguilla?"

"They make them everywhere in the Caribbean. Go somewhere else, Tracey. Jamaica is cheap."

"I don't want cheap. I want exotic and upscale. Like Anguilla."

Not that I know Anguilla from anywhere else in the Caribbean, but it sounds exotic and upscale, and it must be if Jack's sister recommended it.

"You can't afford it."

"I can if I charge it."

"I really don't think that's a good idea," Raphael says darkly, and tacks on a cryptic, "Besides, it might be cursed."

Okay, did I miss something here?

"What might be cursed, Raphael?"

"Hello? Anguilla."

"The entire island?"

He nods. "Brad and Jen went there, and look what happened to them."

"What?" I ask helplessly, because with Raphael, you sometimes get swept along.

"They wound up getting separated before they even boarded the plane home."

"They got lost in the airport?"

"No, separated. As in divorced." He shakes his head wearing a *some-people-are-impossibly-thick* expression.

"Oh." Pause. "Brad and Jen who?"

"Hello! Pitt and Aniston?"

"For God's sake, Raphael." I swat his arm. "I thought you were talking about somebody we know."

"I *was*. Somebody *I* know. Brad, anyway," he concedes when I glare. "I told you I met him last spring during Fashion Week, remember?"

"You told me you grabbed his butt when he walked by you on the street and he threatened to call the police."

"Right. During Fashion Week," he repeats, and I can't help but wonder what, if anything, any of this has to do with me and Jack getting married. Or not.

Horrified inner gasp!

There I go again.

Can Raphael possibly be right about me?

Am I obsessed with myself and Jack and our forthcoming—or not—engagement?

Paranoid, I mentally backtrack over the last few hours...

Then the last few days...

Then the last few *months*...

Can it be?

No. I am not *one of those so-called New York career women whose secret main goal in life is a diamond ring on her finger and wedding date on the calendar.*

Or so I claimed way back in October, when I first found out Raphael got engaged. But things have changed since then.

You know, I'm really scaring myself.

Have I turned into...

The Anti-Bridezilla?

I mean, think about it...

Like I said earlier, what else really matters to me lately?

I should be looking beyond my own little dilemma.

I should be interested in other things. Global issues. Politics. Even Raphael's tabloid fodder.

I must be lousy company.

If I were a true friend, I would probably be asking Raphael about his hopes, his fears, his dreams...

Except that I already know all of them—or most of them, anyway. And what I don't already know, I don't want to know. Trust me. Nobody would.

Still...

"Raphael...?" I ask tentatively, resolving that from this moment on, I will do my best to think about—and talk about—other things.

"Yes, Tracey?"

But I can't think of a single thing to say. Nothing that doesn't involve myself, or Jack, anyway.

Finally, I settle for, "Let's go home."

"But what about Christmas shopping, Tracey?"

"I'll finish it up online," I say. "Or in Brookside."

"I thought Wal-Mart was the only store in town."

"You say that like it's a bad thing."

He laughs and links his arm through mine. "You always do like a bargain."

"So do you."

"Just not from Wal-Mart. We're two of a kind, Tracey!" He smooches my cheek. "I'm so glad you're my maid of honor."

"Me too," I say with feeling.

Then he adds pessimistically, "I just hope I can return the favor someday."

This is God, testing you, I tell myself.

"Tell me about your hopes, your fears, your dreams, Raphael," I say in response.

Without batting an eye, he says, "Well, last night, I dreamed I was the March selection in the Fruit of the Month club..."

Alrighty then. Tune-out time.

I find myself speculating wearily that if Jack would just ask me to marry him, life could get back to normal, which it hasn't been since Labor Day.

Maybe on Christmas Eve, I think hopefully, barely aware that Raphael is continuing to regale me with a tale straight out of a gay-porn movie.

Or Christmas Day...

Or even New Year's Eve...

Or New Year's Day...

Chapter 14

The only thing Jack returned from Toledo bursting to do last night was go to the bathroom—there was snow in Ohio so the flight was delayed, then he drank too much coffee on the plane and got stuck in rush-hour traffic on the way back from the airport.

"That really, really sucks, Tracey," Brenda says sympathetically over her shoulder from the front seat of the cab we're in, headed to the west side for a long lunch. Upper management is at a holiday client reception this afternoon, so we don't have to worry about hurrying back.

Sandwiched between Yvonne and Latisha in the back seat, I say, "Yeah, well, it's that time of year so what do you expect? I'm sure our flight to Buffalo will be delayed tonight, too. And the traffic—well, look at this."

I gesture out the window at the dead standstill ahead of us on West Forty-ninth Street, courtesy of hordes of gawking tourists and child-toting suburbanites making their way to the department store windows, Radio City Music Hall, the Rockefeller Center tree, Saint Patrick's Cathedral.

City sidewalks, busy sidewalks…

Dirty, disgusting sidewalks, I add mentally, watching a vagrant hurtle a loogee onto the concrete in front of Saks.

"No, I don't mean it sucks about Jack's flight and the traffic," Brenda says over the blaring car horns as the light changes and our driver barrels across the intersection, nearly mowing down a cop and a family of five.

Holding on to the seat for dear life, I ask, "Then what—"

"Hello! Tracey! Come on!" That's Latisha. "She means it sucks that he didn't walk in the door and put a ring on your finger so that you can start making your wedding plans the second you get back to your hometown."

"Amen to that, sister." That, of course, comes from Yvonne.

I merely shrug and tell them all, "I'm sure Jack will give me the ring for Christmas, and we're hanging around for a few days after, so I'll be able to at least talk to the priest and book the reception."

"But you'll have to look at places, and taste the food, and hear the bands…" Brenda shakes her head. "How are you going to do all that in a few days?"

"Trust me, Bren, there aren't many options in Brookside. I already know what I want. It's just a matter of nailing down the date."

Please let it be October…

Please let it be October…

Brenda says, "I just wish he would get with the program already. Enough is enough."

She wishes?

If my friends are this frustrated, imagine how I'm feeling right about now.

At last, the cab pulls up in front of Tequila Murray's Midtown, the newest branch of the semi-kosher Mexican restaurant—you'll recall that I had my memorable first date with Jack at their site in the Village.

Ah, memories. They were offering a two-for-one happy hour that night. Jack was late, I had an empty stomach— the better to show off my little black dress—and soon after he arrived, I found myself in the bathroom throwing up my pair of margaritas.

When I think of that night...

Well, it's a wonder that we made it past the first date at all.

It's also a wonder that I'm still fond of Tequila Murray's, though not for happy hour.

Mental note: do not order more than one margarita, no matter how easily it goes down.

Mental note, Part II: do not break diet!

The four of us pile out of the taxi and troop into the restaurant for our celebratory lunch.

What we're celebrating: the holidays, which as far as I'm concerned will commence right after work tonight, which is when the office closes until after New Year's, and Jack and I board our flight to Buffalo.

What else we're celebrating: Latisha's big raise.

Being the jealous type, I can't help wishing we were also celebrating my big promotion to junior copywriter.

Unfortunately, that's not going to happen for a while because as of today, they're still interviewing replacements for Mike.

Meanwhile, he hasn't found a job yet and apparently has a lot of time on his hands. He e-mails me at least three or four forwards a day—ancient jokes, dire warnings, political petitions, instructions to forward his e-mail to everyone I know and Bill Gates will in turn send me a million bucks— that kind of thing.

And he keeps calling me and Jack, wanting to get together for dinner. We said sure the first time he asked, until we realized he meant the *four* of us—as in, me, Jack, Mike and the bitch-on-wheels he married. We've been coming up with excuses to put off the dinner ever since.

The four of us are seated at a nice round table next to a group of cute businessmen who briefly check us out. I can't help thinking that if I were still ten—okay, fifteen—pounds lighter, they wouldn't have gone back to their fajitas and mole sauce quite so quickly.

More inspiration to stick to my diet. Not that I need to be ogled by cute businessmen at Tequila Murray's when I've got one of my very own at home, but still…

"If Jack doesn't give you that rock by Christmas, cut him loose." That's Yvonne's unsolicited little nugget of advice for me, which she plucks out of thin air after ordering a double dirty martini.

"He might be planning to do it on New Year's Eve," I protest, wishing we could just change the subject. "We're having a party, remember? Maybe he'll want to do it with all of my best friends around to witness the happy occasion."

"That's when Derek proposed," Latisha comments. "New Year's Eve. Right at midnight. But we were alone."

"Was that the first time?" Brenda asks.

"No, the fourth."

"That was the time you accepted, right?" I ask, trying to think back over Latisha's series of grand proposals from Derek.

"No, I said yes the *fifth* time."

"Was that when he surprised you with two tickets to Yankees spring training?" Brenda asks.

"You bet." Latisha sighs and shakes her head. "How long did it take him to figure out the way to my heart? Men!"

"I wish Jack would figure out the way to my heart," I grumble as the waiter approaches with our drinks. "I'm a lot less complicated than you are, Latisha. All it would take are four little words."

Yvonne smirks. *"I-won-the-lottery?"*

I smirk. *"Will-you-marry-me?"*

"Maybe you should say no when he asks," Latisha suggests. "Just to keep him on his toes."

"Are you kidding?" Brenda shakes her head vehemently. "She can't say no after waiting for so long. What if Jack changes his mind?"

"What if he already did?" Yvonne asks darkly.

The three of us glare at her.

"I call it like I see it," she responds with a shrug. "Only a real weenie farts around for this long. They've been together two years, he's supposedly had a ring for four months."

I bristle at that, but what can I say?

Nobody calls my Jack a farting weenie but me?

"How are we today, ladies?" the waiter asks, and answers his own question with an annoyingly presumptuous "Everybody merry? Great."

I moodily sip my frozen raspberry margarita, barely listening to the specials as he reels them off…until he gets to the part about the beef chimichangas.

I was going to order a salad, but what the hell? It's Christmastime. I order the beef chimichanga special.

"Lunch size or regular?" asks the waiter, whose name is Sal and who looks like all three of my brothers morphed into one, which makes me fleetingly homesick. Good thing I'll be there tonight.

But back to the business at hand…

Lunch size or regular? Don't you hate when they ask you that? You want to ask how big the lunch size is without seeming like a glutton.

At least, *I* want to.

But I don't. Because it's Christmas, so what the hell?

I say, "Regular."

What, you thought I was going to order the lunch size and take a chance that it's served in a teacup saucer like my salad at Bloomingdale's?

Not when I haven't eaten since the sausage pizza Jack had delivered at midnight.

I'm so famished that I also order a quesadilla appetizer, then graciously agree to share Brenda's shredded chicken nachos as well.

"Did you want sour cream and guacamole on your quesadilla?" the waiter asks me, apparently as an after-thought.

You betcha, Sal.

Sal adds the obligatory dietary deterrent, "It costs extra."

Yeah, bring it on, Sally. They don't call me Hungry Hilda for nothin'.

All right, so they don't call me Hungry Hilda at all.

Yet.

"Extra salsa, too?" Sal is on a roll.

I consider.

"No charge," he adds helpfully—or perhaps, sadistically.

"Sure, okay."

After all, it's free. And anyway, salsa isn't fattening.

But the rest of it…

"Oh my God, why did I just do that?" I ask my friends after our boy Sal has scurried off to alert the kitchen staff re: Hungry Hilda's impending truckload of lunch. "I was supposed to be on a strict diet."

"It's Christmas," Latisha replies.

"Not for another six days," I protest. "If I keep this up, there won't be room under the mistletoe for Jack."

"I bet it's not too late to change your order, Tracey." Brenda is just trying to be helpful, I'm sure.

I probably shouldn't glare at her as I respond, "I just re-ally want that chimichanga. The quesadilla and nachos, too," I tack on quickly, before she can suggest that I skip my appetizer—or my half of hers.

"Don't we all just really want chimichangas, quesadillas and nachos?" asks Yvonne the former Rockette, who maintains her showgirl bod even at this advanced age. Technically, she shouldn't even be involved in this conversation, since she becomes virtually invisible whenever she turns sideways.

"Stay out of it, Slim," Latisha chides.

"Yeah," Brenda and I chime in eloquently.

Our skinny pal gives us the finger.

"I'll skip dinner," I decide. "We're flying tonight and by the time we land, it'll be too late to eat."

Yeah, who am I kidding? When I called my mother this morning, she was making a lasagna, a tray of eggplant parm and a couple of pizzas.

"You and Jack will be hungry when you get here" was her reasoning. In other words, doesn't everybody require a three-course midnight snack?

Not east of the Hudson River, they don't. But back home, you never know when a bubbling casserole dish will magically appear.

Our meals take a while to arrive. Tequila Murray probably had to have more food shipped in from his Village location.

In the meantime, we discuss Latisha's raise, Yvonne's supervisor's rumored extramarital affair and Brenda's fear that she's on the post-maternity-leave mommy track and thus, no longer taken seriously.

I would never tell her that she's right—or that she has *never* been taken seriously.

But in the long run, does it really matter? Brenda is all about being a wife and mother, and we all know that the second Paulie makes NYPD sergeant, she's trading her commuting Nikes and morning *Post* for a pair of terry-cloth scuffies and *If You Give A Moose A Muffin*.

"What about you, Trace?" Latisha asks. "Have you talked to Carol about looking into a junior copywriter position lately?"

"Not lately," I admit. "But there's nothing she can do until they bring in Mike's replacement anyway, so…"

"So meanwhile, you're planning on sitting around twiddling your thumbs?" Yvonne says.

"When I'm not doing Mike's job." I scowl at her.

"Then go after it."

"Go after what?" I ask Yvonne. "I just told you, I can't even think about getting promoted to copywriter until I get a new boss."

Yvonne shrugs. "Why don't you become your new boss, then?"

"She's right. You should apply for Mike's position, Tracey!" Latisha jumps right on board that train. "Why haven't you talked to Carol about it?"

"Because Mike is an account exec, Latisha."

"*Was* an account exec," Brenda clarifies. "And you just admitted you've been doing his job since he left."

"I'm two steps down from account exec," I remind her. "I haven't even been an assistant A.E. yet."

"So maybe they'll downgrade Mike's position and let you step into it," Latisha suggests. "It can't hurt to ask."

She's right. It can't.

Why didn't I think of it?

Because I've been too caught up in thinking about Jack and our future wedding, that's why.

You know, if he would just ask me to marry him, I could focus on other things. Things like advancing my career.

Okay, don't jump all over me. I *know* that's a cop-out.

I *know* that I could just as easily back-burner the whole engagement obsession and focus on other things.

Well, not *easily.*

In fact, it's next to impossible for me to think of anything else because right now, nothing else seems to matter. Including work.

That sounds pretty pathetic, I know. But come on. Is my

longing to get engaged and married really so wrong? I'm in love. I want to spend the rest of my life with Jack.

Until that's settled, I just can't see how I can devote much time and energy to anything else.

"Now isn't the time for me to go asking for a promotion," I tell my friends conclusively. "People are getting laid off left and right."

"Which is exactly why you stand a good chance of getting Mike's job," Brenda informs me. "They'd be getting a competent person who's already been trained, and they wouldn't have to pay an account exec's salary."

"Why should I do an account exec's job for an assistant account exec's salary?" I ask.

"Because you're already doing an account exec's job for an account coordinator's salary," Yvonne snaps.

Oh. Right.

It would be nice to get a raise. Maybe then we could afford better furniture. Or even the rent on a bigger place. And maybe I could pay off my credit card, which is now dangerously close to being maxed out.

"I'll think about it over Christmas," I promise my friends, catching sight of Sal the waiter lugging a huge pile of food our way.

With any luck, things will fall into place any second now anyway, and my engagement worries will be a thing of the past by the time I get back to work in January.

A few hours later, as Jack and I are going through security en route to Buffalo, I naturally can't help wondering if he can possibly be toting my diamond in his back pocket.

I doubt he'd have stashed it in the luggage he just checked downstairs, since his duffel bag doesn't lock and he didn't seem very concerned when the airline employee carelessly tossed it onto the conveyer belt.

"I hope you didn't buy me fine china for Christmas," I quipped, watching the bag land with a jarring thud.

"Huh?"

"You know…if you bought me fine china and it was in that bag, it would be in shards."

"Oh. Right." Pause. "I didn't."

"I figured."

"Did you want fine china?" he asked, looking a little uncertain.

"No!" I said quickly. Too quickly. So quickly that I will probably never receive a piece of fine china from Jack.

I *love* fine china. Love, love, *love* it.

Not that I actually *have* any.

But I'd like some. Wouldn't every woman of a certain age?

Yes, I'm twenty-five.

That's the certain age when a woman's thoughts automatically turn from the snappy convenience of Rubbermaid to the exquisite permanence of fine china. In fact, I've already picked out our pattern in *Modern Bride,* so when it's time for us to register, we'll be ahead of the game.

But as we all know, what I want for Christmas from Jack this year is *not* a Royal Doulton Old Country Roses place setting—or even two.

Now, watching him empty his pockets into the small plastic tub the airport security guy hands him, I shrewdly take note of everything he puts in, wondering if my gift is concealed somewhere on his person.

Keys.

Wallet.

Cell phone.

Pack of gum.

Slip of paper.

Slip of paper?

I peer over his shoulder. Something's written on it. It looks like a phone number.

A craned neck and squint reveals that it *is* a phone number. One with a 718 area code.

Brooklyn.

Or Queens.

Now, of course, I can't help wondering…

Maybe he's involved with somebody else, Tracey, and he's planning on giving her *the diamond*.

Damn that Raphael anyway. Why did he have to bring that up the other night? Now I'm all paranoid.

Well, not *all* paranoid.

But slightly paranoid.

Slightly paranoid enough to ask Jack casually, "What's that?"

Except it doesn't come out casually.

In fact, it sounds like a shrill accusation.

"What's what?" Jack asks, not even pausing as he puts his boots on the conveyor belt and steps into the X-ray archway.

My repeat question is curtailed when an alarm goes off instantly.

I get my hopes up.

A diamond ring in his pocket would definitely make the alarm go off.

So, I find out as the guard waves a hand wand over Jack, would a metal belt buckle.

"Next," the guard says, callously dashing my hopes as he clears Jack's person of explosives and precious gems.

Okay, so Jack doesn't have a ring in his pocket.

No, but he has somebody's phone number.

That's never a good sign. I learned that back in the days of Will the Cheater. Not that I ever caught him carrying Esme's phone number around in his pocket, but that's probably just because I didn't think to look. Back then, when I was naive and innocent—not to mention stupid—I wouldn't stoop to—

"Next!" the security guard says again, impatiently waving me through.

Oops. I was so busy worrying about Jack's secret girl-friend from Brooklyn—or Queens—that I forgot to take off my shoes and empty my pockets. Now the entire line behind me is making exasperated mouth sounds while I unzip and remove my boots, then take out my keys, wallet, cell phone, pack of gum.

No slip of paper with a scribbled phone number in my pocket, though. I don't have a secret boyfriend from Brooklyn. Or Queens. Or any other borough, for that matter.

No, sir. I would never—

My watch just set off the alarm. *Oopsy.*

"Step aside," the guard barks, immune to my charming smile.

I step aside, glaring at Jack's back as he bends to pull his boots on again.

Is he cheating on me?

Is that why we're not engaged?

He turns around to watch me being searched by the metal-detecting wand. Then he smiles, and I melt.

He's so cute, isn't he? And he loves me.

"Ready?" he asks after I've returned my belongings to my pockets and my boots to my feet.

"Ready," I say, and we hold hands as we head toward the gate.

The airport is packed with holiday travelers, which makes it impossible to get anywhere quickly, but we have plenty of time. All is right in Tracey World again.

Until Jack abruptly lets go of my hand.

Now, why would he do that?

It's not as though we can't fit through the crowd walking two abreast.

Did he spot his bridge-and-tunnel girlfriend across the way?

Now you're being ridiculously paranoid, Tracey.

I reach for Jack's hand again, find it, and squeeze it.

He gives me a quick squeeze back, but drops it again.

Okay, so he isn't as into hand-holding as he used to be at the beginning of our relationship. Or two minutes ago.

That doesn't mean he's cheating on me.

Damn that Raphael.

But of course Jack's not cheating. There's a perfectly good explanation for a phone number scribbled on a piece of paper in his pocket.

Maybe…

All right, maybe it's the number for the jeweler from Sheepshead Bay who's designing my ring setting. Maybe he's a little old, I don't know, Austrian man who's been painstakingly trying to finish the job in time for Christmas. Maybe he ran into trouble because his arthritis is acting up and his gnarly old hands aren't what they used to be. Maybe he needs Jack to call him so that he can send the ring via Fed Ex to my parents' house so he can put it into my stocking for Christmas morning.

"Are you coming?" Jack asks over his shoulder.

"Yup."

"This place is a zoo."

"Yup."

I reach for his hand, but alas, it's swept into a moving throng of humanity—insert dramatic sigh—perhaps lost to me forever.

Is that a sign?

Maybe.

I'm starting to think that my getting engaged before the year ends—or ever, for that matter—is about as likely as the actual existence of the little old arthritic Austrian jeweler from Brooklyn.

Jack didn't have a ring in his pocket, so unless he checked it in his luggage—which he wouldn't, because everybody knows you don't check valuables—all I'm getting for Christmas is…

Well, what *am* I getting?

Not a ring.

Not fine china.

Does he even have a gift for me stashed in his bag?

Not that *I* have a gift for *him* stashed in *my* bag.

But I do have the fancy certificate I made on my computer, entitling him to one all-expenses-paid, all-inclusive weekend in Anguilla over Martin Luther King's birthday weekend.

We're going to the Sea Plantation, a resort hotel I found yesterday on Tripadvisor.com. It looked good in the pictures, and it was more affordable than most places there.

Yes, the customer reviews were a little ambiguous—some so glowing you know that whoever wrote them must be related to the resort's owners, others so negative you know that whoever wrote them must have a personal vendetta against the resort's owners.

But at least none of the reviews mentioned bugs in the rooms. I can handle a delayed check-in, a hotel staff that's less than exuberant, even skimpy towels. But bugs are out.

So, yes, I have for Jack a handmade certificate—with fancy red and green font, no less—for a glorious weekend at a bug-free Caribbean resort. Which I can't present to him in front of my mother because she won't approve. She used to give me shit for calling boys in high school…can you imagine what she'd say if she knew I was inviting one on vacation?

Not that I'm in high school, or that Jack is a boy.

But there's something about seeing my mother that instantly erases a decade from my life.

I meet up with Jack again at the gate area, which is packed. No place to sit; barely room to stand.

"We're boarding in five minutes," Jack informs me.

"Good." Time to pop a Xanax, courtesy of Dr. Trixie Schwartzenbaum, who prescribed it last year for potential extreme panic situations like this.

By this I mean getting on an airplane, not finding out my boyfriend might be in love with another woman.

Or not.

By the time we're taxiing out to the runway, I'm not only no longer worried about the phone number in Jack's pocket, I could care less if the plane goes down over the Catskills.

Xanax is a wonderful thing, isn't it?

So, come to think of it, were my little pink pills. Maybe I should make an appointment with good old Doctor Trixie, whom I haven't seen in months, and get back on the meds. Not because I'm having panic attacks per se, but they did wonders for my waistline.

Jack and I rent a car at the airport after we make our bumpy landing in Buffalo, where a blinding snow is falling.

"Isn't it beautiful?" I ask him, gazing serenely past the furiously working windshield wipers at the near whiteout beyond.

"How are we supposed to drive thirty miles through this? And at night?"

"Forty miles," I correct him. "And it'll be fine."

He says nothing, just sits there with his hand clenched on the gearshift, the car still in Park.

"Do you want me to drive?" I offer. "I'm used to it."

"No, I'm used to it, too. I go to Aspen every December, remember?"

"Aspen isn't Buffalo, Jack. This is different. It's lake effect. Really, I can drive."

"I can drive," he says tersely, and shifts into Reverse.

Which would have been fine if we were supposed to be backing the rental car out of our parking spot.

Which we weren't.

"Do you think I dented the fender?" Jack asks, shifting into Drive.

"Nah, I'm sure it's fine," I say, praying he opted for the

extra insurance. I was at the luggage claim when he filled out the paperwork, hoping to grab his bag and sneak a brazen peak inside before he got there.

Apparently, nobody in their right mind—aside from Jack—was renting cars in Buffalo this stormy eve, so he was back in time to pick up his own duffel.

Mental note: get up extra early in the morning to snoop through Jack's luggage.

Mental note, Part II: stop being nosy and obsessive.

The forty-mile drive down the New York State Thruway to Brookside takes us two and a half hours. Jack follows the taillights of the semi in front of us, but there are times when it's obliterated by snow, even though we're creeping along a mere two car lengths behind it.

There are a few harrowing moments when I'm tempted to stage a mutiny, or at least seize the wheel from Jack. But I manage to control myself—and stave off a panic attack, to boot. Probably only because I'm still feeling the effects of the Xanax.

Still, every time I hear Jack's sudden intake of air or feel the car's tires begin to slip, it's all I can do to stay seated and silent.

I find myself wondering if he regrets coming home with me to Brookside. He'd probably rather be winging his way to Aspen right now with the rest of the Kennedys.

I mean, the Candells.

Why didn't I just let him go?

If you love something, set it free.

If it comes back to you, it's yours.

If it goes to Aspen instead, you can hardly blame it.

When we reach the tollbooth in Brookside, Jack heaves a tremendous sigh, followed by a tremendous yawn.

"God, I'm beat," he says. "I can't wait to get into bed."

Bed? Does he actually think he's going to walk into my

parents' house and go to bed? Stealing a glance at the dash-board clock, I see that it's merely ten-forty. He has no idea what he's in for, poor deluded soul.

Why did I insist on exposing him to a Spadolini Christmas before I've even closed the deal with an engagement ring?

If he still wants to marry me after this week, I guess I'll know it's true love.

And if he doesn't, I'll know why.

Finally, we're turning onto my parents' street, where every house displays a spotlit wreath on the door, elegant white lights in the shrubs and single white candles in the windows.

Every house, that is, but one.

"Wow, your parents go all out, don't they," Jack comments, turning into the freshly shoveled drive—which means that at least one of my brothers is here, because like I said, my dad no longer shovels. That job will fall to my unsuspecting boyfriend come sunup.

Not that the sun ever actually comes up in Brookside at this time of year. Ominous snow clouds are pretty much the order of the day, every day.

"What do you mean, my parents go all out?" I ask Jack, pretending not to see the thousands of blinking colored bulbs strung from every limb and rafter, the shiny garlands draped from pillar to post—and a showy new addition this year: an enormous inflated Santa anchored to the front lawn and bobbing wildly in the snowy gusts off the vast expanse of nearby Lake Erie.

"Look at their house. I mean, it just screams hallelujah," Jack says, killing the engine and my last remaining hope for his tolerance of a Spadolini holiday.

Then he adds hastily, "But in a good way," thus endearing himself to me all over again.

"If you like the outside, you'll love the inside."

"Then let's go," he says through a puff of frosty breath, already out of the car. "God, it's cold here."

"I told you." I shiver in my pea coat.

"You're not dressed right," Jack tells me. "You're turning blue. You need a hat."

"I don't wear hats."

"Then you need a hood."

"I'm fine," I say through chattering teeth.

He insists on carrying my luggage and his, leaving my arms free to hug the barrage of family that greets us at the door.

It's almost eleven o'clock on a weeknight, yet the whole Spadolini clan has turned out to greet us.

The crowd includes: Mom and Dad; my oldest brother, Danny, and his pregnant-again wife, Michaela, their two- and four-year-olds, Kelsey and Danny Junior; my favorite brother, Joey, his adorable wife, Sara, and their snoozing eighteen-month-old, Joe Junior; my laid-back brother Frankie and his cute redheaded, freckled wife, Katie; and of course, my only sister, Mary Beth, who is looking more like our mom every day, along with her two boys, Nino and Vince Junior, who unfortunately are looking more like their philandering father every day.

My mother hugs me ferociously, telling me over and over again how worried she was about us driving in from the airport. "It's snowing like crazy out there," she informs everybody, her hand pressed against her ample and presumably palpitating bosom. "I was so afraid something happened to you two."

"We were fine, Ma. Jack drove," I tell her proudly, so that she can love him even more than she already does.

She might not approve of our living situation, or the fact that his parents are divorced and he's not Italian, or Catholic, or from Brookside. But luckily, none of that stops her from treating him like a Chi-chi-bean-loving son. He won her over from the start with his voracious appetite and copious compliments on her cooking.

"Thank you for taking good care of our girl, Jack," my father says, shaking his hand.

I should probably resent the implication that their girl is incapable of taking care of herself, but for some reason, I don't. Not right now, anyway. I'm just glad they're welcoming Jack as warmly as they'd welcome one of their own.

I can't help remembering how wary my parents were of Will—and rightly so, in retrospect.

Granted, they were wary of Jack in the beginning, too, but not for long. Not after they met him. My mother quickly went from calling him a Smooth Operator to FedExing him her homemade pizza.

As I watch Jack greeting everyone in turn—by name, no less, even the kids, and with big hugs—I swear I'm falling more in love with him by the second.

Who else could walk into this madhouse and willingly fit right in?

"Jack, can I get you a glass of pop?" my mother asks lovingly.

"Pop? Ma, get him a beer," Danny speaks up. "I'll have one, too."

My mother looks at me.

"I'll have one too," I say in response—then realize that she wasn't asking me that.

In fact, she wasn't asking me anything; she was giving a silent order: *Go get those beers for the menfolk.*

Okay, she doesn't really say *menfolk.*

But that's about the most progressive thing about her.

Luckily, my newest sister-in-law, Katie, Spadolini Kitchen Slave In Training, comes to the rescue. "You guys go relax. I'll get beers for everyone," she offers.

"Even me?" Vince Junior asks.

She ruffles his hair. "You get pop."

"He gets water," Mary Beth speaks up. "He drank three cans of Pepsi already. I'll never get him to bed tonight."

"Isn't it a little late for them to be up on a school night anyway?" I ask her as we all make our way to the dining room, which is, of course, the center of the house. Countless milestones have taken place around this long table.

Come to think of it, this would be a fine site for Jack's proposal.

"It's not a school night, Aunt Tracey!" says Nino, the proud kindergartner. "We're on vacation!"

I don't reply to that; I'm too busy trying to figure out how to lure Jack to the table with a ring.

But Jack says, "Well, Nino, the thing is, if you don't get to sleep early tonight, you won't get to sleep early tomorrow night, or the next night…and if you're up late on Christmas Eve, Santa Claus won't come!"

By now, the entire family is gazing adoringly at my Jack, because around here, if you like my mother's cooking, small children and Christmas, you're *in*.

Which, come to think of it, would explain why Will was always *out*. He liked none of the above. Especially Christmas. In fact, he's spending the holidays alone in New York again, by choice, supposedly brushing up on his monologue for a January audition.

I presume he didn't get that film role he was so perfect for. I kept meaning to ask him about it the last few times he called—which he still does, from time to time—but he was too busy dominating the conversation to let me get a question in edgewise.

Not that I care about Will's fledgling film career.

Or about Will himself.

I try to imagine him here in Brookside with me for the holidays, sleeping in my brothers' old bedroom and admiring my mother's handmade ceramic Christmas tree and fiber-optic manger scene.

Nope. That would never happen, even if my mother agreed to prepare strictly macrobiotic meals and outfit Danny's lower bunk in Frette linens.

But there's Jack, wholeheartedly complimenting a glowing Connie on everything from the lopsided tree and Vegas-style manger scene to the worn but cheerful vinyl poinsettia-covered cloth that runs the vast length of the dining-room table.

All the table's leaves are in place, as usual. Not because we're expecting to feed a big crowd over the holidays—which we are—but because my mother feeds a big crowd on a daily basis. You never know who might pop in, or at what time of the day or night.

Speaking of which, no sooner have we sat down than the front door opens and a couple of my cousins walk in, dressed, as my father likes to say, to the nines. Here in Brookside, that means designer jeans with spike heels, plentiful cleavage and Sharpie-thick eyeliner.

"Jack, this is Toni and Donna," I say as we shuffle chairs around to make room for them at the table.

"You're the one with the big-shot job in New York City," Donna squeals, tipsy enough from what she and Toni coyly call "Girls' Night Out" to transform Jack's polite handshake into a full-blown bear hug.

"Well, I'm not really a big shot…" Jack extracts himself from Donna's embrace and looks at me, embarrassed.

Maybe he's not a big shot in New York, but…

"Trust me," I say with a bright smile, "you really are."

At least in Brookside.

"So when are you two getting married?" Toni asks, reaching for one of the *cucidati* that are heaped on a platter in the center of the table.

Everybody looks at Jack. Including me.

Normally, I'd be cringing, but at this point, I want to high-five my cousin for putting him on the spot and making him squirm. It's about time he had to answer to some-body for his actions—or lack thereof.

Jack doesn't squirm, though. Nor does he appear to be on the spot.

No, he merely says, wily as Boston Rob, "Hey, are those the fig cookies I've been hearing so much about? They look great," and helps himself to a *cucidati,* thus forever endear-ing himself to the woman who may—or may not—become his mother-in-law.

As for everyone else, they're suddenly busy helping them-selves to the tray of drinks Katie has delivered. Nobody seems the least bit concerned about the fact that Jack and I aren't engaged yet or that he didn't answer Toni's question.

Maybe I shouldn't be, either.

Maybe I should try to just relax and enjoy the holidays.

After all, everybody I love most in the world is right here in this room…how often does that happen? Hardly ever. So I might as well kick back and enjoy it while I can.

Anyway, next year at this time, I'll be married. I just know it.

In fact, next year at this time…

"Who's hungry? I've got lasagna, eggplant and pizza in the oven," my mother announces, even as I tell myself that next year at this time, *Tra La!*—I might very well have a lit-tle Jack Junior in the oven.

Or not, I decide, watching my sister-in-law Michaela turn green and make a beeline for the bathroom at the mere mention of lasagna.

Why rush into parenthood? Being engaged is enough of a goal to start with. Everything else will follow eventually.

Jack catches my eye and smiles.

I don't even pretend he can possibly read my mind as I smile back at him.

Then he mouths, *"I love you"*…

And I realize that he can.

Chapter 15

I'm dreaming of a white Christmas.

Chances are, I'll be getting one. The latest weather fore-cast out of Buffalo calls for bitter cold with windchills below zero, and two feet of snow today—which is Christ-mas Eve—plus a bonus eighteen inches tomorrow. Yay.

I'm also dreaming of a white wedding gown, and a white veil, and a pair of white satin pearl-beaded shoes I saw in the bridal magazine I went out to buy this morning on the pretext of getting the New York papers.

The New York papers aren't available in Brookside, in case you were wondering. The *Buffalo News* and the *Cleveland Plain Dealer* are available, but no *Times* or *Post* or *Daily News*.

"Getting married soon, Tracey?" asked Al, the old guy behind the counter at the local corner store that sells ev-erything under the non-sun.

Everything, that is, but the New York papers.

"Yup, soon," I told Al, because I had on gloves so he couldn't see my bare left hand, and I figured I didn't owe him an explanation even though I've known him forever—he lives a few blocks from my parents' house and goes to our church.

Then again, in Brookside, just about everybody lives a few blocks from my parents' house and goes to our church. That doesn't mean they should be privy to my wedding plans—although when I actually have some, I'm sure I won't be opposed to sharing.

Despite the fact that the forecast for my getting that white gown, veil and shoes is far less certain than the one for snow, I read the magazine from cover to cover when I got home. I had to do it in the bathroom so I wouldn't get roped into helping my mother peel, cube and fry the potatoes for breakfast.

Yes, we're having fried potatoes. For breakfast.

Along with fried eggs, fried bacon and buttered white toast. Typical Spadolini breakfast fare.

Is it any wonder I've had a weight problem my entire life?

I dare to set foot in the kitchen only when my sister, who's dropped by, calls me from the foot of the stairs.

When I get there, I find my father sitting at the table while Mary Beth pours his coffee and my mother fills his plate.

"Where's Jack?" he asks, ostensibly because I need to get busy serving my man, too.

"Still asleep."

"He's tired from all that shopping you two did yesterday," my mother says sympathetically.

"Did you go shopping?" Mary Beth asks with interest. "Where?"

"They went to the Wal-Mart," my mother says on my behalf.

Not that I'd have called it "The" Wal-Mart, which is a strictly local colloquialism.

"Well, that'll wear anybody out," my father concludes,

and puts a forkful of eggs into his mouth. "No wonder he's still in bed. Connie, these eggs need salt."

If I were the one who was still lounging in bed at 9:00 a.m. on Christmas Eve, they would all be calling me lazy. That, or taking my temperature because you don't sleep in unless you've got a bug.

I've passed off many a hangover as a bug in my day.

But Jack isn't hungover, unless it's from milk. Which is all he drank last night, along with the dozen *cucidati* my mother fed him before bed.

We had gone to a movie and he gave my hand a meaningful squeeze during the steamy love scene. When we got back, I was hoping to sneak him into my room for a little preholiday *fa-la-la-la-lovin'*, but there was Connie, waiting up in her flannel nightgown asking, "How about a little snack?" By the time she was finished with Jack, all that was on his mind was a long winter's nap in my brothers' old room down the hall from mine, which is where he's sleeping while he's here.

Oh, well. It isn't like we don't get plenty of *fa-la-la-la-lovin'* action when we're back home.

And anyway, it's hard for me to feel sexy, let alone uninhibited, in my parents' house. Especially when I'm wearing one of my mother's flannel nightgowns, which I was forced to do last night because I spilled lasagna sauce on my pajamas.

But my parents' house is where I am, and where I'll stay, so I've got to make the best of it.

In that spirit I have to admit that it's cozy in the kitchen this morning, just the four of us. An ancient Ray Conniff Singers Christmas album—as in, vinyl—is playing in the next room, and the snow is coming down like crazy beyond the window above the sink.

"Where are the boys?" I ask Mary Beth.

She scowls. "With Vinnie."

"Oh." I pause, then ask because I have to, "How are things going with...everything?" Meaning the divorce, which apparently takes forever to accomplish in New York State.

"Don't ask."

"Sorry, I won't."

Except I already did, and she wants to tell me about it. Her round face, which is normally cute and sweet, takes on that tight bitterness she always gets when she talks about her cheating soon-to-be-ex-husband.

First she tells me that he's been late with his court-ordered child-support payments for months, yet he bought his girlfriend fancy jewelry for Christmas.

"How do you know that?"

"Nino told me. Vinnie took the boys shopping with him to get her gift."

"Wow."

"Yeah. I guess that's quality father-son time."

I shake my head, feeling sorry for my sister. What did she do to deserve this?

Okay, for one thing, she stupidly married Vinnie.

I know it sounds callous of me, but anybody could have seen this whole thing coming from a mile away, even way back on their wedding day. And if not then, anybody could have certainly seen it coming when Vinnie was caught with another woman while Mary Beth was in labor.

But my sister was blindly in love with him, even then. He apologized countless times for cheating on her—which he did countless times—and she took him back countless times. That was on the advice of my mother and Father Stefan, our parish priest, both of whom convinced her that marriage is sacred and must be preserved at any cost, especially when there are young, innocent children involved.

"Plus," Mary Beth says now, per the young, innocent children, "Vinnie still claims he wants shared custody."

"Uh-oh."

"Don't worry, I'll fight him on it in court if it comes to that. And he won't win."

I look at my mother, standing by the stove. She heaves a heavy sigh and shakes her head sadly. I know she encouraged Mary Beth to work out her marriage for the kids' sake, but at this point, she must realize that my sister is better off divorced. Even if it means she can no longer take communion, which, in my mother's opinion, is tragic.

"Do you get the boys back tonight?" I ask Mary Beth.

"Hell, yes."

"Mary Beth." My father doesn't like swearing. Then he says to my mother, "*Bella!* The salt! Come on!"

In our house, it's fine to give orders if they're preceded by an endearment.

"It's coming, it's coming, hold your horses. Here you go, honey, now you eat all of that and I mean it." My mother plunks down a plate that holds enough food to choke one of those horses my father is supposed to be holding.

I watch her obediently return to the stove, retrieve the saltshaker and hand it over to him. He grunts his thanks.

I look back at my plate and say, "I'm, uh, not hungry, Ma."

No, I'm starved.

But not because I haven't eaten. Quite the contrary, in fact. While Jack was feasting on *cucidati* and milk before bed last night, I was downing a large wedge of leftover lasagna. But it's almost as if the more I eat, the more I require.

Mary Beth looks up from her own heap of eggs. "You're on a diet again, Tracey, aren't you?"

"No way!" I say, hoping to head off a lecture on such foolishness.

I pick up my fork.

"Good. You're finally getting some meat on your bones," my mother says approvingly.

I put down my fork.

Meat on my bones? How depressing is that? What am I, a suckling pig?

I proceed to poke at my food while the three of them chow down. In the next room, the Ray Conniff Singers hit a sudden vinyl snag and get stuck singing, *"Oh come let us adore hi—oh come let us adore hi—"*

"*Bella,* the record," my father says, because, you know, she's deaf and he's helpless. "It's skipping."

She sighs and starts to push back her chair.

"Sit and eat, Ma, I'll get it," I say, eager for the opportunity to flee the table.

"You eat," she says, motioning at my plate. "I'll get it."

As she goes into the other room, my father looks at me. "Not salty enough? Is that why you're not eating?"

"No, it's fine."

"Needs more salt." He shoves the shaker across the table in my direction. "Your mother still hasn't learned in forty years that eggs need salt."

"I think they're salty enough," Mary Beth says as the Ray Conniff singers skid all the way to *"Sing, choirs of angels…"*

"You, you're just like your mother, all health conscious," my father accuses my sister.

I hide a snort behind my cup of coffee. My mother and Mary Beth—both of whom swear by good old-fashioned recipes that call for lard—*health conscious?*

Mary Beth decides to change the subject. "So what did you get for Jack for Christmas, Tracey?"

This conversation just gets better and better.

"I got him a, um, gift certificate," I say as my mother returns to the table and resumes eating.

"You got who a gift certificate?" she asks.

"Jack."

"For what? Borders?" asks my father, who received just that from me for Father's Day last year. Not that he ever sets foot in a bookstore. But I had long since run out of gift ideas for him, and I thought he could buy himself some CDs or DVDs if he didn't want books.

I guess he didn't want any of the above, because I spotted the gift card collecting dust on his dresser when I went in to borrow my mother's flannel nightgown after I got the lasagna on my pajamas last night.

"No, it isn't for Borders," I say. "It's for...something else."

"Oh! I get it," Mary Beth says slyly.

"You do?" I ask, betting she doesn't. There's a gleam in her eye, and it's not a Caribbean-vacation gleam. It's an X-rated gleam.

"What?" my mother asks, all swivel headed. "What do you get?"

"Never mind, Ma," Mary Beth says with a lascivious grin.

Needing to set her straight, I begin, "Mary Beth—"

My father cuts me off with an exasperated "What is everybody talking about? Why doesn't anybody ever tell me anything?"

My mother shushes him with a terse "This is girl talk! That's why!"

Then she turns back to me and asks, again, "What's the gift certificate for?"

"Well, it's not for what *she* thinks it's for," I say, bobbing my head at my dirty-minded sister.

"Oh, okay." Mary Beth winks at me.

Naturally, both my parents pick up on that.

My father throws up his hands in confusion, and my mother finishes gulping some orange juice before she does the same—then suddenly clutches her head.

"Oh!"

"What's the matter, Ma? Head freeze?" I ask hopefully.

"Is that gift certificate for something...romantic?" she asks ominously.

"Romantic? I guess so."

"Tracey!" She smacks me in the arm. "I never thought a daughter of mine would go around giving out sex coupons."

"Sex coupons?" my father echoes in disbelief. *"What?"*

I can only imagine what's going through their heads. If I weren't so aggravated, I would probably laugh at the vision of me holed up with a bootleg printing press running off certificates for illicit bedroom services.

As it is, I can only bury my face in my hands and wish that I were somewhere, anywhere, else. New York, Aspen, even the reflexology room at Deux Coeurs Sur La Plage. Anything would be better than this. Why is it that every conversation I have with my parents tends to become an interrogation?

"Tracey, what got into you?" my mother wants to know. "I raised you to be a lady. I raised you to—"

"Ma, I'm not giving Jack a gift certificate for sex, okay?" I glare at Mary Beth, who doesn't even have the decency to look apologetic.

"You're not?"

"No, Ma." *Jack gets sex for free.*

But I refrain from saying that, and she looks mollified until I feel compelled for some reason to add, "It's a gift certificate for a Caribbean vacation."

Pause.

"You're taking Jack to the Caribbean on vacation?"

I nod.

To say that she isn't pleased would be the same thing as saying that it's a little nippy outside this morning.

Clearly, to my mother, my Christmas gift to Jack is a mere step down from doling out sex coupons.

"I really don't think you should be going around doing that," she informs me. Surprise, surprise.

I picture myself "going around" with my Caribbean-vacation coupons. As in door to door. As in, *Hi, my name is*

Tracey Spadolini, and I'd like to whisk you away with me on a sexy island romp.

"You're not even married, Tracey," my mother informs me, because clearly I must have forgotten.

"Ma, come on. They *live* together," Mary Beth speaks up at last.

"Don't remind me." That came from my father, who has resumed shoveling eggs and potatoes into his mouth after dumping salt all over everything.

"If you were married, Tracey, everything would be different."

Yeah, no kidding, Ma. Thanks for enlightening me.

"Married people travel together all the time," she goes on, "and nobody thinks anything of it."

"Jack and I traveled here together," I point out.

"That's different."

"How?"

"This isn't a foreign land."

What the...?

Ah, the old Connie Spadolini logic. It's been a while.

"I'm not sure what you're getting at, Ma."

"It's one thing to fly to Buffalo," she says with a shrug. "It's another thing altogether to go away on a vacation together."

You know, there was a time when I actually valued my mother's infinite wisdom. Either I've changed, or her infinite wisdom has been replaced by meaningless bullshit.

"But we live together," I remind her helplessly. "What's the difference where we go?"

"She wants you to get married," my father interrupts his chewing to say. "Okay?"

I look at my mother, who shrugs.

"I guess I don't get what any of this has to do with my Christmas gift to him," I tell her.

Or what business it is of yours.

"I think Jack is great, Tracey," she says simply. "I just wish you two were at least engaged."

Okay, so we're all on the same page here.

Even Mary Beth is nodding. "I know you probably think living together is the same thing, Trace…"

Who—me?

"…but believe me, it isn't."

"Trust me, I believe you, Mary Beth."

What I can't believe is that they're all sitting here acting as though my marital destiny is in *my* hands.

Tell it to Jack, I want to scream at them.

But before I can, guess who appears in the doorway?

Okay, in this house, you never know. It could be any number of assorted relatives, friends and church ladies.

So I won't make you guess who.

I'll tell you: it's our little adamant-bachelor sleepyhead himself.

Instant smiles all around. Well, I'm not smiling. I'm pissed at him for putting me through this with my family. Why can't he just give me the damn ring and make us all happy?

"Sit down, Jack. I'll get you your eggs." My mother bustles over to the stove. "Tracey, pour him his coffee."

I dig into my fried potatoes, because God knows I can use a little comfort food right about now. "Jack can get his own coffee, Ma."

"Tracey! He's a guest," she chides, but what she really means is *he's a man.*

And I can tell by the way she's looking at me that she now understands why Jack hasn't proposed. It's because I'm not waiting on him hand and foot.

"It's okay, Connie," Jack says easily, going over to the Mr. Coffee on the counter and opening the cupboard for a mug. "I've got it."

Not only does he have it, but he also goes around the table, pouring refills for everyone else, including my mother.

"Oh, Jack, you shouldn't have," she says as though he's just presented her with an extravagant gift.

"No problem." He takes a seat and looks at the heap of food on his plate. "If I keep eating like this, I'm going to have to buy two seats for the return flight."

Everyone laughs.

Everyone except me, that is. I'm too busy trying not to eat everything my mother put on my plate, and then go back for seconds.

But of course, I do.

Stress makes me eat, and being with my family—especially at Christmas—is as stressful as it gets.

After breakfast, Mary Beth goes to The Wal-Mart to finish up some shopping. Jack heads out into the blustery weather to shovel the walk and driveway, which of course thrills my father to no end.

I am roped into kitchen duty, cleaning five pounds of shrimp for tonight's traditional seven-course seafood dinner. As I scrape the gloppy black threads from each shrimp's curved spine, I curse whoever started this tradition back in Italy.

"Why does it have to be seven courses, Ma?" I grumble.

She looks up from the scrod she's dipping in eggs and coating with flour for frying. "For the seven sacraments. Baptism, communion, reconciliation—"

"I know the seven sacraments, Ma," I cut in.

I also know that marriage is one of them.

She insists on naming them all, of course. To prove she's good at religion.

In lieu of applause, I say, deadpan, "Well, I wouldn't want to come up short on my sacraments. I guess if this marriage thing doesn't pan out with Jack, I'll have to go for the Holy Orders one."

"Tracey! Don't joke around about the sacraments."

"I wasn't joking, Ma. Who's to say I might not get the

calling someday? We haven't had a *nun* in the family since Sister Mary Ann."

She was my grandmother's first cousin, and not exactly a fun-loving gal, from what I hear. According to family legend, even the laughing gas she was once given for a root canal failed to make her crack a smile.

Speaking of not cracking a smile, my mother is sternly shaking her head at me and saying, "You don't want to be a nun, Tracey."

"I don't?"

"No. You want to get married and have babies."

She's right, but I can't help saying, "Actually, Ma, anyone can get married and have babies. I want to become a copywriter and win Addy awards."

Which isn't a lie, because I really do want to do that. I just want to get married and have babies—someday—too.

Who should walk in on my poster-child-for-women's-lib moment but Jack?

He grins broadly, and I can't tell whether it's because he assumes he's off the hook with the whole marriage thing, or because he's no longer toiling away with a shovel in sub-zero temperatures.

In any case, he accepts my mother's offer of hot chocolate, and she bustles down to her basement pantry cupboard for some bittersweet cocoa squares to melt.

What, you thought she makes instant?

"So how's it going?" Jack asks, kissing me on the cheek.

I rip the intestines from another shrimp with my bare hands. "Terrific," I say through clenched teeth.

"Is your mother getting on your nerves?"

"How'd you guess?"

He shakes his head. "Holidays are stressful. Try to just take it in stride. And you shouldn't talk about business with her."

"Business?"

"You were saying you wanted to win an Addy. She probably doesn't even know what that is."

"I'm sure she can figure it out. And anyway…that's not what we were talking about."

"It's not?"

I shrug. "Not really."

My mother is back with the cocoa squares, so I don't have a chance to tell him that we were discussing my future with Jack.

Not that it matters now. He's either going to give me a ring in the next twenty-four hours, or he's not. It's beyond my control.

Jack sits at the table sipping hot chocolate and chatting with my mom as she fries the fish, and I can't help but lighten up a little. He's such a good sport. Especially when he offers to hand deliver several tins of cookies to the neighbors, wearing a Santa hat, no less, so that my mother won't have to do it herself in the snow.

"He's crazy about you," she comments, watching him trudge down the driveway, tins in hand, Santa hat on head.

"I don't know…I was just thinking he's crazy about *you,*" I tell her, and I can't help but smile.

Must be the Christmas spirit, because the rest of the day passes in a merry blur of cooking, baking, wrapping and cleaning.

The next thing I know, I'm sipping a well-deserved cup of rum-spiked eggnog—homemade, of course, and served in my mother's cut-glass punch bowl—and the relatives are starting to arrive. Not just my brothers and sister and their families, but dozens of aunts, uncles and cousins.

"Tracey, are you going to eat my sausage this year?" asks my Crock-Pot-toting Uncle Cosmo, invoking Fennel Seed memories of Christmas Past. He pronounces it zau-zage, another odd little local colloquialism.

"As soon as I finish this eggnog," I say, and introduce him to Jack.

"You like zau-zage?" Uncle Cosmo wants to know.

"I love sausage," Jack says.

"That's what you think. You've never *had* zau-zage," Uncle Cosmo informs Jack, who raises an eyebrow in my direction as if to say *save me*.

But it's too late; he's been spirited off to the kitchen with my uncle, leaving me to get reacquainted with my teenage cousins Aldo and Bud, whose real name is Lorenzo.

"How's school going, guys?" I ask, taking in their baggy pants, backward baseball caps and gold chains.

"Yo, it's sick" is Aldo's response, and that clinches it. Hip-hop has come to Brookside at last.

"You're sick?" I inquire, just to get on his nerves.

The brothers—who seem to think they're *brothers*—merely stare at me.

"Huh?" one of them says.

"I asked how school was, and I thought you said—"

"Whatever," the other one says.

Awkward silence.

"So, Bud," I say, determined to show them that I'm cool—if that's what you call it these days. "I really like those jeans. Dude, they're so phat."

My compliment is met with a blank stare.

"Not fat," I say quickly, because apparently he's not up on my hip slang. "You know…phat."

"Word," Bud says, turning to his brother. "Let's go look for some peeps."

With that, they drift off in aimless search of God knows what, but I'd be willing to bet it isn't colored sugar-coated marshmallow chicks.

"How's it going?" Jack asks, reappearing to waft garlicky fennel breath into my face.

I shrug. "I was talking to my cousins. Trying to, anyway.

Next thing you know, these newfangled kids will be doing the lindy."

He laughs.

"God, I feel old, Jack." Old and fat.

Not phat.

"Yeah? Go hang out with your uncle Cosmo. He just told me in detail about his colon issues."

"I didn't know he had colon issues. Is he okay?"

"Yes, when he isn't shitting his brains out."

"Good God." I wrinkle my nose. "Did he really say that?"

"In so many words."

"I'm sorry."

"It isn't your fault."

"It's my family, though."

"So? Look at mine."

I think of Bob, and of Ashley and Not-Mary-Kate.

"Yeah," I say, "but we only see yours in small doses. With my family, we have to move in for a week and see every last living soul who has the slightest drop of Spadolini blood in their veins."

Jack points out, "Well, I don't even have an extended family, really. Now that all my grandparents are gone, we've lost touch with the rest of them."

That's something I can't imagine. It's actually kind of sad, in a way.

Then again, I won't think it's so sad when we're planning our wedding guest list next week. Or whenever.

The fewer relatives on the Candell side, the less chance that the hundred-plus Spadolini relatives I'll be obligated to invite might bump some of our dear friends and co-workers from the guest list.

"Hi, Tracey!" That's my cousin Joanie, whose first communion I missed a few years back, nearly resulting in my being shunned for life.

"Hi, Joanie. Do you remember my boyfriend, Jack?"

"Sure." She smiles widely, revealing shiny braces with an unappetizing hunk of white glop stuck front and center. "Hi again, Jack."

"Nice to see you again, Joanie. Does anybody want some eggnog? I'm going to get some."

"I'll have some," Joanie pipes up.

Jack looks at me. "Doesn't it have rum in it?"

"Sure does."

"But you asked," Joanie pouts.

"How about if I get you some soda?"

She gives him a blank look until I say helpfully, "He means pop."

"Oh! All right. I'll take a Diet Pepsi, Jack," Joanie tells him, and I watch her watch Jack, wearing the same wistful expression I must have worn while watching my older cousins' boyfriends back when I was a chubby preteen with gunky braces.

"He's so cute," she says, turning to me.

"Thanks."

Thanks? Why am I taking credit for Jack's cuteness?

Because when somebody compliments your boyfriend, they are vicariously complimenting you, that's why. It's the same thing as saying, "Congratulations! You landed a real looker!"

Isn't it?

Okay, maybe not. The point is, Joanie thinks Jack is cute, and so do I, and we're both dreamily watching him ladle eggnog out of the punch bowl across the room.

"Are you guys getting married?" Joanie wants to know.

"Eventually," I say, and decide that's the perfect answer. Vague, yet positive, and entirely truthful. I think I'll use it from now on when people ask if we're getting married.

Hopefully, *from now on* will encompass a mere few hours, at which point I'll have a ring on my finger and a date on the calendar, and pesky questions like that one can go away. But between now and then, *Eventually* will suffice.

"Can I be the junior bridesmaid?" Joanie asks promptly.

"Oh…I don't know. I haven't even thought about my bridal attendants yet."

All right, I'll admit that not only have I thought about my bridal attendants, but I've nailed the list of potentials down to a lucky eight—Mary Beth as matron of honor, plus my sister-in-law Sara, Jack's sister Rachel, Raphael, Kate, Brenda, Latisha and Yvonne—and outfitted them in figure-flattering navy velvet sheaths, with a complimentary tux for Raphael.

Just in my head, of course.

But the second Jack hands over that twinkling bauble, my meticulous plans will come to immediate fruition.

"When you think about it, think of me," Joanie says sweetly, and I am struck by a sudden pang.

Maybe a ninth bridesmaid is in order.

But no flower girls. No way.

"I can't wait until I get married."

That's Joanie, of course.

Though it's a statement that easily could have come from either one of us.

"I know exactly what I'm going to wear. Did you see the pictures of Britney's gown?"

"Britney?"

"Spears."

"Oh. Um, I don't think so. Didn't she elope?"

"No, I mean when she married Kevin. They had a surprise wedding, remember?"

"Vaguely."

"Hey! You and Jack should have a surprise wedding!" she says suddenly. "Wouldn't that be the coolest?"

"A surprise wedding?"

"Yeah, you know…where you invite a bunch of people over for a regular party, and then when they get there, it's like, surprise! We're getting married! The celebrities do it that way all the time."

"Sounds great," I say, "only I'm not a celebrity."

"But you don't *have* to be. You can have a surprise wedding even if you're a regular person."

Hmm. I wonder if you can have a surprise wedding even if you're not officially engaged. And I wonder if you can surprise not just the guests, but the groom as well.

I think of the New Year's Eve party Jack and I are hosting next week. Maybe I should—

"One eggnog and one Pepsi," Jack announces, sidling back over to us, unaware that behind my benign smile I'm daydreaming about a forced marriage.

"Thank you, Jack." Joanie sips, then asks, "Are you sure this is Diet?"

"Did you say Diet?"

"Duh," she says with the look of utter contempt only a twelve-year-old girl can deliver quite so effectively.

"I don't think you should be drinking diet pop, Joanie," I say, though I'll admit she's becoming quite the little chubbette. "It's full of chemicals."

"So? Regular Pepsi is full of carbs." With that, she flounces away.

"So much for my winning over Cousin Joanie," Jack says wryly.

"Oh, she thinks you're cute."

"She does?" He grins.

"Yeah, but she also thinks Britney Spears is the epitome of style, so…"

"Hey, look," Jack says, "here comes your grandmother."

I turn around and spot her famous boobage before I even glimpse her face.

"Dolce mia!" she exclaims, and I'm enveloped in said boobage, as Grandma squeezes the heck out of me the way only an Italian grandmother can. Then she pulls me back at arm's length and announces, "You look *bellissima.*"

"Thank you, Grandma. So do you."

She pats her dyed auburn swirl of sprayed hair, which she also has "done" at Shear Magique, but twice a week as opposed to my mother's once. "Oh, I don't know about that."

Oh, cut it out, Grandma, I want to say. *We both know you're stunning.* Not to mention voluptuous. If she were twenty years younger, people would be whispering about implants.

But those babies are one hundred percent real—and hereditary. I happen to know that without the really good bra she's undoubtedly wearing under her tight red sweater, Grandma's nipples would be in danger of getting snagged in her waistband.

Tugging Jack closer, I say, "You remember my boyfriend, Jack, don't you?"

"Of course I do."

That's because Jack was sure to compliment her on her hairstyle and outfit the last time he was in town.

Beauty is to my grandmother as culinary skills are to my mother. Take proper note of either, and you've got a friend for life.

Grandma tells us about her recent shopping trip—to The Wal-Mart, of course—and how, in addition to new muffin tins, a sale on baking flour and her prescription blood pressure medicine, she picked up a new shade of lipstick called Christmas Red.

"I'm wearing it now," she says, puckering up to show us. "Do you like it?"

Jack and I assure her that we do.

Then she points overhead at the clump of plastic greens hanging from the archway and says, "Look who's under the mistletoe!"

For a second, I think she wants to plant a Christmas Red smacker on my boyfriend. Which gives me the creeps. Is Grandma, who's been lonely ever since Grandpa died, moving in on my man?

Then she winks at me, and I realize she's being a true romantic.

"I'll leave you two alone," she says with a smile, and we find ourselves alone as we can be in a fifteen-hundred-square-foot house filled with fifty people.

Jack pulls me close.

"What are you doing?" I ask him, careful not to spill the last rummy swallow of my eggnog.

"Kissing you. We're under the mistletoe."

"Oh, right."

I'm expecting a mere peck, but he plants a soul-stirring kiss on my mouth, leaving me weak in the knees, garlic-fennel breath and all. I find myself setting down the eggnog cup to encircle his neck with both arms, and fervently wishing he weren't assigned to sleep down the hall.

"Hey, I have an idea. Why don't you pay me a little midnight visit later," I whisper in his ear.

"Uh-uh," he whispers back.

"Why not?"

"Creaky floorboards. I tried last night."

"You did?" And here I thought he ate himself into a *cucidati*-induced oblivion.

"I did, but before I could get halfway down the hall, your mother stuck her head out of her room to ask if I needed another snack."

"Oh, God, she's too much."

"I don't suppose she'd consider letting me share your canopy bed instead of sleeping down the hall?"

"Not unless we're married."

That slips out before I can stop it.

I fully expect Jack to frown in response, or make a sarcastic remark.

Instead, he just shrugs, wearing what I choose to interpret as a meaningful little smile.

Call me overly optimistic, but I'm thinking that smile

says, *You might just find yourself engaged before the holiday is out.*

No, really. Call me overly optimistic. Go on.

Maybe I am.

But maybe not.

A few hours later, after we've returned from Midnight Mass and eaten yet another meal, I find myself alone at last with Jack.

My parents have gone up to bed, unwittingly leaving Jack and I to our wee-hour moment of truth: our long-awaited gift exchange.

The living room is lit only by the colored twinkle lights on the Christmas tree. Perry Como is singing "Do You Hear What I Hear?" in the background.

"How late is it?" Jack asks around a yawn as we stretch out on the floor near the tree, side by side, our backs propped against the couch.

"Almost three, I think." I lean my head on his shoulder, wishing I weren't so tired. I don't want to yawn through what could be the most exciting experience of my life.

"That late? Really? It doesn't seem like it."

"That's because it's barely past midnight in Aspen."

"How glad am I that I'm not there?" he asks, giving my shoulder a squeeze.

"I don't know…how glad are you?"

"Very glad." He leans in for a kiss. "I'd much rather be here with you."

"Really? Even with all the chaos?"

"I love the chaos," he says promisingly.

Enough to marry into it? I want to ask.

Instead, I ask, to get the ball rolling, "Ready for your present?"

"Are you?" he volleys back.

"Yes, but…don't you want me to give you yours first?"

"No, you open yours first," Jack says. "I can't wait till you see what it is."

That's encouraging.

Or maybe not.

I can't help thinking that he wouldn't be urging me to go first if his gift to me were a ring. He'd have to know that my gift to him would be a little anticlimactic after that.

But he doesn't seem particularly concerned about the gift-giving order, so...

Not a very good sign, I know.

"Do you want some more wine or some Funyuns or something?" I ask, wanting to stall because...

Well, because suddenly, I'm deathly afraid.

What if this is *it?*

What if this *isn't* it?

I'm not so sure I want to know, either way.

"Funyuns?" Jack is echoing.

"I love them. Don't you?"

"Not particularly. And I've never seen you eat a Funyun in your life."

"It's my guilty pleasure."

"Really." He stares at me for a long moment, as if wondering what else he doesn't know about me, and I wonder if I just blew it. Maybe he's rethinking the entire relationship.

And maybe you've descended to the utter depths of paranoia, Tracey.

Jack shrugs. "If I put another thing into my mouth at this point, I'll explode. Just let me give you your present."

He's already rooting around amidst the packages under the tree, which means my gift has been tucked away here all along, more or less hiding in plain sight.

But how did he get it here? Was it stashed in his checked luggage? Did he have a coconspirator in the household so that he could ship it to Brookside in advance?

I doubt that. Neither of my parents would be able to keep that kind of secret. Jack must have brought the gift with him in his luggage.

"Where the heck is it?" he asks, shimmying under the tree on his belly, his voice muffled.

"I hope it's still there," I call, wondering why I didn't think to snoop around under the tree for a ring-size box with my name on it.

I guess I didn't think he'd be so blatant about it, that's why. I figured nobody puts a highly personal, valuable gift under a very public Christmas tree.

Which is why it probably isn't highly personal or valuable, I remind myself. *So don't get your hopes up.*

As if they aren't already.

"I've never seen so many presents," Jack comments from his distant location.

There are hundreds of wrapped gifts under the tree now, and that's in addition to the dozens of already-opened-ones we exchanged earlier with all the relatives.

Thus, I am able to count among my possessions my very own Love's Baby Soft gift set—who knew they still even made that stuff?—a Garth Brooks CD (?), a twelve-month subscription to *Good Housekeeping* and several polyester-blend sweaters, all size medium—which is too small.

Some of my aunts and my grandmother even brought gifts for Jack. He, too, has a new collection of polyester-blend sweaters, all size medium—also too small.

Mental note: go to The Wal-Mart at an off-hour to exchange sweaters for cash.

Meanwhile, Jack is still hunting for my gift under the tree.

I hope that's because it's such a small box that it got lost in the heap, but I'm starting to highly doubt that.

"Why don't you just open my gift first?" I ask, patting the envelope containing his gift certificate, which is in my back pocket.

"Here it is!" he shimmies backward, dragging with him a...

Huge box.

Not major-appliance-huge.

Not even small-appliance-huge.

But huge enough not to hold my engagement ring, unless it's the Hope Diamond.

Unless...

Do you think he put the small box into a bigger box, and then a bigger box, and then a bigger box, and then...

Nah. Me neither.

Alrighty then. I guess I'm not getting engaged for Christmas.

I comfort myself with the knowledge that it doesn't mean anything other than that Jack decided not to go for the obvious and propose on Christmas Eve, when I would be expecting it.

He probably wants to surprise me.

"Here you go," he says excitedly, handing me the not-my-engagement-ring-box.

The good thing is that it's also the wrong-shape box to hold a Chia Pet, unless it's uncommonly large, rectangular and no more than three inches tall.

"Go ahead, Tracey, open it!"

I rip into the paper, which is the obligatory green and red motif of Christmas trees or wreaths or holly; I don't pause to take note of the pattern.

Beyond the paper is a gift box from L.L.Bean.

"L.L.Bean," I say, because I have to say something.

He grins. "I hope you like it."

"I know I will," I assure him, wondering if it's one of those wool sweaters that itch unless you wear a thick turtleneck underneath. Kate got me one a few years ago and I never wear it.

But if that's what Jack got me, I'll wear it all the time, I promise myself as I lift the lid on the box. I'll wear it, just like I filled the stupid Chia Pet with water even after I knew all hope was lost, because it's the thought that counts.

Inside the box, beneath a layer of tissue, is…

"It's a Gore-Tex Mountain Guide Parka," Jack informs me excitedly.

It sure is.

And it's bright orangy-yellow, or…

"Alpine Gold," as Jack says. "I hope it fits."

It does.

I model it for him cheerfully, even as I wonder what possessed him to buy it. I mean…

Well, I'm not a mountain guide.

Does he want me to be a mountain guide? Does he think we should move somewhere and start a new alpine life together?

"Check out the technical layering system," Jack advises.

I would, if I knew what that was, or where to look. Instead, I pretend to check it out, running my hands over the coat and its lining.

"Pull up the hood," he says, and adds, with impressive used-car-salesman savvy, "See how it's ergonomically shaped?"

Before I can reach for the hood, he's pulling it up over my head.

"It has these great mesh chest pockets for extra gear, see?" Jack asks, showing me.

For a fleeting moment, I'm convinced he's going to pull a diamond ring from the chest pocket. But it's empty. Just waiting for all that extra gear I'll be toting around, um, Manhattan.

"Does it fit right?"

"It fits perfectly."

"Good. I guessed at the size."

"What size did you get?"

"It's a large."

He guessed I was large. This is getting better by the moment.

But he's so earnest, so loving and kind, that I can't be disappointed. And I'm not. Not really.

At least it isn't a Chia Pet.

I muster enthusiasm and tell him, "This is a great coat," because it is. For a mountain guide.

"You're always so cold" is his response as he pulls me close. "And you never have the right kind of coat. I wanted you to be warm for a change."

Okay, that really is sweet.

I smile at him.

I keep smiling even when he pats my head through the ergonomic hood, making me feel vaguely as if I should have a little keg-barrel around my neck, like an alpine dog.

"It's definitely a warm coat," I tell Jack, who seems to be waiting for further glowing commentary.

It *is* warm. Really warm.

In fact, I'm beginning to perspire profusely, so I remove my new parka—did I mention it's bright orangy-yellow?—and fold it back into the box.

"Thank you," I tell Jack again, after jutting out my lower lip to blow a cooling breeze on my sweaty bangs. "It's really a great coat."

And I'm sure I'll use it. At least, here in Brookside.

I daresay it's going to be a bit trickier to blend into the crowd scene in Manhattan, where tasteful black cashmere is as ubiquitous as bulky layers of bright-colored down are in my hometown.

"I'm so glad you like it. I had to get you something that could be mail-ordered and shipped right to your parents' house."

Well, he didn't *have* to.

He could have—

Oh, never mind.

"Your mother was in on it," he informs me.

Why, that little minx.

"She got the package two weeks ago. I'm surprised she kept the secret."

Yeah, well, mothers are good at keeping boring secrets. It's the ones involving diamond engagement rings that are a bit trickier.

"My turn," Jack announces expectantly.

Okay, here's the thing.

I know my parka cost him a pretty penny. Probably at least three hundred bucks, including shipping.

And nobody ever said Christmas-gift expenditures have to be even. In fact, I was entirely prepared to give him this Caribbean vacation even knowing that I might not be getting a present of equal or greater carat value.

But I suddenly feel a bit sheepish about my gift to him.

Don't you think it seems a little...excessive?

Jack is waiting.

My thoughts race wildly.

Maybe I can take my chances and pluck a random gift from under the tree to give him.

It just might work, if I could remove the gift tag without Jack noticing...and if I had a *To: Jack From: Tracey* replacement gift tag all set to swap for it...and if I could be sure the gift wouldn't turn out to be, say, Aqua Velva.

Okay, it just won't work.

There's nothing to do but reach into my pocket and pull out the gift certificate.

"Here you go," I say unceremoniously, and put it into Jack's hand.

"Is this a letter?" he asks, looking down at the envelope.

A letter?

Why would I write him a letter?

"Open it and you'll see," I say, trying not to feel frustrated.

It's just that this whole thing hasn't gone as I envisioned it.

Jack rips open the envelope—and in the process, somehow rips the gift certificate in half.

I watch in dismay as he pieces it together and reads it.

Then he looks up at me in shock. "You're kidding."

Hmm, there's an unexpected out.

I debate taking it. I can agree that yes, I am indeed kidding. Isn't this a great joke? *Ha ha ha ha ha…*

I can then inform him that his real gift is still coming…

But when?

And what will it be?

"Tracey?" he says. "You're not kidding, are you?"

"No," I reluctantly tell him. "I'm not."

But oh, how I wish I were.

"You got me…a Caribbean vacation?"

I offer a shaky smile. "Uh-huh."

"Oh my God."

"Oh my God," I echo, realizing that those are tears in Jack's eyes.

Is he crying because he feels that his Mountain Guide Parka pales in comparison? Not that there's anything pale about Alpine Gold, but—

"I can't believe you did this."

Frankly, I can't either.

"I love you," he exclaims, and pulls me into his arms. "This is the best gift in the entire world."

With that, my misgivings and regrets evaporate. He loves me. I made him happy. Isn't that what Christmas is all about?

"I'm so glad you like it," I say.

"How could I not like it? When are we going?"

"Next month. It's not the greatest hotel in the world, but—"

He interrupts me before I can finish my sentence with *"at least there are no bugs."*

"I'm sure it will be paradise," Jack says, and kisses me.

Then, hand in hand, we steal up the stairs.

And in the end, the best Christmas gift of all is the sound of both my parents' uninterrupted snoring as we tiptoe together past their door to my canopy bed.

Part V

Anguilla

Chapter 16

The weather when we depart JFK Airport early on a mid-January morning is dazzlingly sunny, with a brilliant blue cloudless sky above the deeper blue waters of the Atlantic, and brisk but not cold air.

It's the kind of day that happens maybe once in a typical winter, if you're lucky. The kind of day when you actually want to get outside and breathe, knowing tomorrow the thick gray clouds and intermittent wet snow and dirty slush will once again shroud the city until spring.

But I don't mind missing this day in New York because we're on our way to paradise, where the sun is even brighter, the sky is even bluer, the warm sea is shades of turquoise and the temperature is a good forty degrees higher.

Or so I thought.

Thanks to my trusty Xanax, I'm not even particularly dismayed when we hit some heavy cloud cover somewhere over the Southeast, resulting in major turbulence the farther down we go. In fact, I'm the one sitting here reading *Glamour* while Jack is cringing at every bump.

"Any second now, we'll come out of this," I tell him. "Once we get out over the Caribbean."

"Should we be out over the Caribbean by now?"

"I don't think so. Look at the weather."

Another half hour passes, and I begin to accept that we must be out over the Caribbean—meaning, if this plane goes down, the lovely turquoise sea I mentioned earlier will become my watery grave.

I keep thinking that if we could just reach Anguilla, where the sun always shines, we'll be fine.

In any case, either the Xanax has worn off by the time the pilot informs us that we have begun our descent to the island, or this is one hell of a storm-tossed landing.

I clutch Jack's hand as tightly as he clutches mine, trying not to hyperventilate, wondering why I'm being tossed around a scary charcoal tropical sky on a Friday morning when I could be safely typing some meaningless memo at my desk at Blair Barnett.

Not that life in New York has been much of a picnic these last few weeks. On the heels of our flight home from Buffalo, Jack and I came down with the flu just in time to spend what would have been our New Year's Eve bash feverish and taking turns rushing to the bathroom for three days. Being forced to cancel that party was the first in a string of recent disappointments.

For one thing, in the wake of the holidays, I'm flat broke as always. For another, I still haven't found the nerve—or, okay, the motivation—to approach Carol about promoting me into Mike's old position. For yet another, I still haven't lost the weight I've gained.

And needless to say, Jack and I still aren't engaged.

I can't help but hope that he'll take advantage of this Caribbean getaway and propose at last, but it's getting harder and harder to maintain optimism.

Especially when it's beginning to seem doubtful that we'll even make it to Anguilla in one piece.

"I'm afraid," I tell Jack, on the verge of a panic attack as the plane jolts wildly from side to side.

"It's okay," Jack tells me, looking as though he might require an airsickness bag at any moment. "Just more turbulence. I'm sure once we get below the clouds to the island, it'll be fine."

The wheels touch down a split second later—hallelujah—but oddly, we still seem to be in the clouds.

"I thought you said the other day that it never rains in Anguilla." Jack stares out the rain-spattered windowpane at the tarmac.

No, his tone isn't accusatory, but I find myself bristling anyway.

"I said there aren't *hurricanes* in Anguilla."

Or did I? Well, that's what I meant. I read about it in my Caribbean travel guide.

Then again, maybe that wasn't Anguilla. Maybe that was Aruba.

"But it isn't hurricane season anyway," Jack points out.

You could have fooled me, I think, gazing at the storm.

Oh, well. I'm sure it'll blow over by the time we reach our hotel and we'll be lounging on the beach in no time with those dirty bananas I've been dreaming about.

The line for customs is endless. I can't help but notice Jack doesn't declare a diamond ring, but it's not as if it's foreign produce so I have to conclude it might very well be in his luggage.

At last, we find ourselves careening along winding island roads in a rattletrap open-air vehicle that seems to be a cross between a bus and a van.

Finally, in what doesn't seem like the nicest neighborhood in town, we skid to a stop in front of a three-story purple stucco building. The driver grins broadly and makes what sounds like an important declaration.

"What did he say?" Jack asks me under his breath, inexplicably assuming I must be fluent in the native dialect.

"How should I know?" I murmur.

The driver says whatever he's saying once again, with increased urgency. Then he gestures for us to get out of the cab.

Maybe he doubles as an EMT and just got an emergency call, so he can't bring us to our destination.

The only problem with that theory is that I would have noticed him getting an emergency call since my eyes were vigilantly fastened to him the entire trip, making sure he didn't drive us off the road.

To my surprise—and all right, dismay—I spot a sign on the purple building, one that reads: Sea Plantation.

"Oh," I say, "I think we're here."

Reluctant to step out of the so-called shuttle into the deluge, I stare for a moment at the purple stucco building, wondering why it looks nothing like it did on the hotel's Web site. Nor does it look like a plantation, and I can't see— or hear, or smell—the sea.

"Are you sure this is the right place?" I ask the driver, who erupts in what may be an enthusiastic confirmation of my hypothesis, but could just as easily be a string of profanity.

Minutes later, Jack and I are straggling into the lobby with our waterlogged luggage.

I use the term "lobby" loosely. It's really more of a desk— as in, a regular metal work desk, not one of those tall, elegant hotel-lobby desks—in a small rectangle of a room.

The woman who checks us in has dirt under her nails and a douchy attitude.

"I can put you in a ground-floor room with two doubles," she informs us as she scans her computer screen, looking bored.

"We were supposed to have one king bed."

"We don't have any rooms with kings. They're all two doubles."

"But we only need one bed."

She looks up at me. "Don't use the other one."

"We won't."

So there!

"And, uh, we're supposed to have an ocean-view room."

"They're all ocean view," she says in her island-accented English that might be charming coming from someone with a soul.

"Even the ground floor?" I find that hard to believe.

Not that it would likely be possible to see the ocean even from the beach, given the fact that the island is currently shrouded in clouds. But something tells me that our hostess here is full of crap.

"Here's your key," she says, and hands us…a key. The old-fashioned metal kind that any crazed serial killer can duplicate before turning it in at the end of his stay, and save for future murderous purposes.

I glance over at Jack, wondering if he saw the same *Dateline NBC* special I did.

"Ready?" he asks, picking up our bags, all set to march off to our doom.

"No! It isn't really safe to stay in a room that has that kind of key," I whisper as the woman behind the desk pretends to ignore me.

Or maybe she really *is* ignoring me.

Because when I say, "Um, excuse me, do you have any rooms that use electronic card keys?" she doesn't even look up.

"Excuse me?" I say again, getting pissed.

Jack shakes his head, "Tracey, come on, it's fine."

"Is this the only kind of key you have here?" I persist, in part just because her attitude is getting on my nerves, and in part I'm holding out hope that she's put us in the old wing when she could just as easily have put us in the new wing with king-size beds and those electronic card keys with the codes that are changed after every guest.

"What do you mean, only key?" she finally responds. "There's only one door. That's the key to open it."

It seems that her work here is done, and she isn't the least bit concerned about hotel security.

"I know, but—"

"Tracey, come *on*."

Oh, I give up.

But I'm barricading the door to the room with that useless second bed before we go to sleep tonight.

We head back out into the downpour that blows beneath the covered walkway lined with tropical foliage. It's semifamiliar from the online pictures, but there, the landscaping seemed more lush than overgrown and unkempt. Maybe that's just because of the oppressive gloom.

"Do you think this will turn out to be a beach day?" I call to Jack, then wince as a wind-whipped overhanging palm frond slaps against my face.

"A beach day? I doubt it, but that's okay."

It is? I thought we were eager to sink our bare feet into sugary sand and loll about in tranquil tropical waters.

I was certainly eager to do that.

"This is it," Jack says, putting the key into the lock.

I arrive just in time for him to open the door…and see something scurry out.

Naturally, I shriek, "Was that a cockroach?"

I thought this place was bug free, God help us.

"A cockroach? Tracey, it wasn't a bug. It was the size of a squirrel."

"Oh my God! It was a squirrel?"

"No!" He's laughing at me. "It was an iguana."

As if that's better than a squirrel, or a squirrel-size bug.

"We're in the islands now," he reminds me. "Things are different here."

Yeah, no kidding. We might have bugs in New York, but at least we keep our scary reptiles in the Bronx Zoo where they belong, not running wild in the streets.

You know, I'm beginning to think Jack and I aren't on the same page.

Not for this vacation, anyway.

Maybe not for life in general.

How can I be in a relationship with somebody who thinks it's fine to share our room not just with potential serial killers, but with a creature that looks like a miniature dinosaur?

He looks at me.

I can tell he thinks I'm overreacting, and maybe I am. But I can't help it. This isn't going the way it was supposed to. None of it. And I'm not just talking about the vacation.

"Are you okay?" he asks, softening. "You really look upset."

"I *am* upset," I say, on the verge of tears. "This is awful."

"It'll be fine, you'll see. I mean, come on. We just got here."

He's talking about the vacation. Not the relationship. He thinks the relationship is fine.

I used to think that, too.

But now I think there's something wrong with us. Or, at the very least, with me. Why are we not moving ahead, the way everybody else does? Why is he reluctant to commit to me?

I could understand if it were about not having a diamond, or the means to get one on his salary. But he already took that step. What's keeping him from following through with the rest of it?

Jack holds the door wide open. "Come on, let's go in and change into dry clothes. You'll feel better."

I doubt it, but what choice do I have?

Maybe this really is just about the vacation.

After the post-Christmas letdown of these past few weeks, I really wanted this trip to be perfect—whether or not Jack uses it to finally pop the question.

Mental note: be in the moment. Stop overanalyzing everything.

To my surprise, the room is typical hotel fare—slippery quilted floral bedspreads, generic art, tile bathroom, Mr. Coffee. Not that I was expecting the Ritz. To the contrary, I was expecting an unsanitary dump.

But this isn't bad…as long as there are no iguanas lurking in the tub. I make Jack check, and he reassuringly gives the all clear. Then he turns the air-conditioning on full blast.

"What should we do now?" I ask him, after unpacking my bag into the small dresser, which takes all of sixty seconds.

All I brought is the few pairs of shorts and T-shirts that still fit me, and an old bathing suit that probably doesn't— I couldn't bring myself to try it on back home.

Jack told me to at least add a cute sundress in case we wanted to get dressed up for dinner, which I would have done, if I owned one. I substituted an ancient pair of linen pants and a cute sleeveless black top that makes my upper arms look fleshy, but it was my only option.

He also told me to bring a sweatshirt, because I'm always cold. Needing to prove him wrong—and prove to myself and to him that the weather in Anguilla is perfect at this time of year, as the guidebook claims—I declined.

Now I wish I at least had a jacket with a hood. No, not my mountain guide parka, though the splashy hue is somewhat tropical. A tasteful slicker would be nice; too bad I don't own one.

"Do you think there's someplace where we can get a rum

drink?" Jack asks, tossing his duffel bag on the floor of the surprisingly large walk-in closet, still packed.

"I don't know…I doubt it," I say dubiously. "I mean, this isn't really a resort. More like just a beach hotel."

"Beach hotels have lobby bars."

"'Lobby' is the key word there, Jack. I think a tiki bar tucked into that reception area would have been hard to miss, don't you?"

He laughs. "Then let's go out and walk around. I'm sure we'll find a place where we can get a couple of piña coladas and wait for the storm to pass."

We do just that…except we have dirty bananas instead, and more than a couple—each—and the storm doesn't seem to be passing.

A good few hours later, we're still lounging on stools in a beachside dive bar called the Wet Dog. A burnt-out mainland transplant in a Hawaiian shirt is playing a guitar and singing Jimmy Buffett tunes. When we first got here, I remember thinking he was off-key, but now he's sounding pretty good.

Maybe it's the booze.

Whatever.

All I know is that I'm having a grand old time belting out "Changes in Attitudes, Changes in Latitudes" with my new best friends Gregory and Daniel, a matching-tank-top-wearing, mustachioed, platinum-blond middle-aged gay couple from New Jersey.

"I love you guys!" I tell them warmly as the guitarist takes a break to duck outside in the rain and smoke what doesn't look like a regular cigarette.

Which I could definitely use right now.

I know, I know…and the cravings have pretty much subsided over the last few weeks, except when I have a drink. Or four.

Gazing out the window, watching the guitarist exhale smoke through his nostrils, I momentarily debate sneaking away to bum a smoke—from somebody other than him, as I just want good old-fashioned tobacco.

The only thing that stops me is that down here, you can't be too careful. What looks like a regular cigarette might be laced with, I don't know, whatever it is predatory crackheads lace innocent people's cigarettes with.

What? It *could* happen. I think I saw it on *Dateline* once. No, really.

"We love you, too! And honey, you are *such* the parrot-head!" Gregory exclaims to me, and I could be mistaken, but I think it's a compliment, so I thank him.

"Oh! I know I know I know! We should request 'Let's Get Drunk and Screw' when the guitar guy comes back!" That's Daniel, bouncing around on his stool in excitement. Either he's overcaffeinated, or he's a little hyper by nature.

"Yeah, or we could just get drunk and screw," Gregory says, and we all scream with laughter.

All of us except Jack, who visibly winces.

"Hey, you know what, guys?" I say—mostly to the Fab Two. "I have an idea! We should all get together in Manhattan after we get back home!"

Jack promptly kicks me under the bar.

I shoot him a dirty look. What's his problem? Maybe Gregory and Daniel aren't the most masculine guys we've ever met—all right, they make Raphael seem butch—but I like them.

"We'd love to get together! How does your February look?" Gregory lisps.

"Actually, we have a wedding in February," Jack tells him.

"All month?" Daniel asks, and the three of us crack up. Jack doesn't seem to think it's that funny.

I think it's because he's not drinking enough.

"Oh, barkeep!" I call good-naturedly. "Another round for the table, with an extra Kahlúa floater for my friend Jack here."

No response from the surly male bartender, who might very well be related to the front-desk clerk at our hotel.

"It's okay." Jack gestures at our still half-full glasses. "I don't need another drink yet, and neither do you."

"But we're on vacation, party pooper!" I tell him.

"But this isn't a party," he replies.

"All right then…dive-bar pooper," I amend, and the boyfriends are convulsed with laughter.

Jack shakes his head. I can't tell what he's thinking, but I'm sure he doesn't appreciate being called a pooper of any sort.

C'est la vie.

I'm not going to let him rain on my…uh, rainy day.

I turn back to Gregory and Daniel and pick up where we left off. "So anyway, it's a gay wedding," I say, because that makes all the difference to them, I'm sure.

"When is it?"

"It's on Valentine's Day."

Gregory exclaims, "Oh-my-God-that-is-so-ro*man*tic!"

"You guys really should come."

Why, I don't know. It just seems like a great idea.

But not to Jack.

"Tracey," he says in a warning voice, and kicks me again.

"Jack!" I say, and kick him back.

He says, "They don't even know Raphael."

"Come on, Jack, do you honestly think Raphael would care?"

"Is Raphael the blushing-bride-to-be?" Daniel asks.

"Yup." I proceed to tell them all about Raphael and Donatello and their upcoming nuptials as Jack glowers at me over the rim of his glass.

When he excuses himself to go to the bathroom, Gregory asks, "What's up *his* butt?"

"Hello, I could make *such* a comment right now," Daniel announces, throwing up his hands, "but I won't even go there!"

Ew.

"Danielle!" That, of course, is Gregory's pet name for him. "Please *don't* go there!"

"Yes, please don't," I say. "Jack's really a great guy. I think it's just jet lag."

"I don't know about that." Daniel leans in and says in a singsong lisp, "I think somebody's got a bad case of the homophobic blues."

"Jack? Oh, he's not homophobic."

"Honey, my hand brushed his arm by accident and he jumped out of his chair," Gregory tells me.

"Maybe he thought it was an iguana," I say, and crack myself up all over again, though somewhere in the back of my head, I'm thinking it might not be all *that* funny. Maybe I'm a little tipsier than I thought.

Then again, it feels damn good to be slaphappy for a change, so I giggle away.

Until Daniel says, "Maybe we're cramping your boyfriend's style and he just wants to be alone with *you*."

Hmm. I didn't think of that. I guess double-dating with a strange—all right, in the most literal sense—couple isn't the most romantic way to spend an evening. Still…

"If Jack wants to be alone with me so badly," I ponder aloud, "then why won't he engage me?"

"Engage you in what?" Gregory and Daniel ask in unison, then laugh and say, "Jinx!"

"You know…in an engagement." I tell them about Wilma and the diamond, and they're suitably sympathetic.

When Jack comes back, they glare at him over the fresh drinks I defiantly ordered while he was gone.

Our guitar player is back, too, a little wild-eyed as he does a cover of "Brown Eyed Girl," dedicated from Gregory to Daniel. They get up to dance, leaving me alone with Jack.

"I wish you could just loosen up and have fun," I tell him.

"I am loose."

I snort into my yummy, strong drink. "You're about as loose as…as…"

"As the banana hammock Gregory's wearing?" he supplies.

"That's not a banana hammock," I protest, laughing. I gesture at the elevator-size dance floor, where our pals are cavorting to the music. "See? Those are shorts."

"Well, if he does that high kick again, his dirty banana is going to fall out the leg hole."

Laughing together seems to heal all wounds.

"Come on," Jack says, holding my hand and pulling me up off the bar stool, "it's getting late. Let's go back to the hotel and change so we can go out for a nice dinner."

"Okay, but I just want to say goodbye to Gregory and Daniel."

The only way to do that is to shimmy over to the dance floor, where I find myself instantly roped into their outrageous dance moves as Jack watches from the sidelines.

"You go, brown-eyed girl!" Gregory twirls me around and around, then passes me to Daniel before I can throw up.

"Woo-hoo!" Daniel shouts. "Come on, honey, now do-si-do!"

Do-si-do? I think dizzily, trying to recall my fourth-grade square-dance moves.

Too late.

Daniel is already mincing around me, arms folded across his chest, head bobbing maniacally.

I glance over at Jack, whose arms are also folded, but who is not do-si-do-ing to "Brown Eyed Girl."

He actually looks like he might start tapping his foot any second now—in impatience, rather than in time to the music—so I finally holler, "Boyfriends, I have to leave now! See you on the beach!"

"When?" Gregory wants to know, as they do-si-do around each other, and Daniel asks, "Where?"

"Tomorrow at noon, behind the Sea Plantation. It's down the road!"

"Sounds good," Gregory says, "and afterward, we'll all go to dinner together somewhere."

"Great!"

Jack's going to kill me!

I look over at him. He gestures for me to hurry up, for God's sake.

"Toodle-ooh, Tracey! Bye, Jack!" Daniel calls energetically.

"It's been real," Jack responds dryly, with a Miss America wave.

It's still drizzling out as we walk the short distance back to the hotel, and so humid that everything about me is damp/limp in moments: linen shorts, T-shirt, hair and all.

Now that we're away from the noise and music, I'm feeling conspicuously tipsy. You know, I probably should have eaten the box lunch they handed out on the plane earlier. Despite the turbulence, Jack ate his meal, and then mine. No wonder those drinks didn't affect him as much as they did me.

Anyway, I would have eaten on the plane if I hadn't just watched the guy three rows up gobble down his meal, then promptly upchuck it into his airsickness bag.

"That was fun, wasn't it?" I say to Jack far more loudly than I intended. I hope I'm not slurring.

"Pretty much. Those guys were just a little too over the top for me."

"Over the top? Gregory and Daniel?"

"Tracey—" He looks at me and sees that I'm grinning.

"They were fun, though," I say.

"I would have rather been alone with you."

"Really?" That's sweet. No wonder he was so grouchy. "Well, we can be alone all night."

"I'll take a shower first," he says, unlocking the door to our room, where we're greeted by a refreshing blast of

A.C., "and then I'll go scout out some good restaurants and make a reservation."

"Sounds like a plan."

The only problem with the plan is that there's too much lag time built in. I sit down on the bed to wait while Jack's in the shower, then lie down because I'm a little sleepy, and the next thing I know, I'm out.

Jack wakes me up as he's getting dressed, and I promise him I'll get right on it, but the second he leaves to go scout out restaurants, I'm asleep again.

Maybe it's more like passed out, because when he returns to wake me up again and tell me all about this great seafood place he found by the water, and how we can have a good table if I can be ready in fifteen minutes, I can't seem to rouse myself.

"Do you just want to stay in tonight?" Jack asks, clearly disappointed.

I'm too out of it to do more than nod before drifting back into unconsciousness.

I wake up at three in the morning to find the air-conditioning blasting and the room an icebox. Jack is snoring blissfully beside me in the double bed, hogging the thin bedspread same as he hogs our comforter back home.

For a few minutes, I do my best to repeatedly tug it away from him and get back to sleep.

Then I fool around with the air-conditioning control, but it turns out it's already on the lowest setting. A moment's exploration reveals that the windows are hermetically sealed, so turning the A.C. off and opening them isn't an option. Turning the A.C. off and going back to sleep is also not an option, as it will be a thousand degrees in here in no time.

Finally, shivering, I decide to wrap myself in the spread from the other bed. When I do, it smells like it's been soaked in B.O.

Ick.

Now what?

Too bad I didn't listen to Jack and bring a sweatshirt.

I bet he did, though.

I go to the closet, flip on the light in there and close the door almost all the way so that I can rummage through his bag without waking him.

I have to dig down beneath a stack of T-shirts and shorts before I find a hooded Old Navy sweatshirt. As I open it up to pull it on, something hard and heavy drops out onto my bare foot.

It's all I can do not to cry out in pain.

Looking down, I see what it was.

It's all I can do not to cry out in glee.

It's a ring box, folks.

That's right.

A ring box, not black velvet, as I have oft pictured in my dreams, but a ring box nonetheless. It's that white faux-leather kind.

At the rate things have been going, I'm half expecting to find it empty.

But when I open the box, I find a beautiful diamond ring twinkling up at me.

"Oh my God," I gasp softly, overcome with emotion.

It's a marquis cut, set in white-gold with several baguettes on either side. It's the kind of ring I would have picked out for myself, if he'd given me the opportunity…but he didn't have to, because he knew.

There's no longer a doubt in my mind that we were meant to be together.

I'm about to tug the ring from its satiny slot so that I can try it on when I realize that would be cheating.

I want Jack to be the first—and only—one to put this on my finger.

Now that I know it's here, waiting for me, I can put it back into his bag and wait for him to give it to me.

But was it folded into his sweatshirt, or what?

Maybe it was just sitting on top of it, between the sweat-shirt and the T-shirt above…?

I rearrange the sweatshirt and ring box in his duffel bag a few times, trying to figure out how he would have had it packed.

Wait a minute, why am I stressing? I mean, it's not as though he had the bag booby-trapped, hoping to catch me snooping.

Then again, maybe he did.

I certainly would, if I were him and I knew me as well as he should by now.

Finally, I give up and simply tuck the ring box into the folds of the sweatshirt. With any luck, he just tossed it all in and will have no clue that I went snooping. If he figures it out, I'll just tell him I was cold and borrowed a sweat-shirt.

Except he'll ask why I don't have the sweatshirt on.

And if I put it on now, he'll know I was in his bag.

It's a catch-22 that I can't possibly win, so there's noth-ing to do but zip the bag closed, turn off the closet light and go back to bed.

Naturally, I don't sleep.

I find myself lying restlessly awake, wondering when Jack is planning to give me the ring.

Is that why he went out scouting restaurants? Was he looking for the perfect place to propose?

I certainly shot that romantic plan full of holes with my oblivious alcohol-induced haze.

Mental note: do not drink another drink for duration of trip.

No, my teetotaling will make him suspicious.

Mental note: drink one, and only one, dirty banana per day for duration of trip.

That resolved, I move on to the next problem: ditching Gregory and Daniel.

Why on earth did I have to make beach and dinner plans with them?

Were they really that fabulous?

There's a possibility that their fabulousness was greatly exaggerated by my intoxication. After all that liquor, I would have been asking Mike's wife, Dianne, to be my matron of honor.

If she were here.

And if I were already engaged.

Oh, well, maybe it'll rain.

If it doesn't rain, maybe Gregory and Daniel won't show up.

It doesn't rain, and Gregory and Daniel not only show up, but they're both wearing bona fide banana hammocks this time, along with wide straw beach hats, pink sunglasses—more like goggles, actually—and thick zinc sunblock on their noses. They're also shirtless, and not as buff as one might think. I can see that their guts are pale squishy soft, both of them, even from a distance.

"You've got to be kidding me," Jack says when he spots them sashaying down the beach toward us. "Duck, Tracey. Maybe they won't see us."

I pretend to duck, since I don't have the heart to admit we're a prearranged foursome for the day.

Then the boyfriends are upon us, with kisses all around before they set up camp beneath an enormous pink-and-orange polka-dot umbrella.

"Danielle, can you do me?" Gregory asks, laying out his towel and flopping down on his stomach.

I'm paralyzed with horror until I see Daniel grab a tube of lotion and begin massaging it all over Gregory's white, acne-riddled back.

Relieved, I look over at Jack, and even with his eyes masked behind his black Daggers, see that he's still pretty horrified. Especially when Gregory makes these icky purring noises in response to Daniel's lotion-smoothing skills.

"I just hate tan lines," Gregory comments.

I have to wonder A) how he expects to get a tan using that SPF 60 lotion and B) where he can possibly expect to have tan lines given that Speedo thong he's wearing.

"So do I. You know, it's really too bad nude sunbathing is outlawed on Anguilla," Daniel says, mostly to me and Jack.

I murmur something like, "It is."

Jack mumbles something like, "Too bad."

Then we proceed to spend the rest of our Caribbean afternoon listening to Gregory and Daniel's incessant chatter about their friends back in Jersey, their three dogs, their apartment, which they're remodeling, and their jobs. One of them is a secretary at a travel agency, the other is a veterinarian's assistant. Both perfectly respectable careers, but you'd think they were NASA scientists, the way they go on and on about their work-related adventures.

Several times throughout the ordeal, I'm tempted to flag down the guy roaming the beach selling rum drinks, even with the massive hangover headache I've had all day. But I promised myself that I'd stay lucid, so as not to ruin my engagement moment when it finally comes.

Which it might not, thanks to me and my big mouth.

When the sun is sinking lower and Jack at last asks, "Ready to head back?" I open my mouth to say yes.

But Daniel opens his mouth faster, informing us, "We made a dinner reservation at a great little place down the beach, you guys."

Jack smiles politely, already shaking the sand out of our towels. "That'll be fun. Enjoy it."

"Honey, you're coming with us," Gregory protests. "Tracey! Didn't you tell him about dinner tonight?"

Jack is all, "Huh? What?"

And I'm all, "Dinner? What dinner?"

As in, I must have been smashed out of my mind last night and have no recollection whatsoever of dinner plans that were ostensibly made by me.

"Oh, well, the reservation is for four, at eight," Gregory says breezily. "It wasn't easy to get it, but I gave the cute concierge a big fat tip."

"He probably would have rather had a big fat—"

"Danielle!" Gregory pretends to be shocked. "You naughty, naughty girl!"

The two of them dissolve in bawdy laughter.

Jack looks at me.

Again, I can't see his eyes beyond the lenses of his black Daggers, but…

Well, maybe that's a good thing.

Jack is silent as we walk back to the room.

Ominously so.

I don't dare say anything.

I keep thinking of the ring in the box in his duffel bag in the closet. When was he planning on giving it to me?

Last night, probably.

But when that fell through, he must have decided tonight would be the night.

"Maybe we can pretend we're sick and blow off dinner," I say hopefully as we step into the dim, air-conditioned interior.

"And just not show up? Wouldn't that be rude?"

"No, we can call and tell them that we can't make it."

"Call them where?"

"You know, at their…hotel." It occurs to me that I can't remember which one it is. "Where did they say they were staying again?" I ask Jack.

He shrugs. "I have no idea."

"But they told us last night, and I know they mentioned it again today." I deposit my sandy beach bag on the rug and kick off my flip-flops. "What was it? The Beach-something, I think. Wasn't it?"

"Tracey, I have no idea. And anyway, it would be rude to blow them off after you're the one who set up this whole dinner, don't you think?"

"I didn't set up this dinner, Jack. They made the reservations."

"Apparently, it was *your* plan."

"I really don't think so. I wouldn't have done that."

"Why not? Come on, Tracey. You invited them to Raphael's wedding! Why wouldn't you invite them to dinner?"

"I don't remember doing it," I say, and it's a flat-out lie, but I can't help it. I screwed up big time, and I'm desperate to fix it.

"Maybe," Jack says succinctly, "you were so wasted you forgot."

"I was not wasted!" I protest. "I was just having fun."

Lies, lies, lies. They're all lies. Yet I can't seem to keep them from spewing out.

"Tracey, you passed out!" He tosses the room key on the dresser with a loud clink.

"I went to bed. There's a big difference between that and passing out."

"You're right, there *is* a big difference, and you passed out. Trust me. I'm the one who had to keep trying to wake you up."

"Well, even if I did drink too much, isn't that what you're supposed to do on vacation? Drink dirty bananas and dance and have a good time?"

"Sure it is." He shrugs. "It's fine. Whatever."

But it isn't fine. He's pissed off because I ruined his plans last night, and I don't blame him. Only I can't tell him that, because I'm not supposed to know.

Now I guess we're stuck having dinner with Gregory and Daniel.

"Jack, there's always tomorrow night," I tell him.

"I guess."

"Come on, don't be mad. Let's make the best of tonight, and then tomorrow night, we'll go have a romantic dinner, just the two of us. I'll go shopping and buy something decent to wear so that we can go somewhere nice. We can watch the sunset and have champagne…"

Not that I'm trying to make plans for him, or anything.

I mean, I'm sure he's thought this through. I'm sure he knows exactly how he's going to propose, now that it's actually imminent.

Oh my God! It's actually imminent! I'm going to be getting engaged!

I wonder how much it would cost to call and reserve the banquet facilities at Shorewood from here. Probably a lot. But I really can't waste any time nailing down that October date.

And I'll need to start shopping for dresses right away.

Only, I really should lose at least ten pounds first.

Well, now I'll finally have the incentive.

At dinner, I'm tempted to order the fried-oyster appetizer, but instead go with the raw bar oysters on the half shell. The pasta in cream sauce entrée sounds delicious, but instead I stick with grilled fish. And instead of the fattening—and potent—piña coladas Jack and the boyfriends are drinking, I ask for a white-wine spritzer.

They serve on island time around here, so the meal is leisurely, to say the least. The conversation flows freely, and Jack finally seems to have relaxed around Gregory and Daniel.

By the time we're finished with dessert—a reportedly luscious whipped cream, pineapple-and-coconut cake for the others, plain old fruit for me—it's nearly midnight.

"Should we go out for a nightcap?" Daniel suggests as we stroll into the balmy evening air.

Jack looks at me. I can tell he doesn't want to go.

"Actually, I'm exhausted," I say truthfully.

Gregory makes a pouty face. "Then what's the plan for tomorrow?"

You know, I have to wonder how we've apparently become a tighter foursome than Abba. Was it something I said?

Mental note: in future, do not profess love to total strangers within half hour of making their acquaintance.

"I think we're going to play it by ear," Jack says casually.

"Well, we should exchange cell-phone numbers so we can all meet for dinner again." Gregory pulls out a business card and scribbles on the back, then hands it to Jack. "These are ours. What are yours?"

"Oh, Tracey doesn't have a cell phone, and mine doesn't get service down here," Jack says easily, pocketing the card. "We'll just call you if we're free, okay?"

After hugs all around, we finally go our separate ways.

"That wasn't so bad, was it?" I ask Jack as we walk back down the deserted midnight beach toward our room.

"No, it wasn't," he admits. "But tomorrow night, it'll be just us."

"Right," I say, tucking my hand into his.

He smiles and stops me so that he can kiss me beneath the crescent moon, with the sound of the gentle waves lapping at the sugary shore.

Ah. Paradise at last.

Twenty-four hours from right now, I think contentedly, I'll have that beautiful ring on my finger and Jack's eloquent proposal ringing in my ears.

Chapter 17

"*Then* what happened?" Kate asks incredulously, wide-eyed over the forkful of pasta she's about to pop into her mouth.

We've been in the restaurant more than twenty minutes, and it's taken me this long to work the conversation around from Kate's daily drama report to my legitimate vacation drama, which is now a week old, but just as dramatic in retrospect.

"Then Jack wound up having to contact the U.S. consul to recommend an emergency-care clinic," I reminisce as I push my own lunch around on my plate.

"What did they do for you?"

"They sent us to this hot, crowded place where we had to wait for hours. The doctor said I was severely dehydrated and they hooked me up to an IV."

"Oh my God."

"I know. Then I had to stay overnight and we missed our flight home."

"Wow."

"I know." I shake my head, feeling sorry for myself. "It was awful."

"Well, you can't dwell on it. There are worse things that can happen, so just look at the bright side," says Kate, who has been hospitalized for splinters. And less.

"What bright side? Kate, I got deathly ill and ruined what was supposed to be the most important night of my life."

"Yeah, but you got to spend an extra day in Anguilla."

"Kate, I was so sick I just wanted to be home. And when we finally did get to leave, everything was booked and we had to take three connecting flights—one of them was through Denver."

"What's wrong with Denver?"

"It's a little out of the way, don't you think?" I ask, before she can tell me how darling the Rockies are.

"I guess." She reaches for the Parmesan cheese dispenser and dumps more on her pasta. "What about those guys you met?"

"Gregory and Daniel? What about them?"

"Are they coming to Raphael's wedding?"

"No, they're history. Jack accidentally tossed their phone numbers before we left Anguilla."

"Accidentally?" She snickers. "Billy would never have even taken the card in the first place. So what did the doctor say was wrong with you in the end?"

"Food poisoning, what else? It must have been the raw oysters I ate at dinner the night before."

She stops chewing abruptly.

"What's wrong, Kate?"

She squirms a little. "Oh, gracious."

"What?"

"Just the thought of raw oysters..."

"Are you okay?"

"Excuse me, Tracey..."

I watch Kate bolt from the table and race through the restaurant toward the bathroom.

While she's gone, I toy with my food and relive the rest of last week's ill-fated Caribbean vacation.

Leave it to me to get *thisclose* to Jack's proposal at last, and then screw it up royally with a spectacular forty-eight-hour diarrhea-fest.

If I hadn't eaten those tainted oysters—or perhaps it was that tainted fish—I would be engaged to Jack right now.

But no. Instead of spending the flight—rather, *flights*—back to New York making wedding plans, I spent my time rushing back and forth to the tiny bathrooms as the remains of the food poisoning worked its way through my system.

Even now, a week later, I'm still feeling a little weak and queasy.

The good news is that I've lost eight pounds without trying. Which means I'll be able to go wedding gown shopping any day now…

Well, as soon as Jack gives me that ring.

Which should be any day now.

I keep waiting for him to suggest a fancy date night. Or even just a moonlit walk along the East River. Something, anything other than coming home hours late from the office every night, collapsing in front of the television and falling asleep minutes later.

I know this is his busy Planning season at work, but still…

It only takes a few minutes to get engaged.

Okay, hours, if you do it right.

I can't help noticing he spent more time than that on the football playoff games last weekend.

Kate returns to the table, looking green. "Good gracious, that was ugly," she informs me, pushing her plate away as she sits down. Her Southern twang is always more pronounced when she's being dramatic.

"Maybe you have food poisoning," I say sympathetically. "Or maybe you caught one of those twenty-four-hour—"

"No," she cuts in, "I really think I'm pregnant."

"Kate, you've thought you were pregnant every day for months now, and you never are."

"But this time I have a real feeling about it, Tracey. I think I just had morning sickness."

"Kate, it's afternoon."

"I slept until eleven-thirty," she drawls. "It's morning for me. And I've been craving carbs like crazy."

"You always crave carbs, Kate," I tell her impatiently, anxious to get back to my heartbreaking tale of the Engagement That Wasn't.

"Not like this. I had three bowls of Lucky Charms for breakfast."

I check my watch. It's just past one. "You got up at eleven-thirty and managed to sneak in breakfast between then and now?"

"See what I mean? I bet you anything I'm eating for two."

"That doesn't necessarily mean you're pregnant," I say, having eaten for two throughout most of the fall and well into the winter.

Now here I am, barely eating for one. I'm not complaining about having lost my appetite. But I honestly can't wait to start feeling like my old energetic self again.

We spend the rest of our lunch date talking about whether Jack will propose this coming weekend or next, and why Kate is positive she's pregnant this time, and the decidedly *not* darling gowns we're wearing as Raphael's bridal attendants in less than three weeks.

I take my time walking the ten blocks back to the office. The fresh air feels good, and my stomach is a little queasy again, thanks to Kate's graphic parting description of her bathroom adventure.

It's a nice day for January—not bright sun and blue skies, but at least it's not raining, sleeting, snowing.

I can't believe I only got one beach day out of that long-awaited Caribbean vacation. One beach day and zero proposals. What a bust.

Upstairs, I find Latisha waiting for me.

"Tracey," she says urgently, all hush-hush, "I just heard they're about to make a job offer to somebody for Mike's old job."

"Really? It's about time." I sit down at my desk and open my top drawer in search of the Pepto-Bismol tablets I keep there.

"Trust me, you don't want this to happen. I met this chick when she came in to interview with Carol, and she was a bitch on wheels."

"How can you tell that from meeting her once, in passing?"

"I have a feeling about these sorts of things," Latisha says resolutely. "Listen, you need to go talk to Carol about giving you a shot at that job before it's too late."

"Latisha, what I really need to do is go lie down."

"Why? What happened?"

"Nothing. I'm just still wiped out from being sick." In my desk, I find a fresh shrink-wrapped packet of Post-it Notes I didn't even know I had, and a whole box of rolling-ball pens. I really should go through my drawers more often.

"You mean the food poisoning? That was a week ago."

"I was really sick," I protest.

"Well, pull yourself together, girl, and get your butt in there. *I'm* sick of your wishy-washy attitude."

I look up from the Pepto-Bismol hunt, surprised by her harsh tone. "What do you mean?"

"I mean, take a big step back and look at yourself. You need to stop dicking around waiting for stuff to happen and start taking control of your life."

"I'm in control of my life."

But even as I say it, I realize that I'm so *not*.

Latisha's right. I've been dicking around for months. Years, even.

And not just about work.

After I met Jack, the man of my dreams, I guess I might have slacked off a little, thinking I was all set. That he was everything I needed.

All right, maybe I slacked off a lot.

Maybe, when you get right down to it, I've spent almost two years just going along from day to day, waiting for things to happen *to* me, rather than making them happen for myself.

Where is the Tracey who turned her life around? The Tracey who spent an entire summer losing weight— and, ultimately, a dead-weight boyfriend and a tyrannical boss?

Here I am, stuck in a pathetic rut once again, without even realizing it was happening to me.

And it isn't just about wanting to marry Jack, and waiting for him to propose.

It's about wanting to be something more than an account coordinator for the rest of my life. Wanting to live in a real apartment with real furniture. To take real vacations to real resorts.

You aren't a total failure, I remind myself. *You quit smoking. You even lost most of the weight you gained after you quit smoking.*

Yes, the smoking was a triumph, but the weight loss was a fluke. I don't exercise anymore, ever, and for the most part, I eat crap.

Not only that, but I've lived these last five months thinking that if Jack would just propose to me, my whole life would fall into place just like that.

You know what?

I don't think it will.

I don't think Jack's proposing will solve everything that's wrong with my life.

In fact, it won't solve *anything* other than my being able to get the ball rolling on wedding plans.

A ring on my finger won't transform me into a junior copywriter or a junior account executive. It won't melt cellulite off my thighs, or make my family laid-back, or expand our apartment by a few hundred square feet.

Most importantly, it won't magically erase the everyday problems Jack and I have as a couple. I'm starting to think that he'll never be the kind of guy who would rather go out ballroom dancing than watch a ball game.

Granted, I'm not into ballroom dancing either, but…you get the picture.

We're still going to have issues. Nothing is going to be perfect.

Ever.

Good, yes. Great, even. But not perfect.

Not even good, unless I take Latisha's advice and get off my butt and take charge.

Starting right here, right now, with the job.

"You're right," I tell Latisha, feeling as though I'm coming out of a daze.

"Of course I'm right," she says.

Wondering why I didn't see any of this before, I tell her, "So I guess it's time to do something, then."

"Now you're talking."

But what?

I only have to think about that for a moment. Then I ask Latisha, "Is Carol around?"

She grins. "Last I saw her, she was headed into her office with a bag from the deli."

I'm already on my way down the hall, thinking I should

probably at least figure out how to approach Carol before I go barging in there, but afraid I'll lose my momentum if I do.

Her door is ajar, and she's at her desk eating a sandwich. "Carol? Hi."

She looks up and smiles. She's a round-faced brunette with a cutesy pageboy haircut that turns under evenly all around her head, almost as though she used a curling wand to get it that way. Which she very well might have.

"Tracey. What can I do you for?" She's the type of person who also says hokey things like *What can I do you for?* and *Anyhoo* and *Oh, fudge.*

I think she grew up in the Midwest.

If she didn't, she should go there. She'd fit right in.

Not that there's anything wrong with the Midwest. It's just that folksy people like Carol probably do much better far from cutthroat corporate Manhattan industry, and leave that to icy blondes like Donald Trump's henchwoman Carolyn from *The Apprentice.*

"I was wondering if I could talk to you for a second," I say. "Well, maybe longer than a second."

"Is everything okay?"

"Everything is fine, but…well, everything is actually not fine." I swallow hard over a lump that seems to have risen in my throat.

Do not cry, Tracey.

Whatever you do, do not cry.

Cry at the office, and you're really pathetic.

"What's wrong?" Carol asks, looking concerned.

I clear my throat and say thickly, "I wanted to talk to you about the vacant account exec position."

"Yes? Sit down."

"I was wondering if, uh, you could consider me. For the job." I pause, take a deep breath, recover my professionalism and say, "I'd really like to be considered for that position. I know I don't officially have experience as an assistant A.E. yet, but I know I'm capable of doing the job."

Carol nods, steepling her fingers beneath her chin and watching me.

I can't tell what she's thinking. She doesn't say, *Get out of here.* Nor does she say, *Keep going.*

I do anyway. I tell her about all the work I've done in Mike's absence. I'm tempted to also tell her about all the work I did when Mike was here, on Mike's behalf, but that seems like an unnecessary dig at my old boss.

Anyway, Carol knows he didn't do anything around here. She fired him, remember?

I sell myself. Hard.

But when I get to the part about how she should consider downgrading the position to assistant A.E., she cuts me off.

I know she's going to say thanks, but no thanks.

In fact, I'm already pushing my chair back in anticipation of slinking off with my head hanging in defeat.

Then Carol says, "You're a valued employee around here, Tracey. I'd have to speak to Ron about it—" he's the head of the department "—but I'm not opposed to it. Not at all. In fact, I think it's a great idea."

"You're not opposed to...?" I prod, just to be sure I'm hearing things right.

"I'm not opposed to letting you have a shot at the account exec position."

"Really?" Oh, God, that sounded like a squeal.

I paste a calmly corporate *I'm delighted* expression on my face and lower my voice an octave as I say, "That would be great."

She nods. "You've done a bang-up job these last few months, and I don't see why you can't step in and take over where Mike left off."

So.

Not only is Carol open to the idea of promoting me...but she isn't even talking about a downgraded position.

She's going to recommend me for account executive!

No, it's not copywriter.

Someday, I would still love to be a copywriter.

But...account execs make more. A *lot* more.

Carol tells me she'll get back to me tomorrow, which is my cue to let her finish her sandwich. After thanking her—not too profusely, I hope—I go look for Latisha and the others, so that they can get their *I Told You So's* in early.

It'll have to wait. Nobody's around. They must have gone downstairs for a smoke.

I dial Jack's extension, hoping he picks up for a change. He's been in Planning and he rarely answers his phone when he is.

"Jack Candell."

This, I gloat, is a day in which everything is really going right for a change.

"Jack? Guess what?"

"What?"

"No, guess."

"Give me a hint." He says it hurriedly, and I realize he's in the middle of something, so I let him off the hook and just tell him my news.

"Trace, that's great! I'm so proud of you!"

"Well, it hasn't happened yet...but it looks like it really might. Probably tomorrow. So we'll have something to celebrate this weekend."

Maybe two things, I think hopefully, before reminding myself that this—a promotion—is reason enough for celebration.

"This weekend?" Jack echoes. "Trace, bad news on that."

"What?"

"I'm in Planning. It looks like I'm going to have to work all weekend."

My heart sinks. "All weekend?"

"Probably. You know how it is when it gets like this…"

He's right. I do.

He'll be lucky if he gets home to shower and shave between now and next week.

"Listen," he says, still sounding rushed, "when this is over I'll take you out to celebrate the new job. Okay?"

"Okay."

"Anywhere you want to go."

"Okay," I say again, trying not to be disappointed. "I'll let you hang up. I know you're busy."

He doesn't argue.

I'm sitting staring into space when the phone rings a few minutes later.

"Tracey Candell," I say, picking it up, thinking Jack might have a few minutes to chat after all.

Silence.

"Hello?"

"Did you get married?"

I recognize Will's voice.

"What?" I ask him.

"You said Tracey Candell."

"I did?" I gasp and clasp a hand over my mouth. He's right. I did.

So much for not having marriage on the brain. Thank God it's him and not Jack.

"Tracey, I can't believe you got married and didn't invite me, but congratulations," he says hollowly.

For a split second, I debate letting him think I really am Tracey Candell. After all, Jack has a ring. Sooner or later, I will be.

Then I remember that I am now a grown-up, take-charge person, and grown-up, take-charge people don't lie. Not even to pain-in-the-ass old boyfriends.

"It was a slip of the tongue," I tell him. "I just hung up with Jack, so his name was…you know, on my tongue."

"Oh." He doesn't sound convinced. "Well, anyway, I wanted to tell you about my trip to Belize."

"You went to Belize? When?"

"Over Martin Luther King weekend. It was amazing. I snorkeled in—"

"Really?" I cut in. "Jack and I went to Anguilla that weekend, and it was amazing, too."

There's a pause. Clearly Will is not accustomed to two-sided conversations.

"Did you snorkel?" he asks at last.

I so want to lie, but I don't dare. If I do, the next thing you know I'll be telling Will that we eloped.

"We were so busy with everything else we didn't have time to snorkel."

"Well, I snorkeled in Belize, and it was incredible. I saw the most beautiful—"

"Did you go dancing?" I interrupt.

Again, he seems caught off guard. "Dancing? No, but I—"

"We went dancing in Anguilla," I say, and tell him all about it. Well, not *all* about it. In my account, Gregory and Daniel are much more buff, and straight, and I leave out the part about the do-si-do, of course. My description is like that scene in *Pulp Fiction,* with me in the Uma Thurman role and the Boyfriends as dueling John Travoltas.

Will is quiet, as though he isn't quite sure what to do with this information.

Big trouble in little Willville, folks.

Yet he tries again, stubborn, narcissistic little bugger that he is. "In Belize, the food was unbelievable."

"In Anguilla, it was, too. I had oysters that were to die for."

All right, I know…but, change the *for* to *from* and it isn't technically a lie.

I must say, this is the best conversation I've ever had with Will. Probably because I've decided to take an active role for a change.

It's so much fun that when we hang up—too soon for me, because I didn't get to share the news of my impending promotion, but probably not soon enough for Will—I debate calling my mother, just to check in.

I waited to tell her about my food poisoning until we were safely home from Anguilla, but she's now embroiled in retro-panic. She's been leaving messages a few times a day, needing repeated reassurance that I'm not at death's door.

Still, I decide against calling her now.

My new stronger self is still in the fledgling stages. The last thing I need is to be undermined by Buzz Kill Connie's "See what happens when you recklessly travel to a foreign land?" diatribe.

Anyway, I can hear the girls coming back from their smoke. I meet them in the hallway outside my office, motion them inside and shut the door.

"I've got news," I say excitedly.

"You're pregnant?" That came from Yvonne, obviously channeling Buzz Kill Connie.

"Why do people always think that's what it is when somebody has news?" I ask.

"Because babies are really exciting," Brenda says, and the three of us exchange dubious glances.

No offense to Brenda, but her bundle of joy seems to spend most of his time lying around sleeping, or stinking up the place to high heaven. Not that there's anything wrong with that...

"No, I'm not pregnant," I say firmly. "But now my real news is going to seem less exciting."

"You're engaged!" That's our little doyenne of domesticity again, grabbing my left hand and searching it for a ring.

"No!" I pull my hand out of Brenda's grasp. "Come on, guys."

"Oh! I know what it is." Latisha breaks out into a big grin. "Come over here, baby girl." She opens her arms wide and gives me a bear hug. "You're getting that promotion to assistant A.E., aren't you."

"No," I say again…this time, taking great satisfaction in it.

Latisha's smile fades. "Then what?"

I can't hold it in any longer. "I'm not getting promoted to assistant A.E.—just plain old A.E.! I mean, it's not official, yet, but Carol pretty much guaranteed it!"

Their reaction is all I could have hoped for.

As the four of us dance around, squeal and hug, I remind myself that I am blessed. My girls have been with me from day one at Blair Barnett; they'll be my bridesmaids if—no, *when*—I walk down the aisle with Jack, and they'll be my friends forever.

"Let's go out this weekend and celebrate!" Brenda says. "I'll get Paulie to stay with the baby. He owes me one."

"And I'll make a reservation at Tequila Murray's," Latisha offers. "How's nine on Saturday?"

"Perfect," Yvonne declares. "I'll wear something snazzy."

I grin, teary-eyed. "You guys are the best."

And right here, right now, I don't need anything more than what I have.

Part VI

Valentine's Day

Chapter 18

We've come full circle, me and Jack.

Here we are at another wedding that isn't our own, and once again, I've got my hair in an elaborate updo and I'm wearing a red dress. Just like at Mike and Dianne's wedding back in September.

But this time, it isn't my choice. The dress, I mean. Which is a gown, really: low-cut crushed red velvet and black brocade. It looks like something a character in an Anne Rice novel—or a bordello whore—might wear. It looks pretty decent on me now that I'm back down to my usual weight, thanks to food poisoning, three weeks on Weight Watchers and walking the forty blocks home from the office every night.

Still, it's not a gown I would have chosen to wear, even to a masquerade ball, mostly because it borders on obscene. My bullet boobs have come close several times to popping out of the plunging bodice.

Not that anybody other than Jack and a couple of Raphael's lesbian friends seems to have noticed. The rest of the wedding guests are either gay men or married to Kate.

And Billy would never be caught dead looking at another woman's décolletage. Kate, clad in the same gown only with zero cleavage, would kill him.

Dress complications aside, it's Raphael's wedding, and I'm happy.

I still love weddings.

Presumably, Jack still does *not* love weddings.

Otherwise, we'd probably be planning one of our own by now.

Alas, the only planning he's been doing lately is the media kind.

But I've been busy at work, too. I got the promotion, with a big raise and Mike's window office. Funny how so little has changed, in terms of the actual work—but everything has changed, in terms of my self-esteem.

Just a few days ago, I was presented with a box of business cards.

Tracey Spadolini, Account Executive, Blair Barnett Advertising.

I immediately sent one to Will, tucked into a valentine.

No, I normally wouldn't send Will a valentine. I just needed a convincing vehicle in which to deliver the physical evidence of my impressive new station in life to somebody who never thought I was good enough.

I know what you're thinking, but it wasn't a particularly mushy or personal valentine—just a funny Shoebox one that made me laugh and probably won't make Will laugh because we never did have the same sense of humor.

Jack and I do have the same sense of humor, but I didn't get him a funny card. I bought the mushiest, most personal one I could find; one that read on the front *To the One I Love* and made me cry, embarrassingly, while I was reading it in the Hallmark store.

I also got him a nice boring sweater on winter clearance

at Bloomingdale's, partly because my raise hasn't kicked in and partly because I'm sticking with safe gifts from now on.

I haven't given him the card and sweater yet. There was no opportunity to do it in our mad scramble to get to the wedding on time.

Okay, that's not entirely true.

I was ready for the wedding with time to spare, but I wasn't going to hand over a valentine without some reciprocation. I figure when Jack's ready to give me mine, I'll give him his.

No, I don't expect it to be the ring.

Getting engaged on Valentine's Day is such a cliché. If he didn't do it on Christmas Eve, he isn't going to do it now.

At least, I don't *think* he is.

But maybe I'm wrong.

Who knows? Who cares?

Well, I care, but like I said, I've had other things on my mind. I've been so busy at the office, and helping to throw together Raphael's shower, bachelorette party and rehearsal dinner that I haven't had time to dwell on this the way I had been.

If it happens, it happens.

If it doesn't…

Oh, who am I trying to kid? I want it to happen.

But today isn't going to be about that. It's about Raphael and Donatello.

The loft space they rented for their grand affair is filled with white twinkle-lights, red roses and champagne-sipping guests who are being herded to the rows of chairs set up in front of an ivy-covered *chuppah*.

No, Raphael and Donatello haven't converted to Judaism. They saw the *chuppah* in the caterer's catalog and thought it was "fun." They said the same thing about the baton twirler they hired to entertain when the band takes a break, and about having Donatello's toy poodle Pipsqueak as the best man.

Basically, this has been an Anything Goes wedding from its inception.

As the pianist begins to play the wedding march, and the smiling female minister of God only knows what church takes her place beside the *chuppah,* I adjust the bow tie on Raphael's white tux.

"Tracey, how do I look?"

"Beautiful," I say sincerely.

"Where's Kate?" he asks, looking around in concern. "I could swear she was here just a minute ago, Tracey."

"She was, but she went to throw up. She'll be right back."

"That morning sickness is a bitch," Raphael says, shaking his head. "I wonder how long it'll last?"

"Probably the whole nine months, knowing Kate."

Yes, our little sugar magnolia is pregnant. This time, for real. The doctor said she's due in late September, which means she's barely into her first trimester. But she's already experiencing the aforementioned morning sickness, fierce cravings—mostly for white carbs and colorful candy—and she's been wearing maternity clothes for two weeks. Not because she's gained an ounce, but because they're *darling.*

"Tracey, do I have Gummi Bears stuck between my teeth?" Raphael asks, having eaten most of the bag Kate had stashed in her purse. He bares his choppers for my inspection.

"Actually, yes." I flick a hunk of red from between his front teeth.

"Thanks, Tracey. I promise I'll do the same for you on your big day."

I smile. "I know you will, Raphael, but I'll try and remember not to eat red Gummi Bears beforehand."

"I couldn't help it. I was nervous. Tracey, I'm nervous. This is such a big step."

"Are you sure you're ready to take it?" I ask, grabbing his hand and squeezing it.

"Yes. I love Donatello," he says, gazing adoringly at his black-tuxedoed groom, who, with Pipsqueak trotting at his side, has taken his place at the opposite end of the white runner. "We're meant to be together forever," Raphael says dreamily. "Married."

And so they are, with the power vested in the Reverend Sally Hingleman by, not the State of New York, but presumably by—well, whoever it is who makes these things semiofficial.

I stand beside Kate—who is a Christmassy vision in her red dress, green face—listening to the exchange of age-old vows that never fail to send chills down my spine.

Do you take this man…

I Do.

Do you take this man…

I Do.

As Raphael and Donatello promise to love each other in Good Times and in Bad, For Richer, For Poorer, in Sickness and in Health, I can't help but turn my head slightly to catch Jack's eye, wondering if he's thinking what I'm thinking.

Yes, we've already loved each other in Good Times and in Bad, For Richer, For Poorer, in Sickness and in Health.

We Do.

He smiles and lifts his chin a little, then lowers it just as slightly.

He knows.

With tears in my eyes, I turn back to the ceremony, watching Raphael and Donatello place gold wedding bands on each other's trembling left hands.

Then they kiss, and Raphael crushes a glass with his foot—another "fun" custom they lifted from the Jewish wedding ceremony—and we all shout Mazel Tov. Well, everyone but Kate, who has fled for the ladies' room once again.

I work my way over to Jack, who's sitting with Kate's husband, Billy, with whom he has nothing whatsoever in common. They're having a stilted conversation about something—could be the stock market, could be Billy's looming fatherhood.

All I overhear is him telling Jack, "Yeah, I just have to give it a few months and it'll pay off big-time."

"Wasn't that a beautiful ceremony?" I ask, joining them.

"Really nice," Jack agrees. I slip my fingers into his and he squeezes them reassuringly.

Billy, never the gay-rights crusader, merely shrugs and asks where Kate is.

"One guess," I say, and he sighs.

"Again? She's been puking her brains out all day." He looks at Jack. "You know, this husband-and-father thing isn't all it's cracked up to be."

Way to go, Billy.

Why don't you just buy him a one-way ticket out of town?

"I don't know," I say pointedly, "my brothers are all married with kids and they're all thrilled. Right, Jack?"

"Well, I don't know if *thrilled* is the right word," Jack begins, undoubtedly about to launch into an account of Danny's now-legendary Christmas-morning meltdown on the heels of a four-hour marathon assembly of tiny plastic parts that never did materialize into what I think was supposed to be a Sun-tacular Seaside Villa for Barbie and her pals.

I cut Jack off with a strategic "Oh, look, here comes a tray of bacon-wrapped scallops!" and frantically flag down the waiter.

The reception proceeds rather nicely from there. We witness the spotlight newlywed dance to the Waitresses' "I Know What Boys Like," followed by four hours of dance music, culminating in a rousing rendition of "The Lion Sleeps Tonight" in homage to Raphael and Donatello's safari honeymoon.

I'm *uh-wee-mo-wop'ing* all over the dance floor when Jack, whom I suddenly realize I haven't seen in a good hour and a half, appears to tug my arm.

"Ready to go?" he shouts, because clearly, he is.

"Not really," I say without missing a beat in the song. "This is the last dance. I want to see Raphael throw his bouquet."

"Okay," he says reluctantly. As I start to dance away, he calls over the music, "Do you want me to go down and flag a cab? It might take a few minutes to get one."

I just look at him.

"Never mind," he says glumly. "I'll wait. Go ahead."

Thanks to him, the *wee* has been sucked right out of my *mo-wop*.

I finish the dance anyway, and line up dutifully with the horde of other single gals—none of whom are actual gals—at the base of the winding iron staircase from which Raphael will throw his bouquet.

"I really want to catch it," Raphael's hairstylist friend, Cristoforo, tells me as we jockey for position. "I'm so ready to walk down that aisle with Jason."

I don't want to point out to him that Jason is nowhere to be seen among the would-be bouquet-catchers, and that he spent most of the wedding cozying up to Jones of *Curious George: The Musical* fame.

"No way," an elfin man informs Cristoforo, who's a good eighteen inches taller. "I'm catching it this time. My boyfriend and I are getting married in April."

"Unless you can fly, I'd say it's beyond your reach, little fellow," a bystander says cattily, and the insults are flying fast and furious.

Meanwhile, I'm thinking it's refreshing not to be one of a smattering of reluctant bouquet candidates for a change. I mean, who wants to parade her single status in front of a roomful of couples, and then vie to be the next bride in what is an embarrassingly archaic tradition? Okay I'll admit it. I do. I'm a sucker for old-fashioned wedding traditions.

At Mike and Dianne's wedding, it was me, Dianne's thrice-divorced grandmother and Mike's twelve-year-old niece.

The niece caught it halfheartedly, but not before Grandma attempted to elbow her aside at the last minute.

"Ready, ladies?" Raphael asks slyly from his stairway perch overhead.

"Ready!" we call.

I position myself, then look around for Jack. He's parked at the edge of the dance floor where I left him earlier. But I can't catch his eye. He's too busy looking at his watch.

He really does hate weddings.

But that's too bad. I'm staying at this one until the bitter end.

The bouquet goes sailing through the air.

Our elfin friend must have sprouted fairy wings, because the next thing I know he's waving the bouquet around shouting, "I got it! I got it!"

"Sorry, Tracey," Raphael says, descending the stairs and giving me a hug. "I swear I was aiming for you."

"That's okay, sweetie. Have a wonderful time on your honeymoon."

"We will. Tracey, promise me you won't forget to water my plants and make sure my TiVo is taping *One Life To Live* every day."

"I promise. You're such a beautiful bride." I touch the fierce growth of five o'clock shadow on his cheek, then send him on his way with a kiss for luck.

The bitter end has arrived.

I make my way over to Jack, who pretty much sprints us to the door.

Outside, he surveys the empty expanse of Moore Street, where sleet is beginning to fall in the gloomy February dusk. "No cabs. I knew I should have come down early."

"Do you really think the street was teeming with taxis then?" I ask, stepping over a puddle of slush in my dyed red satin pointy pumps.

I realize that my feet are killing me. How the heck did I manage to dance in these shoes? I can barely walk in them.

"We should head over toward Sixth Avenue," Jack decides. "We'll have a better chance there."

I try not to groan, because he's right. It's just that every step is excruciating and it's going to take hundreds of them to get to Sixth Avenue.

We walk in silence. Rather, Jack walks, lost in thought, and I hobble, lost in a haze of pain.

You know those guys who sell umbrellas on every street corner when the weather is bad?

I think they take Valentine's Day off.

However, Tribeca and SoHo are teeming with every living soul *but* those guys, despite the nasty weather. There are plenty of pedestrians to crowd the sidewalk; plenty of cabs whizzing along the avenue when we finally reach it, though every one that passes is either off duty or full.

As Jack and I stand on the curb getting drenched and cold waiting for a new wave of cars to approach, I shift my weight from one foot to the other.

Jack looks at me. "Are you okay?"

"I'm soaked."

"So am I."

"These shoes kill." There. One-upped him.

"Yeah, they look it. All that dancing couldn't have helped the situation."

"It was a wedding. People dance at weddings."

"I danced," he protests.

"Once. And it was a slow song."

"Did you really expect me to get out there and do the YMCA with you and a horde of guys wearing Village People costumes?"

"They only wore them for that one song. And you always do the YMCA at Yankee Stadium."

"That's different."

"I don't see how."

"It's a ballpark, not a wedding."

My throbbing feet are making me crankier by the second; thus I feel compelled to say, "Look, I know you hate weddings, Jack. But it's over, so can't you just cheer up?"

"I'm cheerful," he says mildly. "You're the one who's not cheerful."

He has a point there.

But who can be cheerful when half a can of Aussie Spritz is plastered to her head in sopping strands?

"And anyway," he goes on, still watching the approaching traffic for a cab, "who said I hate weddings?"

"You did."

"When? I never—"

"Remember Labor Day weekend? Our Lady of Everlasting Misery?"

"Oh, that." He lowers his hand to wave it dismissively at me. "I hated everything about *that* wedding. Mostly the bride."

"Hey, there's a cab!" I say as one races past us.

Jack raises his arm again to hail it. Too late, it's gone.

"I can't believe it," I wail.

"I'm sure another one will be along any second."

Yeah, right. But I need to steer him back on topic, so I say, "Anyway, you were saying…?"

He just looks at me.

"About how you don't hate weddings?" I prod.

"Oh. Right. I really don't hate them. Not all of them. I like some of them."

"You do?"

"Sure, why not?"

"You do not. You complain every single time we get an invitation to one."

He laughs. "Okay, I'll admit that I can think of better ways to spend a Saturday afternoon."

I find myself blurting, "Maybe you'd feel differently if it were your own wedding."

There's no excuse for that comment. I didn't drink more than a few sips of champagne at the wedding, and tight shoes don't force words out one's unwilling mouth.

But it's too late to take it back, so I wait for Jack to tell me not to bug him about getting married.

He doesn't say that, though.

He shrugs and says, "Who knows?"

Well, he sure as hell doesn't.

I sure as hell don't, either.

That does it. I'm so sick and tired of this tiptoeing around the issue when I know damned well he has a ring that he hasn't given me for whatever reason.

Maybe it's not because I ate tainted oysters.

Maybe it's not because he didn't want it to be on a cliché occasion like Christmas or Valentine's Day.

Maybe it is because he changed his mind, or because...

Because, I don't know, he's waiting for hell to freeze over?

Truly, I have no idea why he's waiting, and I don't care.

All I know is that I'm sick of feeling helpless.

So I'm marching over to his court and snatching the ball back, as it were.

I look him in the eye through the curtain of sleet falling between us. "I don't believe you, Jack."

"You don't believe what?" he asks, startled.

"I don't believe you have any intention of ever getting married. To me."

There. It's out there, dangling in front of him like a bully's dare.

What's he going to do with it?

Well, what *can* he do?

What do I *want* him to do?

It's not as though I expect him to get down on one knee

in the slushy gutter and produce that familiar white ring box from his suit-jacket pocket.

No, I don't expect anything like that.

Which is why, when he drops to one knee in the slushy gutter and produces the familiar white ring box from his suit-jacket pocket, I nearly fall off the curb.

"What are you doing?" I gasp.

"What does it look like I'm doing?"

"It looks like you're proposing," I say incredulously.

"You always were quick on the uptake."

He snaps the ring box open. The diamond setting I saw in that closet in Anguilla twinkles invitingly.

But this isn't how it's supposed to happen.

Not here, in the gutter on West Broadway.

This can't really be happening.

"Tracey, I love you," he calls above the noise of the street: honking horns, splashing cars, distant sirens, subway trains rumbling below.

"Oh my God." I close my eyes, shocked.

When I open them again, he's still there, asking, "Will you marry me?"

This is really happening.

"Will you?" he repeats, as another empty, on-duty taxi roars by, this time dousing him with gray spatters.

"Have you been carrying that ring box around all day?" I ask incredulously.

"Tracey, I've been carrying this ring box around for almost two months, trying to find the right moment to do it."

"And this…" I gesture around us at the sleet, the traffic, the passersby, his knee squarely planted in a streaming gutter beside a storm drain. "This is it? This is the right moment?"

"I didn't think so," he admits. "But then I realized, no moment is ever going to be perfect. Nothing ever is. Perfect, I mean."

"No," I say, shaking my head, feeling tears springing to my eyes. "Nothing ever is." I tilt my face up to the sky, and the tears are washed away, just like that.

"I love you," Jack says again. "I want to marry you, Tracey. I've wanted to marry you for months. I would have asked you on Thanksgiving, or Christmas, but Hans took so long to make this setting because he had to have carpel tunnel surgery…"

"Hans?" I echo, my heart beating a little faster.

"He's this jeweler my sister knows. He told me to call him to see if it was done over Christmas so I could at least give it to you for New Year's, but it wasn't, so—"

"His name is *Hans?*"

Jack nods.

"Is he Austrian?"

"German, I think. Why?"

"Does he live in Sheepshead Bay?"

"Flushing. Why?"

I shake my head, grinning, crying at the same time.

Once upon a time, I thought Jack asking me to marry him was about as likely as the actual existence of the little old arthritic Austrian jeweler from Sheepshead Bay.

So the jeweler has carpel tunnel, is German, and from Queens.

And Jack just asked me to marry him.

"What are you smiling about?" he asks from the gutter below.

"I'll tell you someday."

"Why don't you tell me now?"

"Because I have something else to say to you now," I tell him.

"Really?" He grins broadly. "What's that?"

"It's yes," I say. *"Yes, yes, yes, yes, yes, yes, yes…!"*

Yes.

I Will.

Yes.

I Do.

He stands and takes me into his arms, lifting me off my pointy pumps and spinning me around joyfully before he kisses me.

The only thing that could make the moment more complete would be if a chauffeured limousine stocked with towels and champagne pulled up to the curb.

Yes, with Hans at the wheel, I think, and giddy laughter escapes me.

I kiss Jack again: Jack, who has been carrying this ring around for weeks, waiting for the perfect moment to propose.

I think of how I've spent the last few months longing for him to propose at any given moment, and how it never happened.

Life, it turns out, is full of moments. None is perfect; all are fleeting; precious few of them are memorable.

Sometimes you just have to grab one and make it your own.

"Give me your hand, Trace," Jack says gently, and I do.

I Do.

Yes.

I watch through flooded eyes as he slides the beautiful ring over my fourth finger.

I open my mouth to tell him how much I love it, how much I love *him,* but I'm too overcome with emotion to make a sound.

"It was my mother's," Jack says as we both admire it. "The stone, I mean. There are a couple of small inclusions, but Hans said you can only see the flaws when it's under magnification."

I find my voice in time to remind Jack, "Nothing's perfect. Especially under magnification."

His eyes meet mine. "No," he says, "nothing is."

And he kisses me again.

I'd like to say that limo pulls up to the curb then, or even just a cab.

Or that we walk contentedly off into the sunset together, me and my fiancé—my fiancé!

But the sun isn't shining, there still isn't a cab to be found, and my feet are starting to blister.

So we take the subway home, me and my fiancé, holding hands all the way, and you know what?

Some things really are perfect after all.

Part VII

October

Epilogue

Jack and I really do live happily ever after, as you might have guessed.

As for the long-awaited Spadolini-Candell autumn wedding?

Well, that's another story....

New from Allison Rushby

The Dairy Queen

Life for Dicey just can't seem to get any worse.
So, with her best friend, sister and dog in tow,
Dicey returns to her small hometown to find
some peace. What she soon finds out though,
is that moving home isn't the end—it's just
the beginning.

**Visit your
local bookseller**

**RED
DRESS
INK**
™

www.RedDressInk.com   RDIAR574TR

New from bestselling author
Carole Matthews

On sale March 2006

Kate Lewis has it all—but is this all there is? As a
thirty-five-year-old wife and mother of two, Kate
enrolls in a tai chi retreat for some enlightenment,
but will she discover more than she had in mind?

On sale wherever
trade paperbacks
are sold.

**RED
DRESS
INK**
TM

www.RedDressInk.com

RDICM568TR

Who was Tracey Spadolini before she was *Slightly Settled?*

Pick up a copy of *Slightly Single* by Wendy Markham and find out.

Praise for *Slightly Single*

Another "undeniably fun journey for the reader."
—*Booklist*

RED DRESS INK ™

Visit us at www.reddressink.com   RDI0102R-TR

Available now from Wendy Markham,
bestselling author of
Slightly Single and *Slightly Settled*

Mike, Mike & Me

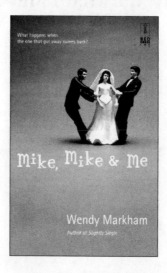

Once upon a time in the 1980s, a girl named
Beau was torn between two Mikes: did she
prefer her high school sweetheart or the sexy
stranger she'd picked up in an airport bar?
One she eventually married, the other she left
behind. But what happens when the Mike
that got away comes back?

**Available wherever
trade paperbacks
are sold.**

**RED
DRESS
INK**
™

www.RedDressInk.com   RDI0105TRIR

Have you met Tracey Spadolini?

If you haven't, you must!

Join Tracey on her adventures as she lives *slightly single* and then *slightly settled* in New York City.

by Wendy Markham

RED DRESS INK ™

Available wherever
trade paperbacks
are sold.

www.RedDressInk.com   RDIMARKHAM05-TR

New from the author of FAT CHANCE

Deborah Blumenthal
WHAT MEN WANT

On sale February 2006

When reporter Jenny George is sent to the
Caribbean to write an exposé, she learns more
about what men want and—more importantly—
what she wants!

*On sale wherever
trade paperbacks
are sold.*

RED
DRESS
I N K
™

www.RedDressInk.com

RDIDB569TR

Are you getting it at least twice a month?

Here's how: Try RED DRESS INK books
on for size & receive two FREE gifts!

Bombshell
by Lynda Curnyn

As Seen on TV
by Sarah Mlynowski

YES! Send my two FREE books.
There's no risk and no purchase required—ever!

Please send me my two FREE books and bill me just 99¢ for shipping and handling. I may keep the books and return the shipping statement marked "cancel." If I do not cancel, about a month later I will receive 2 additional books at the low price of just $11.00 each in the U.S. or $13.56 each in Canada, a savings of over 15% off the cover price (plus 50¢ shipping and handling per book*). I understand that accepting the two free books places me under no obligation ever to buy any books. I can always return a shipment and cancel at any time. Even if I never buy another book from Red Dress Ink, the free books are mine to keep forever.

160 HDN D34M   360 HDN D34N

Name (PLEASE PRINT)

Address   Apt. #

City   State/Prov.   Zip/Postal Code

*Want to try another series? Call 1-800-873-8635
or order online at www.TryRDI.com/free.*

In the U.S. mail to: 3010 Walden Ave., P.O. Box 1867, Buffalo, NY 14240-1867
In Canada mail to: P.O. Box 609, Fort Erie, ON L2A 5X3

*Terms and prices subject to change without notice. Sales tax applicable in N.Y.
**Canadian residents will be charged applicable provincial taxes and GST.

All orders subject to approval. Offer limited to one per household.
® and ™ are trademarks owned and used by the trademark owner and/or its licensee.

© 2004 Harlequin Enterprises Ltd.

RED DRESS INK

RDI04-TR

4/11